out of
NOWHERE

out of NOWHERE

a novel

Jeri Gilchrist

Covenant Communications, Inc.
Covenant.

Cover image © Steve Cole, PhotoDisc/GettyImages

Cover design copyrighted 2003 by Covenant Communications, Inc.

Published by Covenant Communications, Inc.
American Fork, Utah

Printed in Canada
First Printing: June 2003

10 09 08 07 06 05 04 03   10 9 8 7 6 5 4 3 2 1

ISBN 1-59156-208-2

Library of Congress Cataloging-in-Publication Data

Gilchrist, Jeri Lawrence, 1963-
     Out of nowhere : a novel / Jeri Lawrence Gilchrist.
         p.   cm.
     ISBN 1-59156-208-2 (alk. paper)
     1. Mormon women--Fiction. 2. Brothers--Death--Fiction. I. Title.

     PS3607.I4235O94 2003
     813'.6--dc21

                                         2003043465

To my parents, Max and Conni Lawrence,
who inspired me to believe in my dreams
and encouraged me to chase after them.

And to Brad, Tyler, and Bryan
who made them all come true.
I love you all.

ACKNOWLEDGEMENTS

The idea and challenge to write this book came at a point in my life that was full of struggle and trial. Only a couple of months previously, my mom had been diagnosed with multiple myeloma. I tried each month to spend time with her as she was going through chemo. It was a time filled with opportunities and blessings that strengthened my bonds with this beautiful woman and my wonderful dad, who has always been my hero. The idea to attempt my hand at writing this particular book started there. It became our book.

For that reason, the fact that this book will be published is a blessing to me as a remembrance of my time with my parents. So I owe a debt of gratitude to Covenant for its publication, as well as to Shauna Nelson for the phone call that made my gift to my parents a reality. I can't begin to tell you what that call did for me. Thank you to Angela Colvin for your help and especially to Katie Child for your guidance and friendship. When I knew that you would be my editor, I knew I was a lucky girl. It's been wonderful to laugh with you.

For getting me here, I have to especially thank Kerry Blair for being my mentor, example, and friend. I wore her out with all my insecurities. Kerry, you've been so kind. Thank you. I'm grateful to Steve and Lisa Winward and Tim and Julie Langley for their help with the technical information. Hope I got it right, guys! I want to thank my friends and our families who helped make it possible to visit my parents so we could write. Those memories are dear to my heart. I owe you more than I can ever repay. I owe a big thanks to my friends who let me bounce ideas off of them; to Brad, my own personal Prince Charming; to Tyler and Bryan for being my comic relief, especially when my heart needed to laugh; and to my family, who gave me the inspiration for some of the experiences of my characters. I can't forget my good friend Julie Backus for her "lesson" and sweet friendship. Thank you Aunt Helen for your help and input. You made me see things I would have missed. And last, but in no way least, thanks to Judy. You encouraged me and kept me excited. You're the only one I know who can compete with me as a lover of romance.

PROLOGUE

Dazed, Ashlyn Lawrence tried to lift her heavy eyelids. The loud noise seeming to come from her dream suddenly became a reality as her bedroom door crashed open and in walked her older brother, attempting to sing at the top of his lungs.

He flung open the blinds, and bright sunshine burned Ashlyn's sleepy eyes. "Wake up, Ash!" he said. "I have the greatest news!"

Ashlyn looked up, squinting. Her soon-to-be-nineteen-years-old brother stood above her with a silly grin on his face. Feeling a little put out that her wonderful dreams had been interrupted by his so-called singing, she groaned, "Wouldn't your great news be even greater in a half hour or so when I woke up on my own accord?"

"No! No! You won't believe it!" His enthusiasm was so contagious that curiosity got the better of her. Willing her tired muscles to move, she sat sleepily up in bed. "Okay, lay it on me," she yawned. "What's the great news?"

With a twinkle in his eye, Austin replied, "I went in the bathroom first thing this morning and looked in the mirror."

"Yeah, so?" she muttered.

He grinned. "And it's true, Ash! You wouldn't think it possible, but I get better looking each day!"

Before Ashlyn could respond, she found a pillow in her face and Austin was out the door, his laugh echoing in the hallway.

Within seconds he was back. "Oh yeah, Mom said it's time to rouse Sleeping Beauty—her words, not mine! Besides, when I tell her what I saw on the front porch last night, you may want to be there to defend yourself."

Ashlyn's eyes flew open. "You wouldn't dare!" His taunting smile told her that he certainly *would* dare tell—and embellish—the news. In hopes of downplaying the front porch scene Austin referred to, Ashlyn tried to make light of the situation. "Come on, Austin it wasn't a big deal. And besides, it's not a good subject to discuss at the breakfast table."

Austin started to laugh when he saw the panic in her eyes, and she realized he was only teasing. When he turned to leave this time, Ashlyn threw the pillow and missed him by a mile.

"Gee, nice shot, Ash!" He laughed and disappeared down the hallway.

Ashlyn was wide-awake. *Man,* she thought, *Austin can be a real pain!*

Even though she was his little sister, Ashlyn had to admit that Austin was her hero and also her best friend. Nobody called her "Ash" except Austin. It was his term of endearment for her, and she liked it, though she would never let him know it. She could confide in him about her dreams and he would never laugh or make her feel they were insignificant.

It wasn't as if they never squabbled, however. Austin knew how to push Ashlyn's buttons, and when he had pushed his limit with her, she knew how to be the pesky, tagalong little sister who could drive an older brother insane. But there was nobody whom she loved and trusted more. The thing that Ashlyn loved the most was that her brother always seemed to have his head on straight. He knew who he was, where he was going, and, even better, he stayed on the right track to get there.

Although there was more than a year between them, people often thought they were twins since they looked the same age. Austin considered that an insult for the simple fact that he was older and, by all rights and privileges, should have had the title of "firstborn" with its attendant glory. And even though they may have looked like twins, Austin's and Ashlyn's personalities definitely separated them. Her brother was the kind of guy girls swooned over—a real Prince Charming. He was easygoing and caring, with wit and charm to boot. And his never-ending smile complemented his sandy blonde hair, dark brown eyes, and olive complexion. Ashlyn, while outgoing and friendly enough, was a little bit more insecure and all too easily intimidated. No one had given her cause to feel that way. Her insecurities lay simply within herself. She often tried so hard to do things perfectly that anything short of that made her feel inadequate. She longed to have her brother's laid-back style. But instead of resenting him for it, she admired him.

And really, how many older brothers actually gave advice to their little sisters on how to catch "the one"—especially when "the one" was one of his friends? Dave Parker was Austin's friend, but they hadn't known each other long. All Austin knew was that Dave had had a rough family background. His parents divorced after his dad was sent to prison for spousal abuse. Austin knew Dave needed a friend when Dave and his mom moved into the neighborhood six months before, and he had tried to include Dave when he and his friends got together. And through Austin, Dave was even becoming more involved with the Church.

Ashlyn knew what it had cost Austin to give in and help set her up with Dave. He absolutely *hated* the idea of his sister going out with his friend and was never shy about making his disapproval known. Ashlyn refused to listen to reason, and finally, Austin grudgingly conceded. Ashlyn even lost count of the times Austin mentioned that he was doing this "favor" for her in protest. Somehow she knew that Dave got a good talking-to before the actual date took place. Still, that date finally did take place the night before. And what a date it had been!

Ashlyn sat on the edge of the bed, reliving her date with Dave. She had been so nervous at first. Of course, plenty of that nervousness came from the glare her brother gave them as they left the house.

But none of that had mattered to Ashlyn. Every time she saw Dave with his brown hair and eyes, she melted. She had wanted a date with him, and wanted it bad.

Austin's glare may have compounded her nervousness, but once they were seated at the restaurant, she lightened up, and talking came quite easily. Dinner was over before she knew it, and halfway through the movie when Dave held her hand, she was as giddy as a teenage girl could be. Shivers went all the way up her arm and bumped right into her heart, making it skip a beat. On the way home, she didn't anticipate him kissing her, but when he did at the doorstep, she had been caught off guard—pleasantly enough. It had filled her dreams that night.

Most girls would have arrived home to find their parents waiting up, but not Ashlyn. Austin had assured their parents that *he* would wait for her to come home. Once the door was closed after Ashlyn had gone inside, Austin stood across the room with his arms folded across his chest in true "daddy" form.

"We will talk about this in the morning, missy," he said, anger, relief, and humor all playing across his features as he stomped across the room toward his bedroom. "I'm gonna kick his behind ten ways to the sun."

* * *

Shaken from her dreamy thoughts, Ashlyn looked up and saw that Austin had returned. "What?" she asked.

"He's going to answer to me for this one." Seeing Ashlyn's look, he added, "Hello? Are you with me?"

"No. What are you talking about?"

"I saw Dave slobber all over you at the door last night."

Ashlyn laughed until she saw Austin's stern look. "Give me a break. 'Slobbering' is a little exaggerating, don't you think? You're acting worse than Dad." She rolled her eyes.

"I told him he could take you out, but I did *not* say he could play kissy-face with you. I warned him in no uncertain terms that his lips had better not move one inch in your direction. He didn't listen, and now he's going to get what's coming to him. Nobody lays their slimy lips on my sister and gets away with it."

Knowing that Austin was never violent and rarely even confrontational, Ashlyn replied, "Please forgive me, dear brother, for I am but a sinner who was tempted while waiting for my convent application to arrive. Until I become a nun, can you possibly tolerate a mere sinner like me?" She batted her eyelashes. "And by the way, dear brother of mine, I meant to ask you if Jessica had already submitted her convent papers when you planted a big one on her last Thursday night?"

Austin raised his eyebrows in surprise.

Ashlyn continued, "Ha! Found a way to shut you up, didn't I? Maybe we *both* ought to confess our sins to Mom and Dad?"

A long, silent look of truce passed between them before they both started to laugh.

Ashlyn patted the bed. "Sit down. I need some advice." As Austin sauntered in and sat down, she added, "It's about that kiss."

"Don't push it, Ash."

"No really, I have a problem." She hesitated.

Austin looked her in the eye. "I already told you I'm gonna twist his lips off. Problem solved."

Ashlyn suddenly took a keen interest in her fidgeting fingers. "I really liked it," she said softly.

"Oh, geez!" Austin fell back on her bed and stared up at the ceiling. "What advice do you want, then? Apparently you liked his slobbering, so what's to know? It's not like you've never kissed a boy."

"I gave him the 'pat,'" Ashlyn groaned and covered her face with both hands in embarrassment.

"The what?" Austin asked, confused.

"The 'pat'! I gave him the 'pat'!"

"Now I'm really gonna beat the tar out of him!" Austin exclaimed, trying to control his anger. "What the heck is a 'pat'?"

Ashlyn was surprised by her brother's anger, but with a little moan of dismay, she continued. "When he kissed me, he hugged me, and of course I hugged him back—and then I gave him a pat on the back! It was only because I was so nervous! Now what am I going to do?"

Austin's brows furrowed. "So?"

"Don't you see? The 'pat' means you just want to be friends!"

"And . . . ?"

"And I like him a lot more than that." Ashlyn smiled dreamily. "A lot more."

"That's it, Ash. I'm gonna knock him flat." Austin jumped up from the bed and was gone in a flash.

Ashlyn was still seated on her bed—wondering why she'd thought Austin would actually help her—when her mother knocked on the door. Her mother was a beautiful Danish woman with dark hair, soft, dark eyes, and porcelain-fine skin. Her European upbringing had lent her a quiet, inner beauty that left an impression of elegance. She was an intelligent, musically talented woman who worked hard inside and outside the home.

Ashlyn had always felt love and security from her parents. She lived in a strict home with rules and obligations, but with those obligations came freedom and privileges. Trust and respect were taught, and trust and respect were returned. Their mother, Laura, was the disciplinarian while Ashlyn's father, Joe, was the softie. He'd grown up in Heber Valley, Utah, near the base of the Wasatch Mountains. He was a country boy who knew how to work and play hard. A tall, thin man, he had the gifts of communication, affection, and humor. He was well liked, and known as a man who would do anything for anyone. Ashlyn's parents, a Danish city girl and a western country boy, had proved true the statement "opposites attract."

"How did it go last night?" her mom asked, sitting beside Ashlyn and slipping her arm around her daughter's shoulders.

"Mom, I had the best time." Ashlyn beamed. "He took me to dinner and to a movie. We talked a lot, but he didn't open up much about his family. He kept asking me things about myself, and he held my hand at the show."

"It sounds like you had a nice time," Laura said with a smile.

"I hope he asks me out again."

"Honey, Austin seems a little agitated with you dating Dave. Do you know why?"

Ashlyn rolled her eyes. "He's pouting because Dave kissed me good night. Mr. Peeping Tom sat and watched."

"Well," Laura said slowly, "that might be a little hard to take. Not many brothers like it when their friends kiss their sisters." Laura paused. "Was the kiss inappropriate?"

"No, not at all. Well, except I broke the pact I made with Austin that neither of us would kiss on a first date. I wouldn't know if he's kept his word since I don't go around spying on him." *Okay, Thursday was an exception,* Ashlyn thought with a pang of guilt.

"Be patient with Austin. He hasn't known Dave long. But he does know that Dave has had it rough, and that he witnessed some horrible things that went on between his parents. It's my understanding that his court testimony put his father in prison."

"I know, Mom, but Dave doesn't have to pay for his father's mistakes. It sounds like he's already paid enough."

"A person can't go through years of witnessing abuse and come out unaffected. Honey, all I'm saying is that Austin doesn't know Dave too well, so I think he's being extra cautious. He's said that Dave is pretty closed."

Ashlyn was becoming a little angry with her brother. "Mom, do you blame Dave? It doesn't sound like he's had much of a life to brag about. I don't think I'd run around telling everyone about my convict father. He probably doesn't trust a lot of people. It'll just take time."

Ashlyn's mom hugged her daughter. "I'm sure you're right. Now, changing the subject, Austin's mission call hasn't come yet, but we thought we'd go up Big Cottonwood Canyon for a picnic anyway. Up and at 'em."

"Thanks, Mom." Ashlyn smiled.

"You're welcome." Laura rose, then turned back to her daughter. "And Ashlyn? I think the pact you made with Austin is a good one. Kisses mean much more when they're saved for boys who are really special. There may be a strong attraction to a certain boy, especially at your age, but remember to look at him deep down and think about whether kissing him is the right thing to do. Someday you'll meet a boy who will send your heart flying, and once you've kissed him, the other kisses won't mean a thing. Remember that."

Ashlyn smiled. "You just took away the thrill of kissing a boy, but okay, I get the message."

Her mom returned the smile and left the room. Ashlyn smiled to herself. It had still been a great kiss!

* * *

It was a beautiful late-May morning as the Lawrences drove up into the majestic Wasatch Mountains. Austin loved it there: snowboarding and skiing in the winter, and water-skiing, camping, hiking, and fishing in the summer. It was also the place he often came to pray and to think. Some of his biggest decisions were made there, and many of his biggest problems were solved. In those mountains, he felt close to the Savior. He could gaze up and know that the Savior loved him. Because of the beauty of creation and the serenity, he couldn't imagine another place that could bring him such peace. He even went there to accept Moroni's promise after he finished reading the Book of Mormon. It was there that he'd gained his testimony.

It was also there that Austin wanted to open his mission call. He had saved today in hopes of finding out where he would be called to serve—opening the long white envelope from the Church Office Building, surrounded by his family in the mountains. However, the call had not come, but the family had decided to spend the day as planned, enjoying a family outing.

As they drove, Austin continually stole glances at Ashlyn, who looked out the window of the car with a silly grin on her face. He couldn't quite figure out why her infatuation with Dave bothered him so much.

Is it because she likes a guy too much? he wondered. *No. Is it because Dave's a friend? No. I'd probably want to thump any friend who tried to kiss her. I mean, she's my sister!*

He wondered if he was judgmental or just protective. He didn't want to be judgmental, so until he could watch Dave a little closer, he'd settle for protective. *He hasn't done anything to make me question him,* Austin told himself. *He's just a mystery to me. If I had his life, I think I would also try to start clean in a new town. Who wouldn't?* Austin suspected that Dave's mom might not have been the only one abused. Because of that, Austin wanted to help Dave know that things would get better.

Ashlyn looked over at Austin. "Hey, what's up? You're staring at me like I have two heads."

Austin turned back to look out the window and realized he must have been thinking for a while; they were almost to the picnic area reserved for their family.

"Austin, are you okay?"

He turned back to look at his little sister. "Yeah, I'm okay. Just thinking."

"Ooooh!" she teased. "I'll alert the media that a thought may come through any minute."

Austin elbowed her in the ribs and turned back to the window. "At least some of us have a brain to think with. I'm surprised we're from the same gene pool."

Ashlyn laughed. She had chosen long ago to compete with Austin in the "who-got-the-best-grades-in-the-family" game and had given him a run for his money. As it was, Austin had been an honor student from seventh grade on, and Ashlyn would be her class valedictorian at graduation next week. *Who said a little competition isn't healthy?* Ashlyn smiled and turned her thoughts back to the dreamy date with the dreamy guy.

A few minutes later, Joe Lawrence prepared the grill as his wife hummed to herself while unpacking things for lunch. The picnic site was about five miles from the mouth of Big Cottonwood Canyon. Joe's brother worked for Utah Power and Light, and since the company owned a power plant on that spot, the family could reserve the fenced-in area for special occasions. The site had every amenity, including rest rooms, lawns, a volleyball court, a horseshoe pit, hiking trails, and a campfire pit, all among the lush beauty of nature. The river, swollen with the runoff from winter's snow, flowed furiously. Trees mostly blocked the view from the main road that led in and out of the canyon, and the area was right at the foot of the mountains on the south side of the picnic site. Hiking trails led to other camping and picnicking areas, but not within hearing distance of this one. Landscaping, except for the lawn, had been left to Mother Nature. It was a secluded and beautiful little area.

"Hey, Ma!" Austin called. "We're going for a hike, okay?"

Their mother smiled and waved them on. As she thought about her children, she knew that at times they could get on each other's nerves—and hers as a result—but were otherwise so close that they seemed like the twins everyone mistook them for. She knew that their personalities made them unique. Things came fairly easy for her son, and he was much more self-assured than his sister. Ashlyn worked every inch of the way. She was a perfectionist, and it showed in her achievements. She was, however, always a little hard on herself in spite of her work. It wasn't difficult to see that she was a bit jealous of Austin because what took much effort on her part often came natural to him. Still, the two complemented one another, and there was a special bond between them that couldn't be explained other than by their theory that they were meant to come to earth together to conquer the world.

And they could probably do it, Laura thought with a smile. The next two years apart would be hard for them, but it would be good for Ashlyn to grow and learn to be independent of her brother. Austin would surely have a greater appreciation for the little things his sister did for him now that probably, to him, seemed pretty routine. Ashlyn was his greatest fan and constantly did things to show her brother how much she loved him. She never missed a school or church basketball game that he played in, wearing her cheerleading uniform and getting the crowd to cheer him and the team on. Ashlyn brought Austin Slurpies when he was sick. One time she brought him the huge "kahuna" size and mixed all of the flavors together, claiming she wasn't sure which flavor he liked best. She made him cookies when he was up late to study. There were also a few times when Austin reciprocated the deeds. He took roses to school on her birthday and took her to dinner when she was sad.

Laura knew that the lucky souls who became their eternal companions would be blessed. She also knew that to put up with those two, their companions would have to be pretty wonderful also. She looked forward to that phase in her life. But for now, her children were developing hearts of gold. She knew her children weren't perfect, but to her, they were close.

* * *

Ashlyn followed a few paces behind her brother. Austin's chosen path wound around pine trees with sweet-smelling branches sprouting soft, new needles. The trees stood tall and stately, seeming proud to have survived the harsh winter and now feeling the glory of reaching up toward the sun. The siblings wound around quaking aspen trees with beautiful, white trunks and round, green leaves. Along the path were large, jutted rocks. Here and there wild flowers bloomed in an array of color: yellow, white, pink, purple, and blue.

The two were deep within their own thoughts as they came to a large rock and sat to enjoy the spectacular view of southern Salt Lake Valley. The sky was clear blue, and small, ribbonlike clouds drifted through. The sun beamed down as they sat silently, almost afraid to speak for fear of chasing away the perfect vision of endless beauty.

Moments later, Ashlyn broke the silence. "It'll come soon, you know."

"What will?" Austin replied, breaking from his thoughts.

"Your mission call. Isn't that why you're so quiet?"

"Nah, that's not it. I was trying to be really quiet in hopes of seeing a snake that I could catch to throw on you."

Ashlyn stood, intending to run back at record speed the way she had just come.

Austin laughed and grabbed her, and she sat down beside him. "Man, I haven't seen you move so fast since that time you were trying to avoid that 'Trekkie' Jimmy Nolan. Remember how he dressed up like Mr. Spock at school and said he would 'live long and prosper' if you would go to the Halloween Dance with him? Normally I would have thought it was a clever gesture. Problem was, he dressed like that all the time. Scary."

Ashlyn glared at her brother. That day was one of the most humiliating of her senior year at high school. Who would have thought he would show up at a football game to ask her a month in advance to a dance not yet announced to the student body? He had connections and pulled it off during the half-time program. Standing there in the middle of the football field with the other cheerleaders, how could she say no? She wouldn't have anyway, but when he knelt to kiss her feet in gratitude for saying yes, she had almost reached her breaking point. "You're never gonna just let that go, are you?"

Austin laughed. "I'm sorry! It's just that it was such big news that it hit the school paper. How could one possibly forget?"

"One couldn't with one's brother around to remind her," Ashlyn said. "And forgive me if I seem a little jumpy today. After all, I did steal your friend away from you—with a little help from you, of course. And the dagger looks you threw at us as we left last night didn't go unnoticed."

Austin chuckled for a second and looked over at his sister. Growing serious, he said quietly, "You don't need me, you know."

Ashlyn's eyebrows shot up. "What do you mean by that?"

Austin grinned and looked back to the valley. "You didn't need me to get you that date. You could take your pick of any of my friends. They'd jump at the chance to take you out. You may as well know that some of them *are* my friends just in hopes of taking you out."

"Yeah, right," she replied.

"I'm quite serious. The only difference is that most of them took me seriously when I told them I'd break both their legs if they went near you. Dave just didn't think I meant it. Of course, you also begged and pleaded with me to line you up with him."

"So why would you make an exception for him?" Ashlyn asked, surprised.

"Because if you went out with him, you'd see that he wasn't your type," Austin said. "But now, judging by the stars in your eyes, maybe my plan backfired. So much for reverse psychology."

"Hold it right there, big brother. Are you telling me that there have been guys who have wanted to take me on a date but haven't for fear of you? Even more so, you *allowed* me to go out with Dave to get a point across?"

"Hold on, little sister. It's not as bad as it sounds. I haven't ever *stopped* anyone from asking you out. I just know that some of my friends have had crushes on you from time to time but never did anything about them. They didn't need my permission to date you. They just never encouraged me to line them up with you, even though they'd come to the house just to see you. And as far as Dave is concerned, it's not like we're talking marriage here. I just don't think he's your type."

Ashlyn began to calm down, but only a little. "What makes you an expert on 'my type'? And how do you know that someday I won't marry Dave?"

Austin held up his hands in surrender. "I'm not trying to bait you, Ash. Like I said, I just don't think Dave is your type. He's not very open with people, and I'm not just talking about his past. That is his business. But he said he doesn't owe anyone anything. And if you ask me, that's a pretty self-centered comment. Ash, you need open communication. Whoever you marry needs to be someone who wants you around twenty-four–seven, not just when it's convenient for him. He should want to always be there for you because you need and want him to be there. He should also need and want to be with you. Dave won't do that for you. That doesn't mean he won't love you. But right now I don't see Dave loving anyone unselfishly. I guess he could change—it's not my place to say. But I just picture someone a lot different for you."

Ashlyn thought for a moment. "Do you really think my survival is based on my dependence on someone else?" she asked with concern in her voice. "Am I so pathetic that I am no one without someone?"

"No. But you don't believe in yourself to see it any other way."

"Boy, you really know how to sweet-talk a girl."

"You're not just any girl, you're my sister. If you never learn anything else in life, you need to learn who you are so that you can believe in yourself. You know I love giving you my advice, but following your own heart will get you a lot further in life than following any advice I could give you. Being your best self is enough, Ash. You just don't know that yet."

There were tears in Ashlyn's eyes. "How do I learn to do that? There are no books called *This Is You and It's Enough.*"

"It's not something you can read up on, Ash," Austin said. He paused and turned to face his sister. He slipped his arm around her shoulders and gave her a quick squeeze. "I wish I could show you a mirror that reflected the really great you that I see. This mirror would assure you how wonderful you are from the inside out. Then, I would break the mirror that *you* look into every day. Your mirror doesn't show you your true self. The only time you see someone worth looking at in your mirror is if you have perfected some monumental challenge. Your mirror doesn't reflect the whole picture, only the deed."

Ashlyn shrugged. "I hate to make mistakes, and when I do, I'm afraid that I'll look in the mirror and find someone who failed."

Austin smirked. "I've got news for you, Ash. You're going to fail sometimes, even when you do your best. We *all* do. Otherwise, we'd be translated. For some reason, you've gotten it in your head that people won't love you if you make mistakes. But all a mistake means is that you're human like the rest of us."

Ashlyn stared ahead in silence before whispering, "Everyone—except Mom and Dad—compares me to you. It's tough being in your shadow."

Austin was shocked. "You can't be serious! Why would you say something like that?"

"Give me a break, Austin," Ashlyn replied. "The only thing you *can't* do is sing. But even there you can put a coyote to shame."

Austin looked away, deep in thought. After a few moments, he again met her eyes and said, "I had no idea you felt that way. I've always been jealous of you." He paused. "The truth is, I can tell you over and over how wonderful you are, but until you believe it yourself, you will continue to have doubts about yourself." Austin rubbed his face with both hands in frustration and took a deep breath. He looked at her with concern evident in his eyes. "I'm going on a mission, Ash, but I want to go knowing you'll be all right. As soon as you know for certain that you really are a child of God and are of great worth, the easier it will be for you to get through the rough times. But you have to find that out for yourself. I can't do it for you."

"I don't need you to do it for me!" Ashlyn protested. "I just get down on myself sometimes. Besides, it's not a bad thing to try to do your best."

"No. You're right. We *should* do our best, but you've placed such unreal expectations on yourself that no one could ever live up to them. Not even you! That load must be weighing you down. Promise me that you'll ask Heavenly Father to help you. Will you at least do that? I just want you to be okay so I can focus on my missionary work and not be worried that you're home beating up on yourself."

"Yeah, sure," Ashlyn replied hesitantly.

Austin hooked her little finger with his own. "Pinkie swear that you'll seriously seek help from Heavenly Father."

"Pinkie swear," Ashlyn laughed, then was suddenly serious again. "Wherever you go, Austin, they're gonna love you."

Austin grinned. "And I'm gonna love them back. I can't wait! I really want to make a difference."

Ashlyn grinned. "Don't worry, Austin. I'll be fine. Tell you what—while you're gone, I'll make a difference here."

"Deal," Austin said.

"But you sound like you're telling me good-bye now."

"I guess in a way I am," Austin admitted. "Once that call comes, who knows if we'll get another chance to talk like this."

When a tear rolled down Ashlyn's cheek, Austin leaned forward to brush it away. "Come on, Ash. It's only for a little while. And hey, what is two years in eternity? Just don't marry any uncool guys while I'm gone, okay?" He considered his statement for a moment. "Maybe I'd better help you in that department myself. I'm really good at choosing, you know. 'Course, you'll probably be too stubborn to take him."

Even though she knew he was teasing, Ashlyn bristled. "I'm not getting married in the next two years! I mean, even if I wanted to, I need you here to give your stamp of approval." She chuckled. "But when you're picking him out, remember I want somebody who kisses good."

Austin groaned and jabbed her in the ribs.

"Austin, you'll be the best missionary," Ashlyn said fervently. "I wish I was going with you."

"You are going," he said, patting his heart with his hand, "in here."

Ashlyn leaned over and hugged her brother. "I love you. You've always been my best friend."

"I love you too. Keep me that way."

"I promise to make a difference while you're gone. I'll do it for you."

"No, Ash, do it for yourself, and for Heavenly Father."

* * *

Picking up momentum as they ran, Ashlyn and Austin stumbled down the trail toward their parents, laughing and trying to see who would reach the table first. Laura and Joe sat under a shade tree talking and holding hands.

"Aren't you guys a little old to be acting that way?" Ashlyn asked, secretly thinking how cool it was that they were still affectionate with one another. "It's embarrassing the way you two are always holding hands and kissing."

"I'll *never* be too old," Dad said, smiling at his wife.

Austin rolled his eyes at his mother's silly grin and tried to appear disgusted, but his broad smile gave him away. "Okay, okay, enough. Can we eat?"

Laura kissed her husband on the cheek and rose, laughing. "Have a seat. It's all ready."

After Austin blessed the food, the family ate, laughed, and talked to their hearts' content. The river swished and babbled its way down the canyon, and a slight breeze cooled their skin while the sun beamed brightly. The weatherman had predicted a perfect day, and he had been right.

All too soon it was time to pack up and prepare to leave. While Joe and Laura cleared the picnic site, Austin and Ashlyn played a game of Frisbee.

"Come on, Ash!" Austin yelled as he once again missed the Frisbee. "You throw like a girl!" He paused for a moment, catching his breath. "Are you doing this on purpose or do you really stink?"

"All right, buddy, let me show you just how bad I am at this," she taunted. "Your ego is going down!" With a full swing, she threw the disc hard and fast.

Austin ran back as fast as he could. Jumping high in the air, he caught the Frisbee and turned around in a victory dance. Suddenly, a shot rang out. The force of the shot pushed him back, and he fell to the ground.

Ashlyn screamed as Joe and Laura ran from the parking area to find her hovering over his body, crying and screaming. Austin lay on the ground, covered with blood, the Frisbee still in his hand.

Ashlyn held his other hand while Joe called 911 on his cell phone. Laura grabbed the picnic blanket and used it to cover her son, then sat cradling his head in her lap while crying. After finishing the call, Joe laid his hands on Austin's head and gave him a blessing, then stood over his still body with tears rolling down his cheeks.

Ashlyn didn't hear the police and ambulance arrive, but as they pulled her away from him, she knew her best friend, her brother, was dead.

Ashlyn's whole world went black.

* * *

The next few days were a never-ending nightmare. The police questioned her over and over again. Did she see who had done it? *No.* Where had the shot come from? *The trail where they had walked.* Did anyone have it in for Austin? *Absolutely not.*

The police's questions seemed endless while Ashlyn's went unanswered. *Why? Who?* And again, *Why?*

Ashlyn was frustrated that she couldn't give the police the information they were looking for. They asked the same questions so many times that Ashlyn felt they wanted her to change her answers. She knew she should be grateful that they were trying to solve the crime, but she felt angry instead. Her brother had been shot in cold blood, and here they were asking her the same questions.

Joe's best friend, Bob Bradley, worked for the Salt Lake Police Department in the Criminal Investigation Bureau, and he finally persuaded the investigators to stop the questioning and focus elsewhere. The forensics report came back showing that the bullet had come from a .45 and was a clean shot to the heart. Austin had died immediately. Whoever had shot him knew how to handle a gun.

The report also showed that the shot had come from the direction of Austin and Ashlyn's hike. But no clues were found in the secluded area, and since the ground was so rocky, no footprints were found. The authorities concluded that either someone had purposely shot Austin or had mistaken him for someone else. Either way, they told the family, it would be difficult to find the shooter.

On the morning of the funeral, the long-awaited white envelope arrived. Austin was to serve in Denmark. Since Laura was the only member of her family who had joined the Church, she had always hoped missionaries would one day touch her family's hearts as they had hers. She wept as Joe called the Church mission office to let them know the situation.

Ashlyn could hardly contain herself as they closed the coffin. Joe said a family prayer, the last they'd have with Austin. Tearfully, the family slowly made their way into the chapel, where Austin's friends sat together. They, too, were in tears. She glanced at Dave. He sat with his mother and stared straight ahead, a look of pain on his face. His mother cried.

After the family was seated, the congregation sang "How Great Thou Art," one of Austin's favorite hymns. The funeral continued with a eulogy given by Ashlyn—a beautiful talk that touched the congregation with laughter and tears—and with moving talks, songs, and testimonies. Another one of Austin's favorite hymns, "Abide With Me," closed the service, and the funeral was over.

Later that night, after friends and family had left, Ashlyn clung to the thought that her family would be together forever. She knew she would see Austin again. But that comfort always led her back to a whole trail of "whys," "what ifs," and "if onlys."

If only I hadn't thrown the Frisbee so far or *What if it had been me? Why him? Why not me? He had so much to give.*

The trail went on and on, but it always led to the same question: If someone was out to kill, why take one of the sweetest, purest people on earth when they could have taken her, a person with so little to offer anyone?

Late that night when the sorrow was unbearable, Ashlyn quietly made her way out the door and to the car. Hardly able to see through her tears, she drove to the cemetery and walked to her brother's grave. As she sat by the graveside, her body was racked with sobs.

"I'm so sorry, Austin," she cried. "So very, very, sorry. You deserved to live and I should be lying here. It was my fault. I never should have thrown that stupid Frisbee. I was trying to show off, and you paid the price for it. Please forgive me. Austin, you're the best friend I've ever had. Please don't leave me here."

Suddenly, Ashlyn remembered the words Austin had spoken the day he died.

"You have to find out for yourself. I can't do it for you."

Ashlyn lay by her brother's grave, trying to remember every detail of their last talk. It seemed like a lifetime ago. She cried until her body gave in to exhaustion and finally, with a tearstained face, she slept.

CHAPTER 1

After Austin's death, Bob and Janice Bradley had moved to Monroe, Colorado, where Bob had been promoted to police captain. His new job was a step down from aggressive police duty but allowed a quieter life than the Salt Lake Police Department had to offer. Although Bob kept close contact with Joe and Laura Lawrence, he had still found it difficult to leave—especially because Austin Lawrence's murder had never been solved.

Although it had now been a decade since the incident, Bob still felt he had failed the Lawrence family. Austin and Ashlyn Lawrence had almost been like his own kids, and he was frustrated that the case had gone cold. He'd exhausted all his resources, and still nothing turned up. He didn't know if the murder had been a random act of violence or if maybe someone out there still had a plan to carry out. He'd seen the forensics report. Considering the distance and accuracy of the shot, the shooter knew what he was doing. Yet the crime remained unsolved, and it was beyond Bob how Austin could have fit into a scheme of hate.

The family had been devastated by their loss, and yet their faith held them all together. Even Ashlyn had learned to work through her pain—more or less. The tragedy had struck her hardest of all. Bob knew that although she had accepted Austin's death, something inside her wasn't quite settled, a thought that concerned him deeply. Maybe one day she would find someone to confide in who would be able to help her work out her feelings. Until then, he knew she'd continue to hold something back.

Ashlyn made friends easily and had several who were close, but as far as Bob knew, she hadn't had a boyfriend since shortly after Austin's death. She had dated Dave for a little while until the day he came by and told her he was moving. He'd said he'd call her, and occasionally he still did. But she hadn't needed to lose someone else at that time. She'd been forced to deal with so much in her young life, but she rose to the occasion and succeeded. She had Bob's respect.

Ashlyn had loved Monroe the moment she moved in. It was a beautiful small town on the outskirts of Denver—far enough away from the city, yet close enough to have its own conveniences nearby. It was a pretty town with a main street that ran the length of the town, and it reminded Bob of a modern-day Mayberry. Although the town was fairly small—forty thousand—and had a fairly low crime rate, it still had a well-staffed police force. Ashlyn was one of the police detectives.

Bob was thrilled the day he got a call from Ashlyn inquiring about a detective position with the unit. She'd gone through the academy immediately after high school graduation, and it wasn't hard to guess that her brother's death had played a vital role in her career choice. She'd worked hard with many crime-prevention programs and had made a good name for herself as a detective. Bob had highly recommended her, but knew her merits got her the job. She had now been with the force almost three years and was a valuable asset to their close-knit team. She had a knack for detail and a keen instinct—two talents that had already served her well in her career.

Bob watched her from across the room and thought about his upcoming retirement. He knew she was taking the news of it a little hard; there was no question why. He was the only one besides her best friend, Kerry, a dispatcher, whom Ashlyn had confided in about her brother. Nearly everyone knew she had a brother who had been killed, but that was the extent of their knowledge. Only he had been there and understood, and now she was worried about him leaving the force.

Leaving *her* was more accurate, though it wasn't as if they wouldn't see each other again. Janice had taken Ashlyn under her wing the moment she moved to Monroe. The two women were very close, and Ashlyn had become the daughter Janice never had. Bob and Janice had secretly hoped that one of their four sons would have taken Ashlyn as a bride, but they knew that Ashlyn still needed time, so the opportunity never came to be.

As if his retirement wasn't bad enough, Ashlyn would also get a new boss. Bob tried to talk her into applying for the sergeant's position herself, but she had refused. Now the force had done a lateral hire, and Ashlyn would be working under Tyler O'Bryan, a guy Bob really liked and had met with on several occasions during the hiring process. O'Bryan was a driven cop who had more than earned his way to a higher position than a sergeant. He'd said that he wanted to leave the Los Angeles Police Department to live someplace safer. Monroe was that someplace, and he felt confident he could someday safely raise a family there. Bob respected him for that.

In going over Tyler's file, Bob realized that Tyler had seen his share of ugliness. In fact, Tyler had seen more in his thirty years of life than a lot of these cops probably would in their whole careers. Bob knew Tyler could handle the job.

Only the fact that Tyler was still single and possibly ready to settle down was cause for concern. With only one of the secretaries married, Bob worried about the other three, who were hot on the trail of a man.

But if Tyler could handle his one and only female detective, he could handle just about anyone. Bob attributed several of his gray hairs to supervising Ashlyn. She stuck to the rules, but she could find so many amazing ways to stretch them. He knew

Ashlyn wouldn't be chasing after her boss since she wasn't a flirt like the secretaries; her career was first in her life. She was a go-getter, but then again, Tyler's file indicated that he was too. Bob hoped he would give Ashlyn the freedom she needed to do her job well.

He'd love to be a fly on the wall when those two met. If Ashlyn would give Tyler a chance, Bob knew it would all work out just fine. But, as it was, she wasn't happy about his retirement, let alone a new change in office management. Luckily, she knew the others filling in the different positions, and they all respected and liked her. She'd be fine, and Bob knew it. He just had to get past this parental instinct that he had. Tyler was a good man and would be fair. At least he *hoped* he would, or Ashlyn would give him a good piece of her mind, which could possibly put her job on the line. Maybe he'd better warn Tyler. Or was it Ashlyn who needed the warning? He'd warn them both and leave with a clear conscience.

* * *

Ashlyn looked at her coworkers with dismay and thought, *I don't believe this!* True, in her line of work one needed all the laughter and celebration one could find. Law officers saw so much hatred and crime that they looked for any excuse to celebrate, but a party to celebrate the captain leaving seemed . . . well . . . wrong!

Okay, Ashlyn thought, *not having a retirement party would have been disrespectful, but celebrating when a person leaves . . . isn't that a little harsh? Besides, I just don't think he's ready to retire. I'm not ready to have him retire!*

But she knew she'd see Bob and his family often. In fact, she would see him and his wife the next day, since Janice was throwing a retirement party of her own and had invited most of their close friends. Yet still, Ashlyn had found strength and comfort in knowing Bob supported her in her job. Now, not only would he be gone, but she also had a new boss coming in because the old lieutenant was stepping up into the captain's position. She was less than thrilled with the idea.

Reluctantly, Ashlyn's thoughts returned to the moment at hand. Everyone knew the captain was a member of the Church, and in respect to that—and to all the officers on duty—punch and soda were the only beverages served. Only a handful of the force was LDS, and Ashlyn felt grateful that religion didn't separate this group.

When everyone raised his or her paper cup to salute the captain, Ashlyn felt as if it were a twenty-one-gun salute. Tears threatened in her eyes, and she looked toward the ceiling, a trick she'd learned to keep from crying. Although it was a good idea, it wasn't a very effective one, since it failed more times than it succeeded; one tear escaped the corner of her eye. She tried to make a quiet exit to the rest room, but someone tapped her shoulder.

"Oh hi, Shirley." Ashlyn suppressed a moan. "I didn't see you coming."

Shirley would be the new sergeant's secretary and was far from being one of Ashlyn's favorite people. Shirley had sent an e-mail to all the single women in the force that said she had dibs on the new sergeant. After all, she would *work closely with him, and it's only right.*

Remembering the memo, Ashlyn laughed at the thought of Shirley's desperate attempt to get a man.

"You just answered my question," Shirley said with a forced smile.

"How did I do that? I never even heard the question."

"Well, honey, you looked like you were really close to tears, but then you just laughed, so I assume you're all right."

Ashlyn forced herself not to roll her eyes. Shirley was the queen of gossip. She had a clever way of finding out everything about anything, and any tidbit of information she could find became breaking news.

"Of course I'm all right," Ashlyn said. "My contacts are getting to me. I think I need to rewet them. Excuse me."

Now that was a good excuse. I wonder if she'll buy it. Ashlyn looked at the expression on Shirley's face. *Nope, she didn't.*

Shirley spoke in an accusing voice. "I wasn't aware that you started wearing contacts. I thought your eyes were perfect, like the rest of you."

Ashlyn bristled. She had come into this job looking forward to meeting new faces. But the instant the two women had met, it was obvious Shirley disliked Ashlyn. She was often cold and sarcastic, throwing little digs and sarcastic comments at Ashlyn any chance she had. But Ashlyn had made it a goal years ago not to cower to anyone or let anyone make her feel inadequate. It was a self-preservation tactic. She found it interesting that the hoodlums she had arrested would call her every name in the book and it never bothered her. But for some reason, Shirley's behavior did. Ashlyn figured that perhaps the criminals were merely lashing out at being caught, whereas Shirley's behavior was personal. True, it did bother her to be on the receiving end of Shirley's hatred, but then again, Ashlyn realized they had a definite personality clash and therefore spent little time dwelling on it.

Ashlyn had a second thought. She was known to be one of the Mormons in the office and therefore had an example to live up to. Perhaps telling the truth was the better way to go. To have the Church misjudged on account of her behavior was the last thing Ashlyn needed on her shoulders.

"Actually, Shirley," she said, "I don't wear contacts. I'm just feeling a little sentimental with this retirement party, and a little embarrassed that I can't control my emotions."

Ashlyn was pleased at Shirley's reaction to her honesty. She appeared to be taken aback by it, as well as a bit disappointed that her game plan to gossip about "the emotionally imbalanced Ashlyn" had been thwarted. "Uh, Shirley," Ashlyn probed, "did you need something? The water faucets in my eyes seemed to have turned off now. You stopped me from making an exit, so what did you want?"

Shirley's eyes narrowed. "I did want to talk to you about something, but before I forget, Captain Bradley wants to see you in his office before you leave. You *are* leaving, aren't you?"

Ashlyn smiled. "Of course I am. Unless you want me to stay?"

Shirley shifted from one foot to the other. "I just thought you might want to get some sleep before you go on shift tonight. We wouldn't want anything to happen to you because you weren't wide awake, now would we?"

Ashlyn chuckled. "Well, I don't know about you, but I certainly don't. Think of all the paperwork you'd have to do!" Ashlyn paused. "Shirley, let's not play any more games here. You don't think much of me, and I know it. I don't know what I've done to offend you. Maybe someday you'll tell *me* instead of everybody *but* me. Either way, you must have stopped me for something important, so what is it?"

Shirley's eyes narrowed. "I do too think highly of you. You're one of the best women cops I know."

"Oh, come on, Shirley, that's not going to fly with me."

"Okay, you're right. I don't like you. You walk around here thinking you're Miss High and Mighty. Sorry to break it to you, honey, but you're the only one thinking it."

"I'm sorry you feel that way. Now that we have that squared away, just tell me why you stopped me." Although Ashlyn put up a good front, Shirley's words had truly hurt.

Shirley glared at Ashlyn. "I heard something about the new sergeant coming in from L.A. I thought you'd be interested."

"If it has nothing to do with my job," Ashlyn said with a shrug, "I'm not."

"Oh," Shirley said snidely, "I think it might affect your work."

"Alright," Ashlyn said, losing patience with Shirley's attempts to bait her, "but first tell me your sources of information."

"I can't do that."

"Then how do I know it's reliable?"

"I promise it is. But it's also privileged."

Shirley obviously wanted Ashlyn to hear the tidbit of gossip she had picked up. Ashlyn turned to walk away. "I'm concerned about you, Shirley. I really am," she said with a smile.

"Wait! I'll tell you what I know! I heard that our new Sergeant Tyler O'Bryan is a real looker and that he's coming here to look for a wife!" Shirley could scarcely contain her excitement.

Ashlyn rolled her eyes. "And this concerns my job . . . how?"

"I didn't say it *concerns* your job, I said it may *affect* your job. I'm here to help you understand that it doesn't *concern* you or your job."

"Why, Miss Shirley, I do believe there is a hidden message here. Could it be you're telling me that you have first dibs on the new sergeant, so all the rest of us poor, single females must keep our hands to ourselves until further notice?"

"See? I knew you were a good detective!"

Ashlyn burst out laughing. "Shirley, what makes you think anyone would listen to your warning? Even more, who in their right mind would come to Monroe of all places to search for a wife? And last, what makes you think I would be interested in all this gossip anyway?"

"You're absolutely right, Ashlyn," Shirley said angrily. "You wouldn't be interested in this news because you *have* no love life. Not one man here even *looks* at you as anything other than one of the guys. There's not a feminine bone in your body. But hey, I'm not judging. One less single female on the market means less competition for me—"

A deep voice from behind Shirley cut off her tirade. "That's enough, Shirley! Go somewhere and retract those claws."

Ashlyn looked up at her good friend, Eric Christensen. Eric was one of three sergeants from the unit, and he had trained

Ashlyn when she first moved to Monroe. Eric was a good man and the secret love interest of her best friend, Kerry.

Shirley recovered quickly. "Oh, Sergeant Christensen! I was just talking to Ashlyn about the difficulties we women have in this man's world."

"Don't take me for a fool, Shirley," Eric responded sternly.

Shirley looked sheepish and stomped off as Ashlyn smiled at her friend.

"Thanks, Eric," she said quietly.

Eric shook his head. "She can be pretty vicious. The sooner she gets her man, the more peace we'll all have."

"You're telling me!"

"Her words were pretty harsh. Are you okay?"

"Yeah, sure. The day Shirley breaks me is the day I put in for a transfer!" Ashlyn laughed, trying to lighten the mood.

"Hey, the elders have a service project tomorrow. Someone bought the Jones place out on Riley Lane, and we thought we'd help them move in. I realize you've got the night shift, but if you have any extra energy, we could use the help."

Eric was the elders quorum president in their ward. He had welcomed Ashlyn into the ward the first Sunday she attended church and introduced her to others. When she arrived at work the next day and realized he was also her colleague, she felt like she already had a friend in the force. He'd then introduced her to Kerry. She and Ashlyn had hit it off so well that when Kerry's rent went up and she started to look for another apartment, Ashlyn invited her to move in with her. The house they rented, though small, was plenty for the two of them. They were now best friends.

"I'm so jealous! I love that house!" Ashlyn exclaimed. "But I'll see what I can do about helping them move in. How much help do you have so far?"

"Well, let's see. Brandon Hooper, Chris Jacoby, Danielle Franks, Landon Frost, and Kerry. Landon and Danielle can only help for a short time, though."

"How big is the family moving in and what time will you be starting?"

"About the family I don't know. And then we'll probably be there from ten until whenever."

"Okay," Ashlyn said. "Plan on me bringing lunch for everyone. I'll show up as soon as I can."

"Thanks, Ashlyn." Eric smiled before turning to walk away.

It would be nice if he and Kerry could get together, Ashlyn thought, but if they hadn't by now, she wondered if they ever would. Eric didn't seem to see Kerry as more than a friend, and Kerry refused to be the pursuer. *Still, they'd be good for each other,* Ashlyn thought.

As Ashlyn looked back at the party, she wished she hadn't come. She wanted to leave now and be alone with her thoughts. As she turned to go, she remembered that the captain wanted to see her.

CHAPTER 2

Ashlyn followed Bob into an office that seemed awfully cold and empty now that he was leaving it. Most of his things had already been packed away into cardboard boxes.

Bob closed the door behind them. "Ashlyn, I probably should have taken this opportunity long before now, but I didn't quite know how to bring it up. I don't have much of a knack for words, but I'm talking to you as a friend now, so I hope you listen with your heart and not your head."

Ashlyn noticed that he was beginning to sweat. "You're worrying me. Are you all right?"

"I'm fine."

"Janice?" Ashlyn's concern rose.

"She's fine."

"The family?" Now she was almost panicked.

"Ashlyn, everyone is fine," Bob said with frustration. "Everything is fine except my nerves! I'm worried about you."

"That's it?" Ashlyn asked, incredulous. "That's what you're so nervous about?"

"I'm trying to tell you!" the captain snapped, then stopped, drawing in a deep breath. "Are you happy? I mean, is your life in line with what your goals always were?"

"Bob, do you feel all right?" She eyed him closely.

"You know what? Never mind. Have a good day, and I'll be sure to see you tomorrow at the church for the party."

"This must really be something big," Ashlyn said. "Now that you've piqued my curiosity, I'm not going to just dismiss it. Let me make it easier for you. I guess I'm happy. Why? Am I being suspended or something? Does the force want me to transfer?"

"Good heavens, no!"

"Then, Bob, just tell me." Ashlyn's lips turned up in a slight grin.

"I'm just concerned that you don't have a special someone in your life."

"Now you're starting to sound like Mom. Has she been talking to you about wanting to hear the patter of little feet around Grandma's house?"

"She's mentioned it. But this has nothing to do with her. I'm worried about you, and I want you to be happy." Suddenly, he showed great interest in the thin layer of dust on his desk.

"Is this really a talk for the office? Maybe we can continue this . . . this interrogation on the home front?" Ashlyn shifted nervously in her seat.

"I just want to know why you're putting your career first."

"I don't know. Maybe Mr. Right figured I was Ms. Wrong and found Ms. Right in the wrong place." Ashlyn smiled. *How clever was that?* In reality, this conversation made her feel uncomfortable. She didn't want to analyze this part of her life, and she didn't want anyone else to do it either.

"You know that's not right. You have half the single men in this unit, not to mention those in four other districts, drooling when they see you, and unless they're a doped-up criminal, you don't even notice they exist."

"That's not true. I date, but it does take two, you know."

"But you never date the same guy more than two or three times."

"Bob, you're out of line here. My love life doesn't concern you—or Shirley, for that matter. I don't want to seem disrespectful, but I don't care to discuss this with you."

"Shirley? What does she have to do with this?"

"Nothing, except that like you, she has taken an active interest in my love life," Ashlyn answered defensively.

"If you at least were trying to find someone," he muttered, "I wouldn't be worried."

"Bob, where is this little talk of ours going? Because I'm getting a little offended, and I'm ready to walk out."

Bob took a deep breath. "Here it is, straight. I watched you as a child and a teenager try to go after the things you wanted most in your life. You had such ambition, and you always got what you wanted. Then life took a tragic turn and changed us all a little bit. Not a bit . . . a lot."

Bob lowered his voice, and Ashlyn winced at the pain in his voice. "When Austin died, I suspect so did some of your dreams. I remember when you married everything off from your Barbies to the dogs. Your life, you said, would be inside a white picket fence. That life has never come to pass, and I wonder if it's because of your pain. But you need to remember that our Heavenly Father wants us to be happy and not go through life with a heavy and burdened heart. I think your heart is heavy, Ashlyn, and that worries me."

"How else was I supposed to react?"

"Like you always have—with ambition and determination. Remember that our Heavenly Father knows us perfectly and knows what's best for us, including Austin. Surely His knowledge is greater than ours. We just have to have faith in Him. If we don't, well, that doesn't change what happened, it just makes us more miserable because we refuse to trust His will." Bob walked over to the window and stared in deep thought.

He turned to Ashlyn and continued. "Our Heavenly Father wants us to have joy. And happiness. But we need to look for those opportunities that give us joy. If we don't, what would be the purpose for existing?"

Without waiting for an answer, he continued, "I know you became a cop out of respect to Austin. This would never have been your original career choice, and we both know it. But you're good at it, and the captain in me commends you. But the friend in me who loves you wants to tell you to go home and follow your original dreams. It is more honorable to Austin's memory to live than it is to build up some kind of monument because he died."

Ashlyn had been listening so intently that she didn't realize she was crying. "I don't know how," she whispered. "What right do I have to be happy when he never got the same chance?'

"What makes you think he's not happy? Do you really believe that if God's plan was to take Austin for a special purpose that only Austin could fulfill, that God would have taken his happiness away?"

"I never saw it that way." She was comforted a little, but still, her heart was heavy. "Do you really think that Austin has found true happiness?"

"Sweetheart, how could he not have? It's part of the eternal plan. Why do you think it's sometimes referred to as the great plan of happiness? So live well and be happy. Life can be extraordinary if we allow it to be." He smiled through his tears and whispered, "I miss him too."

"That's a lot to think about." Ashlyn wanted to absorb everything Bob had said, but it was all a little overwhelming.

"Well, if I know you, you'll give it some thought. You'll analyze it, dissect it, but I also ask that you ponder, fast, and pray about it."

"Why are you telling me this here and now?" Ashlyn asked, confused.

Bob shifted slightly by the window. "I guess because I won't be here to look out for you. To tell you the truth, I'd like to see you leave with me. I know that won't happen, but I wanted you to think about the direction your life is going and consider if this is what you want. If it is, you have my full support, and you know that. If it's not and you're doing this out of some misguided duty to your brother, I think you need to examine your priorities. If this is what you truly want, then please, for your own sake, create happiness, because that will sustain throughout life. Think about it. Will you do that for me?"

"Yeah, I'll do that. I still wonder why you brought this up, though."

Bob rubbed his face with both hands. "Ashlyn, I honestly don't know why. I've thought about it in the past and considered talking to you before, but it was never the right time. For some reason, it seemed important today. Maybe I felt prompted. I don't know. I'm not even sure I've said everything I've meant to say. I just want you to know that you don't have to do it all alone."

"Are you trying to arrange a marriage for me?" she asked, trying to lighten the mood.

"No! Can't you just take the advice for what it's worth?"

"I guess I've never known you to play Cupid."

"And I'm not about to start now. Can't you trust me? I've no hidden agenda or ulterior motives. I'm just worried about you."

"And that's it? Nothing else to it?"

"Now *you're* beginning to get on *my* nerves. That's it, Ashlyn. That's all there is to it. Think about what I've said, and I won't bring it up again."

Ashlyn stood and hugged her very dear friend. "Thank you. You can tell my parents you did your best and gave me a few things to think about."

Bob laughed. "This talk is between you and me and doesn't leave this room. One more thing. You know the new guy, Tyler? He's a good man, and if you will allow the hand of leadership to have some influence over you, he could probably teach you a few things."

"Are you trying to tell me to be nice to the new kid on the block?"

"Yeah." Bob grinned. "Something like that."

"Okay, Daddy." She hugged him again.

"Hey, I take that as a compliment."

"Thanks, Bob," she said sincerely.

"For what?"

Ashlyn smiled. "Everything. Thank you." Ashlyn turned and left. It had been a good talk, and she knew she'd have some thinking to do. Despite Bob's retirement party, the day hadn't turned out so bad after all.

* * *

At 1:00 A.M. on Saturday, Ashlyn found herself driving to the scene of an accident. Officer Jeff Thomas was the first police officer on site and called for Ashlyn's backup. The driver of the car was obviously drunk and had passed out. When Ashlyn stepped beside the driver, the strong smell of alcohol nauseated her. The driver had thrown up at some point, and it took everything Ashlyn had in her not to follow suit. The ambulance arrived, and the paramedics removed the driver from the car while Ashlyn investigated the scene of the accident.

Idiot! Ashlyn fumed. *The guy tried to take out the light pole by wrapping his car around it. He's lucky he didn't take himself or someone else out in the process!*

It wasn't hard to gather the evidence for the accident. After supervising the routine blood-alcohol tests at the hospital, Ashlyn decided to head to the tavern that she suspected the driver had come from to talk to the bar owner, Sam Murphy. Sam was in his midfifties and was short and stocky with thinning gray hair. From all appearances, he had a rough exterior and tried to run his business with as few problems as possible. He obviously didn't like cops and wanted them to stay away because they were bad for his business. Ashlyn liked him though. She didn't like his business or the deadly effects it could have on customers. But she couldn't fault Sam for the choices his customers made. Every once in a while she thought she'd see a soft spot in him. But she knew very little of him. He would never speak unless spoken to and wouldn't give information willingly.

Once she arrived at the tavern, she made her way through the crowd over to the bar. The tavern was small and dimly lit. Square wooden tables and chairs sat around the room. The bar, where Sam always stood, ran along the distance of the far wall. He was at the opposite end of the counter, so Ashlyn sat up to the bar and took a look at the scene around her. People laughed and some even slept, passed out in a drunken stupor. The room smelled of stale smoke and alcohol. Music played loudly over the speakers.

"What'll it be, sweetie?" Ashlyn turned to look up into Sam's eyes. "Now what do you want? We're all on our best behavior, minding our own business, so how can I help to make your visit brief?"

"Hi, Sam!" she said, unaffected by his dismissal. "It's a thrill for me to be back. I need to ask some questions."

"Shocker," Sam grumbled.

"Why, Sam, if I didn't know better, I'd say you're still a little irate with me over citing the place for not abiding by alcohol laws."

"Wow, you're wise beyond your years."

"If you'd be a good boy, I wouldn't have to slap your hands. Now, to change the subject, does the name Charlie Wilson ring a bell?"

"No." But his eyes narrowed in thought.

"Liar. He just tried to eat a light post. Was he alone?"

Sam shrugged. "Don't know."

"What did he drink and how much?"

"I don't know." He leaned a hip against the counter and folded his arms across his chest.

"Come on, Sam. I'm not the enemy here. Help me out or I'll just have to go around flashing my badge and talking to anyone and everyone to get some answers. Hate to spoil all of your fun here, but I've got a job to do. So I am going to ask you one more time. Do you know a Charlie Wilson who may have come in here tonight?"

Sam looked at Ashlyn reluctantly and answered, "Yeah, he was here. The guy had a death wish. Drank straight whiskey and added up a big bill until I told him he'd had enough. I told him he wasn't leaving until he sobered up. I even offered him some coffee. He laughed and said he had a designated driver. I refused him service, and he got mad and started running off at the mouth, so we booted him out the door. Contrary to what you may think, I don't want my customers dead or to take a chance at getting some lawsuit slapped on me."

"Does he come here often?"

"First time. I remembered the name because the credit card he gave me to pay the bill was declined. He said I was ripping him off because he knew dang well the card worked because he'd just deposited some big money. He finally paid cash, though, and he had a big wad of that. That's all there is to it. You're bad for business, so will you go now?"

Ashlyn smiled. "I'm out of here. Thanks, Sam."

"When you decide to lighten up, come back and I'll fix you up with something that'll make you feel real good."

"Sorry, Sam," she replied. "Somehow I think that any drink you might offer me would be mixed with arsenic. Good night."

"Come back when you can't stay so long," Sam said with a laugh and went back to wiping down the counter.

Sam isn't a mean person, Ashlyn thought on her way out the door. He just felt like the law was for everyone but him. He tried to ignore the liquor laws every chance he could, but he was right in saying that he tried to avoid lawsuits and trouble. He also tried to stay on the good side of the police by cooperating as he had tonight. Thanks to Sam, Ashlyn could go back to the precinct and finish up the reports, hopefully by the end of her shift.

CHAPTER 3

Tired and grateful to be home at last, Ashlyn was pleased that she was getting more used to the graveyard shift. Since it would be hers for the next two months, the sooner she adjusted to it, the better. She dressed for bed and snuggled gratefully under the covers. Still, as tired as she was, sleep evaded her. Her talks with Shirley and Bob kept running through her head.

Where does she get off making comments about my love life? Ashlyn fumed. *What did she imply? It couldn't be over the new boss coming in. I've never given Shirley cause to believe that I'd compete with her for a man, let alone for my boss, for crying out loud. What did I do that gave Shirley the impression that I think I'm so superior?* She scrunched the pillow under her neck and stared up at the ceiling. *Forget about what Shirley said. What was Bob implying?*

As hard as it was to explain, even to herself, Ashlyn was touched by Bob's words. They helped return the peace of mind she'd lost so long ago and gave her new ideas to consider.

If Austin were here, what would he say to me? Ashlyn wondered. *That he's disappointed in the way I've lived my life, or that he's pleased at what I've tried to accomplish in his behalf? Would he tell me Bob's right—that I shouldn't go through life alone?*

Ashlyn sat up in bed. *Even if I wanted to open my heart to someone, I wouldn't know where to begin. I've tried so hard to live my life in a way that Austin would be proud of. The problem is,*

I've stopped living my life so that I could keep Austin's alive. In the process, I've lost sight of everything I've ever wanted.

She pulled her pillow into her lap. *If they'd only caught the guy, then . . . then what? Justice would be served? If the person had been caught, would the darkness and loneliness that consumes me go away? There is nothing . . . nothing that could fill the emptiness inside me, not even an eternal companion. It's been a pain for too long. I wouldn't know how to begin to change the path I've chosen or lessen the hurt inside. No matter how much I wish I could.*

The day Austin died was the day she stopped living, and now she was just going through the motions. The murder had been ten years ago, and since then she had wanted to be alone. Now she wanted people around her. Her emotions were so conflicting. Inevitably, the tears began to fall.

She was in such deep thought that she didn't hear her room-mate come in. Suddenly she felt Kerry's arm around her, and Ashlyn leaned into her friend's shoulder and cried. Kerry was such a good friend.

She didn't say a word until Ashlyn gained some control of her emotions. Then she asked gently, "Hey, did you have an ugly night?"

Ashlyn tried to smile. "It wasn't so bad, actually."

"Then why so glum, chum?"

"I guess I'm just overly tired," Ashlyn said evasively.

Her friend looked at her with obvious disbelief. "Yeah, I buy that. You don't have to tell me if you're not ready to. Just tell me that you'll be okay."

Ashlyn nodded. "I'm fine. Are you headed somewhere?"

Kerry grinned. "To see Eric."

Surprised, Ashlyn blurted, "He finally asked you out?"

The smile disappeared. "No. He won't do that until donkeys fly. But thanks for the reminder." She flipped her strawberry-blonde hair behind her shoulder. "He set up a few people to help somebody move in to the Jones place and I said I'd help."

Ashlyn grimaced. "Oh, I forgot! I said I'd help too."

Kerry shrugged. "I wouldn't worry about it. I'll tell him you had a long night. Have you even been to bed yet?"

"No, but I have too much on my mind to sleep." She glanced at the clock. "It's almost ten now, so go ahead without me. I'll shower and pick up some lunch at the store. I'll meet you there."

Ashlyn thought about what a good friend Kerry was. She constantly did small, thoughtful deeds and had a warm personality that made one feel immediately accepted. She could find the bright side in anything, and she was good for Ashlyn's morale. Like herself, Kerry was twenty-seven and a fitness guru. The roommates often lifted weights, ran, and did aerobics together.

The biggest difference between them was that Kerry accepted dates as often as Ashlyn turned them down. Sure, Ashlyn dated now and then—and they had even double-dated once or twice—but so far the only eternal feeling Ashlyn had experienced was the eternal boredom on last Saturday's blind date with Grant Farlow, the nephew of her well-meaning neighbors, Ray and Issie.

By the time Ashlyn had showered and dressed and was on her way to the house, it was after eleven. The smell of the pizza on the back seat of her silver Pathfinder made her mouth water. She hadn't eaten since the retirement party the day before, and her stomach was growling. She had stopped off at the store for drinks, salad, doughnuts, and paper goods before stopping at the pizza place.

The Jones place was down a narrow, quiet lane on the outskirts of town. Ashlyn had always loved the house, but when it had come up for sale, it was sold before she had a chance to even check the asking price. But it didn't matter. She'd never be able to afford this beautiful home with the rock front and wide, wraparound porch. The yard was beautifully landscaped with shade and pine trees in a natural setting. The Rocky Mountains rose in the distance. Certainly the sunsets would be something miraculous to behold from the porch.

As she pulled to a stop in front of the house, Ashlyn wondered about the family who had bought the large home.

Eric and Chris came down the ramp of the moving truck carrying a large, heavy dresser. Two men she didn't recognize followed with king-size box springs.

"Hi!" Ashlyn called. "Anyone ready for a lunch break?"

Eric smiled. "Man, did you come at the right time. Please tell me you brought some drinks." Without setting down the dresser, he made introductions. "Ashlyn, this is Rory and Conner, friends of the new owner. This is Ashlyn."

The guys put down their box springs to walk over to shake her hand. Rory spoke first. "For some reason, the water didn't get turned on. A few of the other guys went into town to find out why. In the meanwhile, we've been dying of thirst."

"Well, you're in luck," Ashlyn said. "I brought drinks, ice, and cups. If you're ready to take a break, I'll get it all from the car."

"Let me help," Conner offered, heading in that direction before she could protest.

Soon everyone had their fill of pizza, drinks, salad, and doughnuts and headed back to work. Ashlyn sat in the kitchen admiring the view out the back window.

Kerry joined her. "Deep in thought again. Now you're really starting to worry me."

Ashlyn cupped her chin in the palm of her hand with a deep sigh. "I'm dreading Monday morning is all. I don't want a new boss."

"Um, Ashlyn—"

She cut her friend off. "No, let me finish. I know what you're going to say—give him a chance, blah, blah, blah. But why does he think he can walk in and take over? He's not even from around here, and he knows nothing of our unit. He'll probably have the personality of a wet noodle and live for his authoritative little title. He'll come in and change things that don't need changing just because Mr. Big is from the LAPD. To top it off, he probably wears a toupee and has smelly sweat stains under his arms."

Ashlyn felt the hair rise on the back of her neck as she saw the horrified look on Kerry's face. Slowly, she turned toward the open doorway. There stood the most gorgeous man she had ever laid eyes on. His arms were folded across his broad chest as he leaned his hip against the kitchen counter.

He looked Ashlyn in the eye, raised an eyebrow, and said, "Gee, I hope my deodorant doesn't fail me."

Ashlyn felt sick inside. *What have I done?* she thought. *Open mouth, insert not only my foot but my entire body!*

The look on Kerry's face mirrored her embarrassment. "Ashlyn, this is the new home owner, Tyler O'Bryan. That would be *Sergeant* O'Bryan, to you. Your new boss."

Ashlyn tried to force a weak smile but failed miserably. All she could think was that now would be a good time to discontinue the use of her spot on the planet. After turning three shades of red, she at last found her voice. "Welcome to Monroe, Mr. O'Bryan."

"Am I?" he asked. "I wasn't under that impression."

Kerry quickly excused herself, and Ashlyn finally managed a weak smile. "I'm afraid you caught me at a disadvantage."

"I'm afraid you're right. I'm waiting to see how you'll squirm out of it." Tyler walked over to join her at the table, his midnight-blue eyes sparkling.

Ashlyn was quiet, trying to think of an intelligent comment.

"You seem suddenly to have become a woman of very few words."

"Yes," was all she could think to say.

"Then allow me to talk. Thank you for bringing us lunch. Things haven't run as smooth as I'd hoped this morning, so lunch was a pleasant surprise. Can I reimburse you for the cost of the food? I certainly don't expect you to pay for it."

"You think *you've* had a bad morning?" Ashlyn responded weakly. "How would you like to be in *my* shoes right now? If I say lunch is my treat, is there any chance you'll let those few tiny comments you overheard fly by unnoticed?"

"No. I'd rather buy lunch and watch you squirm."

He smiled and Ashlyn melted. "Would it help if I apologize?"

"Only if you mean it."

"Okay, I'm sorry I accused you of wearing a toupee. I can clearly see I was mistaken."

"Wow," he said sarcastically. "That was sincere."

"And I don't see any sweat stains," she continued.

"I believe there were a few other things you mentioned. Something about pasta?" he questioned, raising an eyebrow.

"Yeah, well, I can't *sincerely* apologize for that one. I still don't know if you have the personality of a wet noodle or not."

"Fine," he said, obviously enjoying his advantage. "I'll let that one slide on a technicality for now. Anything else?"

"Not that I can think of," Ashlyn said innocently.

"Think harder."

His eyes narrowed, but all Ashlyn noticed was how expressive they were. "Maybe there was a little something in there about a Mr. Big from the LAPD."

"Something like that."

"Oh, fine!" she said, and paused, thinking of the right thing to say. "I guess I'm just worried about what changes you'll make and if I'll be back to square one at the precinct. It's nothing personal to you, although you may have gotten that impression."

"I can't imagine what would have given me that idea."

"I'm sorry. It was uncalled for," she relented. She couldn't help but smile. This man made her knees weak.

Rory walked in before Tyler could respond. "Get your lazy body off that chair and get to work," he said. "Although I hate to interrupt, we'd hoped to get you moved in before the winter snow sets in. Besides, you said this would be fun and I'm *not* having fun."

Ashlyn laughed as she stood. "Where do you want me to work?"

"Wait a minute," Rory replied. "I meant him, not you."

"Yeah," Ashlyn grinned, "but if you don't put me to work I'm going to fall asleep."

Tyler looked up at her. "Gee, thanks. I didn't realize I was such great company—in addition to all the other shining attributes you mentioned."

Ashlyn blushed. "It's not you. I just came off the night shift, and it's catching up with me."

"Oh yes, the beloved night shift," Tyler said ruefully. "Is it luck that *my* first shift is graveyard, or is that the way the unit welcomes me to Monroe?"

"Why, Sergeant, Monroe welcomes you! Well, everyone but me, that is. But really, it's purely coincidental." Ashlyn tried to keep from laughing at the look on Tyler's face. It was a cross between offense and disbelief.

"Yeah, right."

"No, really," she said. "You have three single secretaries counting down the hours to your arrival. But Shirley has first dibs on you. The rest of the unit is thrilled that you've joined us. Except maybe for Terry Thornhill. You stepped on his toes when you got the position and he didn't. He's a real forgiving man, though. A couple of doughnuts and some hot chocolate as a peace offering and he'll be good as new. Then there's me. How you treat me will determine whether or not I welcome you." Ashlyn smiled.

Rory chuckled. "How does ol' Tyler have to treat you to be welcomed?"

Now Ashlyn turned beet red. The men stood biting their lower lips, trying to contain their laughter.

"I mean how he treats me on the job, not me personally." Ashlyn couldn't contain her own laughter. "I can see that I'll have to keep on my toes around here."

"I knew what you meant," Tyler said, "and you don't have to worry about Rory. He's going back to L.A. along with Conner. I only brought them with me because they're cheap labor. That's about all they're good for."

Rory turned in mock offense. "Now I *am* leaving. If I want this kind of abuse, I can go home and get it from my wife. At least she's a lot prettier than you, Tyler."

"I'm sure she appreciates your loyalty," Ashlyn laughed. "If you two will excuse me, I'll go help the movers while you two argue over who is the prettiest." She walked out the door.

Tyler watched her retreat. "Rory, old pal, you were right, she is beautiful!" Tyler had every detail of Ashlyn's face engraved in his memory. Her nose crinkled when she laughed, her cheeks turned red when she was embarrassed—and she embarrassed easily—and she had slight dimples in her cheeks when she smiled. There was also something about her eyes. They reflected . . . he didn't know what they reflected, but he wanted to find out. Tyler noticed she was tall, probably about 5'8", with finely toned arms, long legs, and a trim figure. In short, she was breathtaking.

"Hello? Earth to Tyler."

Rory's words brought Tyler back to his senses. "What did you say?"

Rory laughed. "Oh, man, you're whipped."

"What are you talking about?"

"We're in Monroe all of five hours, and the first female you lay your eyes on, you're smitten with. Have you two set a date?"

"A date for what?"

"A date with destiny, you dope. What do you think? I walked in here and found ol' Tyler, a confirmed bachelor, drooling over one of his employees. It was disgusting!"

Tyler groaned and rubbed his eyes with the back of his hands as he stood.

"What's wrong?" Rory asked. "All of a sudden you look like you just got smacked."

"I did," Tyler said. "Right between the eyes. She's a cop, Rory. She's under my authority. I can't touch her with a ten-foot pole."

"Why? Don't tell me you're sticking to that pathetic rule of yours not to date cops. I know your relationship with Jessica was stressful, but she's not even in the same league as Ashlyn. Besides, no dating within the force varies from unit to unit, and here you're the boss. Just ask her out."

"No."

"You make simple things complicated," Rory smirked.

"And you make complicated things seem too simple."

"What is so complicated?" Rory shrugged. "You like her, you ask her out."

"Then what? Take her out a few times, then break up and still have to work together? Too complicated."

"Or," Rory said, "you take her out a few times, fall in love, and set a wedding date. No mess."

"I'm not about to lose my focus and get shot again. Next time the guy might have better aim. I'd like to be around to see my children grow up."

Rory raised an eyebrow. "What children?"

"End of subject, Rory. I said no."

"Then you're a fool. You liked her immediately."

"She doesn't even want me here."

"Okay, so let that be your excuse. Everybody will buy it except you and me." He turned toward the door then back to his friend. "You know what your problem is? You're scared. You're scared to fall for somebody because you don't want to lose her. You know what? I was right where you are a year ago—until I met Kate—so I know where you're coming from. But I was wrong and so are you. There's nothing in the world like coming home to a wife who loves you. Going home to a big, empty house is a lousy way to live and you know it."

"Back off, Rory," Tyler said, but he looked at the doorway Ashlyn had walked through moments before. "I don't intend to stay single all my life. I just haven't met the right one yet." He hoped it was true.

"Yeah, whatever," Rory replied as he led the way back out of the kitchen toward the moving van.

CHAPTER 4

Ashlyn carried a box labeled "bathroom" from the moving van up onto the porch. As she entered the front door, she almost ran into Tyler. Her heart skipped a beat. "Hey, Sarge," she said. "This box says 'bathroom.' Would that be the one upstairs, downstairs, or at the back of the house? You've got a very nonspecific box here."

Tyler grinned. "If it's the box with deodorant in it, it goes in the bathroom upstairs to the left."

"Very funny," she replied as she pushed past him and headed for the stairs. Despite herself, she sighed. She'd never forget the way they met in a million years. When she'd turned and had seen him leaning against the counter, her heart dropped to her stomach. She'd never had such a reaction to a man. On the other hand, she'd never seen such a man. His hair was such a dark shade of brown that it was almost black. His eyes were dark blue, his nose was slender, and he had high cheekbones. He had long, dark eyelashes, and he always seemed to be smiling. The dark blue T-shirt he wore enhanced his eyes, and his jeans were well-worn and fit perfectly on his trim body. She figured he was about 6'4" and could tell he was lean and muscular.

You noticed all this at first glance? she asked herself as she climbed the stairs. She hoped she hadn't been staring. *Please tell me I wasn't staring!*

Ashlyn walked through the doorway that led to the master bedroom and saw Kerry handing Eric various tools. It looked

more like they were performing surgery than putting together a
bed frame. "Well," she said, "if it isn't the sea captain who
jumped ship when the seas got a little rough."

Kerry looked up at the sound of her roommate's voice, but
Eric looked studiously at the tip of his screwdriver, trying to
hold back a grin.

"Oh, that's just great," Ashlyn said sarcastically. "I see she's
already told you all about my first encounter with the boss man.
Good. That will save me the trouble of trying to save face."

Eric laughed and within moments Kerry joined in. Ashlyn
walked past them. "That's just great, live it up at my expense!"

"Do you want me to try to do some damage control and talk
to him?" Eric asked.

"You're just the guy I would trust to do that for me. Two
seconds ago you were laughing so hard you were ready to choke
up a lung. Now you want to help?"

"Is that a 'no'?"

"That's a not-if-my-life-depended-on-it no!"

Ashlyn walked through the bedroom, past the walk-in closet,
and over to the bathroom. It was bigger than her whole kitchen!
Thou shalt not covet thy neighbor's bathroom, Ashlyn, she
reminded herself.

She walked over to see if the water had been turned on. As
she turned the tap, she could hear the gurgle of the air and water
being forced through the unused pipes. It didn't seem to be
enough pressure. She turned the taps a little further, noting
nothing. Turning the tap full blast, she still noticed nothing. As
Ashlyn knelt down to get a closer look, the water came bursting
out in squirts as the air pockets ran through the pipes, sopping
Ashlyn. As she jumped back, she slipped on the water and
knocked her head on the wall behind her.

Eric and Kerry were the first to arrive on the scene. Split
seconds later, Tyler and Rory followed. There sat Ashlyn,
soaking wet in a puddle of water, rubbing the back of her head.

Tyler rushed over to turn off the water and kneeled down by Ashlyn on the tiled floor. "What are you doing?"

"Just checking my plumbing skills. Thanks to me, your water works fine."

"How about you?" he asked, trying to conceal a grin. "Do you still work fine?"

"Oh, I'm peachy, thanks."

"You look like—"

"Don't even say it."

"I was just going to say you look like you could use a hand getting up."

"Oh. Who said chivalry was dead?" Ashlyn felt the heat rise to her cheeks. *Well,* she thought, *if my big mouth doesn't impress him, perhaps my knack for making a fool of myself will.*

Eric jumped over to help and asked, "Are you okay? We heard a loud thud and then a yelp."

"I'm fine. My pride has taken a beating but the rest of me will recover. By the way, I don't *yelp.*" She looked over at Kerry, who nodded. "It was a yelp?" Ashlyn asked her friend. Again, Kerry nodded.

She looked back at Tyler. He was smirking, trying not to laugh. "What's so funny?" she asked.

"Nothing! Is it a bad thing to yelp?" He grinned.

"Not if you're a seal!" Trying to diffuse the embarrassing situation, she asked, "Where are some towels so I can clean this mess up?"

"In one of my nonspecific boxes." He turned and left the room and was back seconds later with a couple of sweatshirts. He handed one to Ashlyn and then used the other to mop the floor in front of the sink. Ashlyn glanced up and caught sight of herself in the mirror. She looked like what her mother lovingly referred to as "something that the cat dragged in."

Ashlyn was determined to find some humor in the situation, though she had to dig deep. She looked at those who had gathered in the bathroom. "Okay, everyone, let's break it up. The party is over. Everyone go back to where you came from." She turned to Eric and Tyler, "I think I've done as much damage as I can for one day. Maybe I'd better go home and forget this day ever happened." She didn't want to just *go* away, however. She wanted to *run* away—far, far away.

Both men smiled, looking incredibly handsome. She and Kerry had good taste in men, she thought. Ashlyn stopped dead in her tracks. *Where did that thought come from?*

Her face must have mirrored the horrifying thought because Kerry jumped up and asked, "Ashlyn, are you okay?"

Trying to make a quick recovery, she said, "Yeah . . . fine . . . super."

"Do you need me to drive you home?" Kerry persisted.

"No, really, I'm fine."

She turned to leave, but Tyler gently grabbed her wrist. She felt shivers all the way up her arm. "Will you be okay? You don't look so hot."

"Oh! So chivalry *is* dead." Ashlyn smiled as he tried to correct his words. "I'm fine. Really."

* * *

Ashlyn woke to the sound of the front door slamming shut.

Kerry made a beeline to Ashlyn's room. She tapped on her door and, without waiting for Ashlyn to bid her welcome, flew into the room and pounced on Ashlyn's bed.

"Oh my gosh!" Kerry exclaimed. "I was torn between following you home and following Eric around like a little lost puppy. Sorry. You came in second." She giggled. "Tell me everything that happened after I left the kitchen. By the way, I'm sorry that I left."

"How warm and sincere," Ashlyn muttered.

"Aw, come on, don't be mad. I get nervous in those kinds of situations. Besides, I tried to warn you that he had walked in, but you wouldn't listen. I don't suppose you noticed how gorgeous he is?"

"Notice? How could anyone *not* notice?" Ashlyn grinned at the thought of her new boss.

"Well . . . he's no Eric, but he could sure give him a run for his money! He was so nice to you! Even after you were so rotten to him!"

Kerry brought her back to reality with a thud. "Gee, thanks."

"So, tell me! I'm dying to hear!"

"After he rubbed it in a little, he made me apologize. It was like pulling teeth to get me to do it, but he succeeded." Ashlyn smiled at the memory.

Kerry started laughing. "You should have seen yourself on the bathroom floor. It was pretty funny."

"Well, I'm just happy to have been the comic relief for the day." She couldn't bear to think about it anymore, so she changed the subject. "Are you going to the retirement party? It's time to get ready, or we'll be late."

"I overheard Eric talking to Chris. Looks like a few of the people from the force are invited, so I've got to look good. Somehow I've got to get Eric to notice what a great catch I am. If you're not wearing your red dress, can I borrow it?"

"Sure. I think I'll wear my new black one." Ashlyn knew Kerry looked great in red. Perhaps Eric would notice her, and Ashlyn wouldn't have to come right out and tell him to get a clue.

"Thanks. Oh, and I promise not to leave sweat stains in it." Kerry laughed and left the room.

"Ha, ha. Very funny," Ashlyn called to her friend.

* * *

Within the hour, both women met in the front room ready to go. Ashlyn smiled at Kerry as Kerry walked into the front room. "You look great tonight. You do for that dress what I could only dream about. Keep it. I could never wear it now."

"You're good for my ego. Thanks. I'll bet you capture the new sergeant's attention tonight as well."

"He'll be there? Why didn't you warn me?"

"What do you need warning about? You like him, don't you?" Kerry asked slyly.

"No, that's not it. He makes me nervous, that's all. I'm going to see this guy practically every day between work and now at church functions. I'd just like to get my bearings before seeing him again," Ashlyn said defensively.

"Knocked you off your feet a bit, hasn't he?" Kerry teased.

"Will you stop? You know how I feel about my career."

"It's a woman's prerogative to change her mind. Especially when it comes to Tyler O'Bryan."

"He's good-looking and fun. There, I've said it. He's also my boss, and I've got a job to do, so don't try any matchmaking. It just may come back to haunt you. You mustn't forget that I am good friends with Eric," Ashlyn teased, "and I'd hate to be the one to reveal your love for him. Besides, Tyler is taken."

"I'm to the point that if Eric hasn't figured it out yet, he's not going to. As for Tyler, how do you know he's taken?"

"If some woman hasn't already claimed him, Shirley is next in line." Ashlyn felt her anger with Shirley rise, and she took a deep breath to calm herself.

"Are you talking about that ridiculous e-mail she sent? I showed it to Eric. He laughed and said, 'Poor guy won't know what hit him.' Shirley is no competition for you."

"This isn't about competing. I've no interest in Tyler. He was really nice, especially after what I said. And yes, he's pleasant for the eyes, but that's it. Now, let's go or we'll be late."

As they walked to the door, Ashlyn added, "Speaking of Shirley, I had an interesting conversation with her yesterday. Come on. I'll tell you on the way."

* * *

The stake center was lit up as the two women made their way through the front doors. After hearing Ashlyn's story about Shirley, Kerry had become quite angry, and Ashlyn was trying to calm her down.

"Who does she think she is?" Kerry fumed. "I mean the nerve of that . . ."

"You're more upset than I am. Consider the source and forget it." *And you'd do well to follow your own advice, Ashlyn.*

"There's the belle of the ball," a deep voice called from behind them.

"Daddy?" Ashlyn was shocked. "I didn't know you'd be here! Why didn't you tell me you were coming?" She gave her dad a big hug and a kiss.

"We drove here early this morning, but I'm afraid it's a quick trip for us this time. We wanted to surprise you, and we couldn't miss Bob's party. How are my girls?" He turned to Kerry and gave her a hug. Kerry kissed him on the cheek.

"It's been too long since I've seen you, Joe." Kerry grinned. "You're just as handsome as ever."

"The road runs in both directions, you know. When will you be home to visit, Ashlyn?" He eyed his daughter.

"I am getting a little homesick, so I'll come soon. I promise. But why does it have to be a quick trip?" Ashlyn asked, disappointment apparent in her voice.

"It's your mom's turn to teach tomorrow."

"So is she still a Relief Society teacher?"

"She is, and loving every minute of it. Janice is introducing her around. Go find her. You're the biggest reason she came."

* * *

Across the room, Tyler sat at a table with Eric. Tyler thought Eric was a nice guy, and they seemed to get along well. Eric probably made friends easily, Tyler thought.

Janice approached their table as the two men stood in gentlemanly manner. "Eric, you remember Laura, Ashlyn's mother, don't you? I believe you met her when they came to town for a visit during last year's softball fund-raiser against the fire department. That was such a hoot! Remember how Officer Barney split his pants sliding into third base? Poor rookie."

"Unfortunately for him, the unit won't let him forget. How are you doing, Mrs. Lawrence?" Eric shook Laura's hand.

"Please call me Laura. I feel so old when people call me Mrs. Lawrence. At my age I can't afford to feel much older." Laura smiled.

Tyler stood by, listening and thinking that Ashlyn had her mother's eyes. *For the millionth time, quit thinking about Ashlyn!* he berated himself. *She's a* cop! *You're her boss!*

Janice turned to Tyler. "Laura, this is Mr. Tyler O'Bryan. He is the newest sergeant on the force. Tyler, I don't know if you know Ashlyn Lawrence or not. She's a detective in the unit. This is her mother, Laura. She and her husband are our dearest friends. They've come from Salt Lake."

Tyler took Laura's hand. "It's a pleasure to meet you, and actually I met your daughter today. She was part of the moving crew from the ward that came to help me out. I see where she gets her beauty."

Laura seemed to be blushing. "The pleasure is mine. Thank you for your kind words. You may change your mind when you have to work with her. I'm afraid my daughter is a bit obstinate. Takes after her father in that respect, I'm afraid. Her good traits come from me." Laura laughed.

Tyler liked her immediately, and he smiled. "I got a hint of that today. But the compliment still stands."

Janice broke in. "Could I impose on you two young men to check on the refreshments? The Young Women are supposed to be tending the table, but I'm afraid they're, well, young. I've just a few more people to introduce Laura to, and then I'll be in to help."

Both men agreed and made their way to the refreshment table. Tyler glanced up and spotted Ashlyn a few yards away. She looked breathtaking. She stood tall in a formfitting black dress that showed off her thin figure. Her hair was pulled up and twisted at the back of her head with a few tendrils falling down.

"Tyler? Hello?" Eric interrupted his thoughts.

"I'm sorry, what did you say?" Tyler looked at Eric, hoping he hadn't noticed why he'd been distracted. Luckily, Eric appeared oblivious.

"I said we could probably stock up on some of this food and the punch bowl is almost empty. I think it's a slush with Sprite in it or something."

"Okay, I'll see about the punch bowl if you'll restock. Sound good to you?"

Eric nodded and both men headed for the kitchen.

On his way out of the kitchen, Tyler stole one more glance in Ashlyn's direction. Disappointed to find her gone, he made a mental note to look for her later. Maybe he could even steal a dance or two.

Ashlyn looked all over for her mother but couldn't find her anywhere. As she walked around the church, it suddenly occurred to her that she knew right where she'd be—in the kitchen. That was her domain.

Coming from the opposite direction, Kerry met up with her. "No luck. I haven't seen your mom. Have you found her yet?"

"No. Did you check the kitchen?" Ashlyn asked hopefully.

"I walked past but I didn't look in. Let's try there." Ashlyn was so wrapped up in their conversation as they walked to the kitchen that she suddenly ran into something that reminded her of a brick wall. She hit so hard that she fell back a step and landed on Kerry's foot with her heel.

In a split-second reaction to the pain, Kerry pushed Ashlyn off her foot and back into the supposed brick wall. The next thing Ashlyn knew, there was a loud crash and she was dripping wet with a freezing cold beverage spilled down the front of her and dripping into her shoes. She was shocked as she looked up and saw that the brick wall had been Tyler.

When she crashed into him the second time, Tyler, who had tried to catch Ashlyn and had instead dropped the punch bowl, stood absolutely astonished, trying to figure out what had just happened. He had slush in his hair, and punch was dripping from his chin. The front of his white, newly starched shirt was completely soaked with slush, and the rest of the contents from the bowl oozed all about his feet. Red slush dripped down the kitchen walls and flooded the kitchen floor. Kerry sat on the floor behind her friend, rubbing her bruised, swollen foot and glaring at Ashlyn, who stood shivering and speechless. No one moved or said a word as they began to realize what had just happened.

Tyler spoke first. "Oh my gosh, that stuff is so cold!" He tried to brush the drink from his suit jacket and from the front of his once-white shirt.

Ashlyn surveyed the scene and burst out laughing. Tyler looked at her as though she was from another planet, which made her laugh harder.

"I'm trying really hard to see the humor in all of this," he said incredulously, "but do you see what you've done here?"

"Me?" Ashlyn gasped. "I don't think so! It was your fault!"

"Really? How do you figure? No, on second thought, let's ask the eyewitnesses." He glanced in the direction of the three young women who stood, unmoving, in the corner of the kitchen. Tyler turned toward the girls and flashed them a charming smile. "Young ladies, who would you say is at fault here, and therefore does the cleaning? Would that be me, who was only trying to help you, or this person who came carelessly barreling around the corner? There is a candy bar in it for the one who answers correctly."

The three girls answered in unison, pointing at Ashlyn. "She did it."

"Oh sure, use the power of bribery. Here, let me ask them. All right, girls, I know your parents, and I know where you live. Who's at fault here? Think carefully."

The girls whispered and turned toward each other.

Tyler looked at Ashlyn with an amused smile in his face. "Oh, I get it! The power of intimidation is much more effective than the power of bribery! Let's just say it's a draw and get to work." As Tyler sloshed around the kitchen looking for a towel, Ashlyn walked a few feet down the hall to the janitor's closet to get a broom and mop. By the time she got back, Kerry, Eric, and her mother had joined the ranks of the cleanup crew.

"Good heavens, Ashlyn, what have you done?" her mother inquired.

"Me? Why does everyone automatically assume it's my fault? I didn't do it—he did." Ashlyn pointed to Tyler, whose eyebrows shot up at the accusation.

"What do you mean *I* did it? Here I am, minding my own business, and you come barging around the corner."

"If I'd known you were there, I wouldn't have slightly bumped into you!"

"*Slightly bumped* into me? What was I supposed to do? Blow a fog horn and yell, 'Look out anyone who might be *barreling* around the corner, I'm coming through'?"

They started laughing again while Laura looked at both of them and shook her head in disbelief. Everyone worked together to get the mess cleaned up, and soon the job was complete.

"There might not be enough drinks for everyone now," Kerry logically surmised. "There was a lot of good slush that went to waste here, not to mention somebody's punch bowl."

"Why don't you and I go buy some sherbet and Sprite?" Eric asked Kerry.

"Good idea." Kerry smiled and looked at Ashlyn, grinning.

"I'll pay for it. Get what you think we might need. Shouldn't we get another punch bowl too?" Tyler offered as he reached into his back pocket, pulled out his wallet, and handed some bills over to Eric. "Oh, and would you pick up three candy bars?"

Eric looked at Tyler with confusion. "Three candy bars? Why?"

Ashlyn rolled her eyes. "He's trying to charm a biased jury. The case was won before both parties had a chance to speak their cause of action," Ashlyn replied sardonically. "There won't be a store open that sells that kind of punch bowl. I'll replace it Monday. I have one at home that we can use. I need to go home to change, so I'll pick it up while I'm there."

"I guess I'd better change as well. I feel like rigor mortis is setting in my suit. I'll be back, so if that money doesn't cover it, let me know," Tyler offered again. "Thanks, Eric and Kerry, I appreciate your help." He looked at Ashlyn and grinned.

CHAPTER 5

Ashlyn only lived a few blocks away from the church, so it wasn't long before she arrived home. The phone rang as she walked through the door. The caller ID showed "unavailable" so Ashlyn picked up the call. "Hello?"

A deep, creepy voice came over the line. "Remember your brother? You better back off or you'll be next." Then the phone went dead.

Ashlyn's face went white, and she dropped the phone, staring at it as if it were poison. She started to shake, and soon tears were falling freely. She knew this wasn't a sick joke. Somebody knew about her brother, and somehow he considered Ashlyn to be some sort of a threat.

She ran to the front door, locked the dead bolt into place, then crashed into the overstuffed chair. Her deepest fears came to the surface. Austin's death wasn't an accident nor was it a random shooting. Someone had been out to get him, and she would be next if she didn't back off.

But back off from what? What was missing in this scenario? As a cop, she knew she should be able to figure it out, but this time she couldn't. Fear started to take over. If she left, would he be outside waiting for her? Was he watching her now? She felt like a time machine whipped her back ten years ago to that dreadful day she had tried so hard to put behind her. She went through every detail of the day of the shooting and the following months. Fresh tears flowed. Why now? Why after all this time? She'd moved to Colorado to escape. Would the fears and anger always follow her? She was deep in thought when she felt a hand on her shoulder.

Ashlyn screamed before she realized that Kerry was in front of her. The look on Kerry's face showed that she was terrified by Ashlyn's reaction. "Ashlyn, look at me! What happened? Tell me what happened!" Kerry was almost in a panic.

Ashlyn looked at her friend as she slowly began to focus. Then she grabbed her friend and hugged her tight. Ashlyn tried to move, but her dress had gone stiff from the slush. How long had she sat there?

Kerry studied her friend. "You've been gone for an hour and a half. I tried to call, but the line was busy. It's not like you. I got worried."

Ashlyn stood on wobbly legs and tried to smile. "I'm sorry. I didn't hear you come in. I guess I took longer than I should have. I don't think I feel well. Maybe you could take the punch bowl back to the church for me."

Ashlyn looked over and realized that Eric was with Kerry. He stepped over and hung up the phone that was still dangling by the cord from the table. "What happened here tonight?" he asked in a no-nonsense manner.

"Nothing, just a silly prank phone call," Ashlyn answered evasively.

"It's not 'nothing' if it upset you this bad," Eric persisted. He looked at the caller ID and muttered, "Figures," when he saw "unavailable."

Ashlyn stood and glanced out the big picture window. "I just overreacted a little. I'm really tired, and I'm so sticky that I'm beginning to feel like duct tape. What I need is a good, long bath and a year's worth of sleep. Just go ahead without me, and please give my apologies to everyone."

Kerry looked doubtful as she reminded Ashlyn that her parents were in town.

"Oh, fine," she gave in. "Give me two minutes to clean up and I'll be right over. Go ahead. I'll meet you there."

Kerry looked her friend over. "Maybe you shouldn't be alone."

Ashlyn rolled her eyes. "I'll be all right. It was a prank call that caught me off guard, that's all. Go. I'm right behind you." With great reluctance, both of her friends turned and left.

Ashlyn showered and changed in record time, and was out the door before she could ponder the call too much. She needed to think this through and clear her head, but there wasn't time for that now. Later, when she was alone, she'd figure out what to do. This wasn't the first prank call she'd received telling her to back off, but it was the first one to mention Austin.

Why? her heart screamed.

* * *

Ashlyn stepped back into the dimly lit cultural hall where many people had gathered. Several were police officers, both active and retired, who had become Bob's friends in the past, while others were friends and family of the Bradleys. Music was playing softly as some used half of the room to dance while others used the other half to mix and mingle.

Ashlyn slowly scanned the room, looking for her parents, and spied them dancing together as if they were the only two in the world. She envied the relationship they had. They were anchored and drew strength from each other.

As she watched them, a longing began to ache somewhere deep inside of her. At one time she wanted that for herself, more than anything. To be honest, she still did.

Someone tapped her on the shoulder. "Ashlyn? Pesky little Ashlyn? You grew up!" She turned, recognizing the voice immediately. "Trevor Bradley! How have you been?" Ashlyn reached up and gave Bob and Janice Bradley's youngest son a hug.

"You look like you were longing to dance. Need a partner, or has someone already claimed you for the evening?" Trevor asked.

"Nope, no claims here. Care to join me?" Ashlyn tried to grin, also trying to forget the call that haunted her thoughts.

Trevor took Ashlyn's hand and chuckled. "Then allow me. I do believe we have about three years of catching up to do."

"Lead the way." Ashlyn smiled.

"Seems to me the last time I tried to lead was at my wedding reception when I stepped on your toes." Trevor's eyes sparkled with humor. "Sure you want me to lead?"

"You're in luck. I wore my steel-toed shoes in hopes of stealing a dance with you."

"Why, Ashlyn, you flatter me. Lead on."

Ashlyn pulled Trevor across the room to the dance floor. As they started dancing, Ashlyn felt herself starting to relax a bit. Soon they were laughing and talking as though it had been only yesterday that they had seen each other last. The dance melted into another one, and during the third number, they traded partners with her parents.

Ashlyn looked up at her dad. "What's got you sad, sweetie?" her father asked, trying to read the emotion in her eyes.

"Nothing," she answered brightly, hoping to dismiss the subject. "I'm working the night shift, so I'm tired, and I'm a bit sad Bob's retiring. I guess I've just had a long day."

Joe listened to his beautiful daughter. She was his pride and joy, and he hurt knowing she'd never been truly happy since Austin had passed away. He continually wanted to mend her broken heart, but he didn't know how. No one did. But he prayed that she'd find strength and comfort through the Savior.

Trying to keep the mood light, he commented, "I've met your new sergeant. I liked him right off the bat. He seems to have a good head on his shoulders."

"You could tell that in one brief introduction?" Ashlyn was surprised to find her father so open-minded to a stranger.

"Well, no. I actually sat and talked to him for about a half hour. He's an outdoorsman, likes sports, is career oriented, and he's got smarts. I like that in a man. Not married though. He's thirty and single. I don't know what he's waiting for."

The song ended and Ashlyn hugged her dad. "I love you so much," she whispered.

"I love you too, honey." He hugged her back and then said, "We really need to hit the road before it gets too late. We'll be driving all night as it is. Let's go find your mom."

As they left the dance floor, Kerry walked up to join them, carefully watching her friend. She knew better than to say anything that would alarm Ashlyn's father. The three walked away in search of Ashlyn's mother, visiting as they walked.

* * *

Tyler had watched Ashlyn walk into the cultural hall and begin dancing with Trevor Bradley. Even though he knew Trevor was married, Tyler envied Trevor's opportunity to dance with Ashlyn.

When he had returned to the church, he was surprised to find that Ashlyn wasn't there yet. He started to wonder if she'd decided not to come back. It bothered him that he would even care. He had only met her that morning, under less than favorable conditions, but he was immediately attracted to her. She was beautiful—he'd never deny that—but she also made him laugh, and she was easy to be around. He was frustrated because he knew that nothing other than friendship could ever exist between them. He would *never* date another cop. He'd learned his lesson with Jessica. He'd always been so stressed in their relationship because she was continually taking stupid risks just to prove what a good cop she was.

He had heard of Ashlyn's merits when he was applying for the job, so he knew she was good at what she did. She obviously appeared worried about what he'd do with her position, yet it was beyond him why. He had no intention of changing anything to do with her job.

He also wanted to avoid Ashlyn because he *was* her boss. He figured that once he got to know her better, his attraction would fade, and then a friendship could form. Until then, he'd keep his thoughts to himself, and in time, his attraction would go away.

It has to, Tyler thought. *The sooner, the better.*

Tyler then noticed Kerry and Eric talking in the corner. There were looks of concern on their faces as they both looked up and watched Ashlyn dance with her father. It was obvious that she was their topic of conversation, and Tyler wondered why. When the song ended, Kerry made her way over to Ashlyn and her father, and the three then turned and walked out the door.

Eric joined Tyler a few seconds later. He sat down with a heavy sigh.

"Something wrong?" Tyler asked Eric nonchalantly.

"I don't know for sure. When Ashlyn got home, she got a prank call. She's trying to pass it off as nothing, but you should have seen her. Whatever it was about, it got to her. She doesn't usually let small things upset her, so something tells me it was 'something' and not 'nothing.' Either way, she's not talking."

Tyler felt an uncomfortable feeling in the pit of his stomach. "Was she threatened? Has it happened before?"

"Not sure. Like I said, she's not talking. That's not unusual for her, though. She's not too open with her feelings. But she doesn't sweat the small stuff. She's had plenty of people talk smack to her, especially since she often has to testify against criminals. I've never seen it get to her before, so whatever happened tonight got her good."

Tyler sat and looked at his refreshments. "Is there someone she would have told if this had happened to her before? I mean, besides Kerry?" Tyler realized that he was asking Eric if she had a boyfriend. He'd analyze that one later.

"She's close to the Bradleys, and of course to Kerry, and I'd like to think Ashlyn would tell me. We're good friends, but I've never heard her mention anything."

"How long have you known her?" Tyler wondered if Eric had ever pursued a relationship with her, but refused to ask outright.

"I've known her since her first day on the job three years ago. I was surprised she was a cop. You know, meeting and greeting thugs and druggies. She's good at what she does, though. The best I know."

"You talk highly of her. Did you ever go after her?" *Man, you're pathetic!* Tyler thought.

"I'm sure I dreamed of it, but we've always been too good of friends. Anything more than that wouldn't have felt right. However, I could point out about twenty guys who would love to go out with her."

"And?" Tyler prompted, not sure he wanted to know the rest.

"And they're still hopeful. Tyler, my man, you're asking a lot of questions about her. Any particular reason why?"

"Nope."

Eric laughed and patted him on the back. "Yeah, sure. Either you think I'm buying that, or you've left someone behind in L.A. I wouldn't worry about being curious about her. I'd worry about you if you weren't. I mean, look at her! But you know what? She's even better on the inside."

"So, what about Kerry? How available is she?" Tyler looked at Eric, trying to bait him a little just to see his reaction. He had a hunch and wanted to test it.

Eric shifted in his chair and sat up a little taller, then reluctantly answered, "She's available, but there's some pretty stiff competition out there for her too."

"Is that why you act like there's only friendship between you two?"

Eric fell silent. He looked at Tyler and asked hesitantly, "What are you talking about?"

"Come on, Eric. I'd like to think we're becoming friends. Remember, I'm trained to look out for suspicious behavior. Today during the move I was checking out members of my new ward. That's all." Tyler smiled, and they both looked at each other and chuckled.

"That's not all you were checking out. Ashlyn was getting her share of your observations."

"Guilty as charged." Tyler shrugged. "It won't ever mean anything, though, so let's keep this conversation between us. I'll return the favor to you. Deal?"

"Deal. One thing though . . ." Eric paused.

"Yeah?"

"What's stopping you from ever letting those looks mean anything?"

"She's a cop."

"So?"

"There's more to it than that." Tyler stopped. "This is between us, right?"

Eric nodded.

"I thought I was in love with this woman back in L.A. who worked in the same force as me. She was so competitive. It was the whole 'anything you can do, I can do better' thing. I kept trying to tell her to stop because she was going to get herself killed taking so many dangerous risks. One night we were called out on a drug bust that resulted in a shoot-out. She just *had* to get her man, so she took off in the line of fire to get closer. I went after her. She got her man all right, and I got shot. Then she had the nerve to come to the hospital all worried that I would do something so crazy as to go after her. She said it was my fault I got shot. She got suspended for not following her commanding officer, and I was made to look like some sort of hero for being so brave. It was ridiculous. I wasn't doing my job. I was looking after her and her immature behavior. I felt like I had betrayed everyone who had counted on me to do my part.

After that, I decided I would never take that risk again. Not only that, but I need to know that when I go home at night, my wife will be there for me. It takes a strong and brave woman to be the wife of a police officer, and I'd be a wreck if I had to wait to see if my wife came home alive each night."

"But what if you met the woman of your dreams? You'd give her up because of the job she loves to do?"

"I wouldn't ask that of her. That's why my policy is no personal contact with women officers. Ashlyn seems great, but I've got a job to do. End of story." Tyler leaned back in his chair.

"Okay. You probably wouldn't get her anyway. She's a beauty, she's smart, and she's got a good heart, but she's got a mission to accomplish, and there's no way she'll let anything or *anyone* get in her way of doing that."

"What kind of mission are you talking about? Don't tell me she's out to prove something too!" Tyler groaned.

"Only to herself. She's not a fool like your friend. Ashlyn puts everyone ahead of herself—so much so that she rarely lives for herself. I think it has to do with her older brother, who was killed when she was young. I don't know a lot of the details—it's not an open topic of conversation—but it's why she became a cop. Her bosses have always allowed her the freedom to go by her gut instincts because she usually hits the nail on the head. She never crosses the line, but she stretches it."

"Is that why she'd be worried about a new boss?"

"If she is, I'm sure that would be it." Eric looked his new friend in the eye, but Tyler seemed deep in thought.

"Interesting," Tyler said at last, returning to the conversation. "Now, what's your story?"

"I don't have a story," Eric said, confused.

"Yes, you do. Come on, the whole Kerry thing and all. I mean what, is there some kind of interoffice dating rule?"

"Not really. There's never been a need for one. Your secretary, Shirley, and two other secretaries are on a man hunt like

you'd never believe. But other than some of the dispatchers and
Ashlyn, there are no other single women in our force. Consider
yourself warned that Shirley is hot on your tail. I'll have to let
you read an e-mail sent to all the single women in the unit. It
was . . . interesting."

Eric's expression made Tyler curious. "Is that what Ashlyn
meant when she referred to Shirley today at the house?"

"Yup. Gave Ashlyn a personal warning. I heard the tail end
of it. She was vicious."

"Could Shirley be behind the call?"

"Maybe, but I thought she said the caller was a man. As far as
Kerry is concerned, we're no more than really good friends. She dates
so much that I'm not even sure she wants to settle down, and I'm
too old to play chasing games. She's beautiful and fun to be around,
but I've never even seen a hint of interest on her part. I've been
tempted a couple times to ask Ashlyn about her, but I wasn't so sure
I wanted to hear the answer. So I figure that friendship is better than
nothing. So, in the words of a famous cop, 'End of story.'"

"We're pathetic, you know that? Speaking of the devil . . ."

Both guys watched as Kerry weaved her way through the
crowd to their table.

"Hey, guys. Can I join you for a second?" She smiled, but it
didn't reach her eyes.

"Sure," Tyler answered. "Let me go get you some refreshments. What would you like?" He stood as if in a hurry to go.
Eric shot him a look.

"Anything, thanks, except the slush. I've had enough of that
to last a lifetime!" Kerry laughed at the smirk on Tyler's face.

He looked at her and asked, "Is Ashlyn coming back? I
mean, should I get her something too?"

"She just walked in. Why don't you ask her?" Kerry indicated toward the door where her friend had just entered.

Once Tyler was gone, Eric leaned over to Kerry and asked,
"Did you find out anything more from her?"

"No. I get the feeling it hit a little close to home though, because there are only a few things that would have upset her like that. I'm not so worried about a prank call. Kids do that all the time. I'm more concerned that it was a threat of some kind, either to herself or someone she cares about. I've racked my brain trying to think of someone who would have it out for Ashlyn, and I can't come up with a single soul."

"Could Shirley be behind it?"

"Maybe. I don't think she's up to something like that, but I guess it's possible. I think our best bet is to see if the person calls us again."

"What do you mean?" Eric looked at her with the worry evident on his face, which made Kerry feel good. At least she knew he cared.

"Well, maybe the call was for anyone who answered and not particularly for Ashlyn. I'll talk to her tonight and see what I can find out. Knowing Ashlyn, she's probably over it now. She's a pretty tough cookie."

"That's not going to fly with me. You're worried and I can see it, so keep me posted."

Kerry *had* brought up something Eric hadn't thought of. Maybe the call wasn't specifically for Ashlyn. But he'd seen Ashlyn's reaction. He'd seen her angry and even upset in the past, but he'd never seen her like this. He was worried.

* * *

Ashlyn got butterflies as she watched Tyler move toward her through the crowd. He had changed into a black suit, white shirt, and red tie, and he looked absolutely handsome. She had to admit it—she liked him. He had a sense of humor and a nonarrogant self-confidence like Austin had. She was intrigued, but she didn't want to be. She couldn't allow herself to be. The thought of Austin brought a chilling reminder of her phone call and sent shivers up her spine.

Tyler slowly stopped in front of her. "I wondered if you were coming back. Kerry, Eric, and I are over there at a table. Care to join us? I'm getting a plate for Kerry now."

"Sure. I think I'm about ready to call it a night, but I'll sit for a minute. Knowing those two, I suppose they told you I got a phone call that less than thrilled me. Correct?"

She was blunt and honest, and Tyler liked that. "Eric mentioned it. Ever had prank calls before?" Tyler asked as he filled a plate for Kerry.

"I've had prank calls before, and I think I just overreacted. I guess it's just been a long day."

Tyler considered the smile that didn't reach her eyes. "I don't know you very well, but for some reason, I don't buy what you're telling me. You don't seem to be a person who overreacts. Eric and Kerry feel the same way. We're your friends, and we'd like to help if we can. Maybe I should say I'd like to be your friend as well. If you don't want to talk about it, I'll respect your wishes, but if it truly upset you, we'd like to know what happened."

Ashlyn smiled up at him, appreciative of his gesture. He wasn't overbearing, and she liked that. *Great! Like I need another reason to like him!* she thought.

Ashlyn followed behind Tyler as he led the way to the table. As they sat down, Kerry and Eric suddenly became quiet. Ashlyn looked at them all watching her.

"Why do I get the feeling that my ears should be burning?" Ashlyn smiled but tried to hide her true feelings.

Eric shifted uncomfortably. "I'll get right to the point, Ashlyn. Was the call a threat? Was it meant for you, or just anyone who answered the phone? We don't know what to think. We're worried."

Ashlyn was a little taken aback by his bluntness but realized they had every right to worry. Trying to keep her emotions in check, she continued cautiously, "The call was definitely for me. Apparently someone is unhappy with me and offered me a one-way ticket to see my brother if I don't back off. Back off to who or what, I don't know." She paused. "But I'm fine."

Kerry sucked in a deep breath when Austin was mentioned. Everyone else sat and stared at Ashlyn. She continued, "This is supposed to be a party. So let's party. Someone ask me to dance."

Everyone sat, stunned, until Tyler stood and reached for her hand. "May I have this dance?" he asked quietly.

"Good idea. Thank you."

He took her hand and led her to the floor. He turned and took hold of her right hand in his left, then put his hand on her waist. He was thrilled to have her in his arms but knew it was only for a fleeting moment. He looked into her eyes. "I have a million questions, and I don't know where to begin or if I should even try," he spoke quietly and hesitantly.

"I thought you might. I'm sorry. I don't usually talk about my brother. It's just that that darn call really threw me."

Tyler looked at her, a bit confused, so she began. "Here, let me make it easier on you and I'll explain. My brother, Austin, was shot and killed ten years ago. The shooter was never caught, and the police figured it was some random shooting. I've never believed that, and neither has Bob Bradley, who worked on the case." Unwanted tears started to stream down Ashlyn's face, though she tried to avoid it. "I loved my brother, and tonight someone told me he was murdered as I'd always suspected. The murderer's out there somewhere, and he knows where I am."

By now Ashlyn was crying so hard Tyler took her hand and led her out of the cultural hall and into the hallway. Looking for a place where she could talk and cry openly, he led her into a classroom and turned on the light. He set two chairs across from each other and helped her into one. Ashlyn sunk down and tried to gather her emotions. Tyler handed her his handkerchief.

"I am so sorry. I can imagine what you must think of me." She smiled through her tears.

"You have no need to apologize. I can understand how painful it must have been for you." He sincerely wanted to comfort her but didn't know how, so he just listened.

"The call brought it all to the surface, you know? I mean, it was chilling to talk to the person who killed—or at least knew who killed—my brother. My fears are confirmed, but I have no more answers now than I did back then."

"Why would they go after your brother? Was he somehow involved with the wrong crowd?" Tyler asked hesitantly.

Ashlyn grinned. "Are you kidding? He was the closest thing to an angel I've ever known. He was waiting for his mission call. It was all he wanted to do."

Tyler gazed at Ashlyn. "I'm sorry for your loss. I really mean that."

Ashlyn nodded her head soberly and wiped her eyes. "Look at me, I'm a mess." She smiled grimly.

"You look beautiful."

"Yeah, if you go for the type who has a runny nose, red, swollen eyes, mascara smeared across her face, and is an emotional puddle of tears." Ashlyn smiled weakly and shifted in her chair, preparing to leave when Tyler grabbed her arm.

"Let me help you figure this out." When Tyler looked in her eyes, they were soft but disbelieving. If she would ever let him in, now would be the time. He tried again. "You're too close to the situation. Maybe a second opinion will open new insights. Let me help you." Again, he looked into her eyes. They intently studied him back.

She paused for breath and spoke quietly. "Every one of my brain cells tells me not to trust people. I'm afraid because of that, I don't let too many people get close to me. It's my own survival technique." Tyler looked crestfallen. Ashlyn continued, "I'm usually a cautious person, and I hardly know you, but for some reason I do trust you. I can't begin to explain it, let alone understand it. For ten years, I've tried to figure Austin's death out on my own, and I'm no closer today than the police were back then. I'm not very good at asking for help, but I . . ." She choked the next sentence out between sobs. "I'm starting to see that I can't do this alone."

Tyler was thrilled that she trusted him. He leaned over and gave her a quick hug. "I'll do my very best to not let you down. We'll see if we can figure this out."

CHAPTER 6

Sunday morning came bright and early as Ashlyn and Kerry prepared to go to church. They had talked late into the night after staying to help the Bradleys clean up from the party. Ashlyn had only gotten a few hours of sleep since before her shift on Friday, and she had a pounding headache to show for it.

When Kerry and Ashlyn got to the meetinghouse, Kerry turned toward the Primary room to teach the three- and four-year-olds' class as Ashlyn walked into the Relief Society room.

In class, Ashlyn listened intently as Sister Hales gave a wonderful lesson on the importance of family home evening. Normally a lesson like that would have caused Ashlyn some unease since she didn't have a family, but this time she reflected on what she had been taught in her youth and the importance of the topic. Sister Hales's lesson inspired her to talk to Kerry about the two of them trying to have it in their own home. Maybe having family home evening would get them into the habit with their own families when it came time.

Where did that thought come from? Ashlyn thought as she stepped into the cultural hall to go to her Gospel Doctrine class. *I set my path long ago, and it didn't include a family of my own.* As she sat down and pulled out her scriptures, she prepared for the day's lesson. Rick Adler was the teacher and had been forever. He had been an English professor at the community college and sometimes spoke above everyone else, making it difficult for

Ashlyn to understand. Judging from the lack of people paying attention, Ashlyn wasn't the only one who had a hard time following him.

An opening prayer was said, and class began. Ashlyn glanced across the room and saw Eric and Tyler sitting together. Stephanie Hutchinson, a single, pretty schoolteacher, whispered something in Tyler's ear and laughed. He looked at her, smiled and nodded, then turned his attention back to the teacher.

Rick asked all the newcomers and visitors to stand and introduce themselves. As Tyler stood up, Stephanie gleamed with pride as if he were there on her behalf. Ashlyn suddenly felt jealous and didn't want to know the reasons why, but she wasted the rest of the class time mentally listing them anyway. She didn't feel any better by the time class ended. She swiftly made her way toward the chapel for fear of running into Tyler and lecturing him on flirting with the likes of Stephanie. His social life was none of her concern, and she wasn't about to make a fool of herself again in front of him. Tomorrow he'd no longer be a friend, but her boss. Until then, she needed to bide her time thinking of other things.

The thought depressed her. How would things change once they got to work? She'd find out the next day at a staff meeting at 11:00 A.M. at Grizzly's, a local restaurant that was one of Ashlyn's favorites.

She was brought out of her thoughts when Tyler approached her just before the last meeting began. She looked up at him and smiled.

He smiled back. "If I weren't so self-assured, I'd think you were trying to avoid me." She smiled but didn't say a word. His smile faded. "You *are* trying to avoid me, aren't you?" Ashlyn grinned but still remained silent. "So much for being self-assured," he muttered. Still, Ashlyn said nothing. "Okay, this is the part where you boost my ego and say something, because I'm drowning here."

Ashlyn couldn't resist. She burst out laughing. "You're weak."

"Only when it comes to some things," he answered quietly, looking at her intently. "I was wondering if you've gotten any more calls."

"No, but the more I think about it, the more I think I was making a big deal out of nothing."

"Well, I was thinking about it last night," he said, mentally recalling that he was thinking more about *her*, "and I think we ought to start with the present and work our way back. Maybe we should check out the cases you're working on and see if there is a connection somewhere. I've been invited to join someone for dinner today, but we can look into it when our shift starts tomorrow night. Sound good to you?"

Ashlyn didn't trust herself to speak, so she nodded her agreement.

"Great. I'll see you then." Tyler turned and walked over and sat by Eric. Ashlyn clenched her jaw as she watched him walk away. The thought of him having dinner with Stephanie—or so she assumed—frustrated her—not only because Stephanie was a flirt, but also because she let it bother her. She scowled.

By the time she got home, her mood had blackened. She told Kerry she was going to sleep and not to interrupt her for any reason. Kerry nodded as she walked into the kitchen to fix herself some lunch. Ashlyn was asleep almost before her head hit the pillow.

Ashlyn awoke to the sound of a ringing doorbell and some talking. Glancing at the clock, she noticed that she had been asleep for almost six hours. It was eight o'clock, and her room was getting dark. She rolled out of bed feeling better than she had for days.

She slowly made her way down the short hallway to the front room. Kerry sat reading a very thick novel.

"I thought I heard some talking in here," Ashlyn said.

Without taking her eyes off the book, Kerry replied, "Annie brought us over some cookies. She said we could use some fattening up. They're really good, unfortunately. They're on the table if you want any. Eat them fast. My girlish figure can't handle those sinful things." Kerry laughed.

"I hope when I get to be fifty, I'll remember to be as kind as her. I feel sorry for her. She's all alone." Ashlyn thought about Annie Long, a widow in the ward who had never remarried. She suddenly had the depressing realization that her choices in life might lead her down the same path. Trying to shake it off, she asked Kerry, "Feel like going for a ride?"

Kerry put down her book, placed a bookmark in it, and set it aside. "Anywhere in particular?" she asked.

"Nah. The weather is still so wonderful. It won't be long until the first snowfall, so we may as well enjoy it now."

"You love the snow. Where do you really want to go?"

"Spying," Ashlyn answered disappointedly.

"Eric lives down a private lane. We'll get caught."

"Eric? Eric who?" Ashlyn asked innocently.

"You really are pathetic." Kerry giggled.

The two women drove here and there for a while, then turned into the neighborhood that the Christensen family lived in.

"There he is!" Kerry screamed.

Thinking fast, Ashlyn exclaimed, "Duck!"

Kerry responded quickly but not too gracefully as she bumped her head on the dashboard. "Ouch!" she cried, diving to the floor of Ashlyn's Pathfinder.

"Kerry! He's waving me over to stop." Ashlyn's voice revealed her panic.

"Ignore him!" Kerry exclaimed, the same panic rising in her voice. She could feel Ashlyn slowing the vehicle down to a stop.

"I can't! He saw me and he's walking out to the curb!"

Eric walked over to the Pathfinder, looked in, and was surprised to see Kerry bent over. Suddenly she sat up. "Found it!" she cried as she lifted up a sticky old quarter from under the seat.

"Hi, Kerry," he said, confusion evident in his voice.

Kerry wanted to fade away into parts unknown, never to return and face Eric again. She looked over to see Ashlyn and Eric staring at her. "Fancy meeting you here, Eric," she said weakly, feeling the heat rise up her neck and onto her cheeks.

Finally, after what seemed like hours, Ashlyn gathered her wits about her. "Uh, did you need something? You stopped us."

"Oh," he answered still looking at Kerry questioningly, "I was wondering if you've had any more calls."

"Nope. All is quiet today," Ashlyn answered a little too enthusiastically.

"A little too quiet," Kerry mumbled under her breath.

Eric, overhearing her comment, asked, "What did you say?"

Kerry's reaction to being caught was instant. She stuttered, "I . . . said . . . a little true diet. Ashlyn and I decided to go on a true diet and really stick to it this time. Just started it today. Didn't we?" She shot a look at Ashlyn, who wanted to disappear.

"Yeah," was the best she could do.

"I was going to invite you in. Mom made some German chocolate cake. I guess that's not such a good idea."

"That's a great idea." Kerry perked up with excitement. "Park the car," she quickly ordered her friend.

Ashlyn looked at her as if Kerry had just lost her mind. "What about our 'true diet'?"

"Like I always said, never start a diet on Sundays. That's what Mondays are for." Kerry grinned and jumped out of the car.

* * *

Eric and Ashlyn sat on the couch cheering as Kerry and Eric's teenage brother, Neil, played a game of Nintendo. It had come down to the third game, best out of three wins, and they were tied one to one.

"Come on, Kerry. Women worldwide are counting on you to bring the victory cup home!" Ashlyn cheered her on.

Eric laughed. "I'd hardly call the last piece of cake a 'victory cup.'"

At that second, there was a loud whoop and holler as Kerry broke into a victory dance.

"Careful, Kerry. We don't want to be sore *winners!*" Ashlyn shouted as she got up and joined Kerry in the victory dance as Eric brought the last piece of cake forward. He then slumped onto the floor next to a dejected Neil.

Kerry stopped. "Oh, here, you big babies. You can have the trophy. But with every bite, let us not forget who rules!" She handed the cake over.

"We don't want your charity. We challenge you to another duel at a later date," Eric dared.

"Fine. Can we get this wrapped to go?" Kerry said triumphantly.

Eric stood to carry out her wishes. "What happened to your true diet?" he asked as he left for the kitchen without waiting for Kerry's reply.

* * *

Heading down Main Street at ten-thirty that night, Kerry was still going on about the great time she'd had. They were coming up on Sam's place when someone out in front of the tavern caught Ashlyn's attention. She whipped her car into the empty gas station parking lot across from the bar, then turned off the engine. The station was already closed for the day, allowing Ashlyn some darkness to see what she was looking at without being caught.

"What are you doing?" Kerry asked.

"Sshh!" Ashlyn answered hastily. "It's Carl Wadsworth. He's at Sam's. I want to see if he's up to something. Stay here and don't make a noise, okay?"

"Be careful," was all Kerry had a chance to say before Ashlyn was out the door and peeking around the corner of the station. She had a clear view of Carl, a man she had arrested for selling drugs about a month ago. Someone, however, had put up an astronomical amount of money to bail him out. She knew that the drug bust was only the tip of the iceberg, but it was merely a gut instinct and nothing she could prove. She knew he was dealing, and she wanted not only to get him, but his supplier too. She had exhausted all her leads and was waiting for him to make a false move. She knew he would because criminals like him always did. It was just a matter of patience, but hers was wearing thin.

She sat and watched him. She could feel the evil around him. She knew he was ruthless. She thought of the time she was called to a scene in the alleyway behind the housing project where his brother Terry lived. Someone had found Terry half dead, and when asked who had beaten him, Terry had whispered, "Carl." But Carl had been let go when Terry insisted that he was asking them to call Carl, not pointing a finger at him. Consequently, Carl was let out on a lack of evidence.

Carl was thirty-eight years old, six feet tall, and weighed 210 pounds. Ashlyn knew his stats from his police records, but she didn't need records to tell her who he was. His hair was a greasy, mousy brown that would hang in his eyes, giving the impression that he was hiding behind it. His nose had obviously been broken a few times but never set, and he was missing a front tooth. The teeth he did have were stained from chewing tobacco. He was one of the very few people Ashlyn truly feared.

He stood out front talking to two other men. One was Terry, but the other she couldn't recognize because he had his back to her most of the time. Carl looked around suspiciously as if he sensed someone was nearby. He quickly drew out three pieces of white paper and handed one to each man and kept one himself. They quickly put them in their pockets, talked a few minutes, and walked away. Carl and Terry got into Terry's old pickup truck, and the other man went into the bar.

Once the coast was clear, Ashlyn got back into her car, where Kerry was waiting. They headed home.

"What was that about?" Kerry asked.

"I'm not sure. Carl's up to something, I can feel it. I don't know what it is, but I've got to find out, or he'll be my undoing." Ashlyn had an eerie feeling and tried to shake it off. Her hands were cold and chills ran down her back. As the two women drove home in silence, she wondered how true those words would be.

CHAPTER 7

By the time Ashlyn woke up, Kerry had left for work. During the week they didn't see much of each other since Kerry was on day shifts and Ashlyn worked nights.

Ashlyn lay in bed, a feeling of disappointment creeping over her. Today Tyler became her boss. She knew better than to let it bother her. After all, she had wanted the day to come so she could quit worrying about becoming too good of friends with the handsome man she'd spent far too much time thinking about. She needed to be professional because professionalism would help her reach the goal she'd set long before she knew that a man like Tyler existed.

To help pass the time before her staff meeting, Ashlyn decided to catch up on her laundry. She'd let it go for a while and didn't realize how much she had. Eleven o'clock rolled around before she knew it, and she found herself walking through the doors of Grizzly's a couple of minutes late. Luckily for her, the meeting was just starting. Looking for a place to sit, she found a chair at a table that sat three other officers and offered a great view of Tyler. *Not that it matters,* she reminded herself.

He wore jeans and an officer's uniformed shirt. It was a dark navy blue that enhanced his wide shoulders as well as his eyes. Ashlyn sighed, and as she looked back at his eyes, she noticed they were looking at her! She was sure she'd turned ten shades of red as he smiled at her. At that moment, she also noticed Shirley sending her an icy glare. She pretended not to notice.

The tinkling of a glass caught Ashlyn's attention as Lieutenant Don Jamison stood to get everyone's attention. "We want to thank everyone for coming today. There are some who have pressing matters to attend to, so we'll make this brief. We want to introduce you to your new sergeant, who comes to us from the metro drug unit out of the LAPD. He has quite a list of accomplishments, but he asked that I make his introduction brief so that he doesn't break out into a sweat." At this everyone chuckled except Ashlyn. She dropped her fork with a clang that surely echoed through the Rockies. She looked over at Tyler as he did his best to suppress a grin. "So, without further ado, let's give a warm welcome to Sergeant Tyler O'Bryan."

Everyone applauded, including an overly enthusiastic Shirley. Tyler stood and looked at Shirley as if he thought she should be committed. Ashlyn rolled her eyes. Shirley didn't notice but instead kept applauding until someone discretely asked her to sit down and let the sergeant speak. She giggled so annoyingly that Ashlyn cringed. Shirley continued to look at Tyler with stars in her eyes.

"Thanks to everyone. Being the new kid on the block, I wasn't sure what to expect. Following Lieutenant Jamison gives me some pretty big shoes to fill, and I hope I'm up to the challenge. I've already been briefed on how things have been run in the past, and I think most things will stay the same. We all know 'sergeant' is only a title, not who I am. You're welcome to call me Tyler except when my bosses are around." He looked at Captain Sinclair and laughed. "And of course during official business. I'd like to help out any way I can. I'd like to join you in your cases. For the next several weeks, I'd like to work with each of you individually so that I can learn your areas, cases, and problems. I admire Lieutenant Jamison's admonition to adhere to all rules. I expect that too and will not allow insubordination. This is for the safety of your team as well as yourselves. I look forward to getting to know each of you and joining your team. Thank you."

Ashlyn watched Tyler as he sat down and the lieutenant patted him on the back. She realized she was truly impressed with Tyler, and it had nothing to do with those broad, muscular shoulders or dreamy blue eyes. He had the courage to pick up his life and step into uncharted waters to take command. Where did it land him? Looking at her fellow employees, she knew it had landed him a place of acceptance and respect.

Why couldn't she have that strength? Would she ever get to the point in her life where she would feel that she'd done enough? She felt herself sinking. She wasn't happy; she hadn't been truly happy for years. She wanted to be, but Austin's death weighted her shoulders, and she couldn't escape. Until she solved Austin's murder, she would continue to carry the blame.

Ashlyn was shaken from her thoughts as she watched Shirley fawning all over Tyler. He didn't seem to mind Shirley's attention either. She sat closely by him, talking to him often and giggling constantly. He sat and smiled back at her. Suddenly Ashlyn had the urge to run. Run where? Far enough away that he would never know how much she wished it was her that he smiled at? No. It never would be her.

Ashlyn stood abruptly, apologized to the officers at her table, and headed for the door. She never looked back to see the triumphant look on Shirley's face.

"Good-bye, angel," Shirley murmured.

* * *

Heading down Main Street with a load of groceries in her car, Ashlyn noticed Sam sweeping the front steps of his tavern. Without putting much thought into her actions, Ashlyn pulled into the parking lot and cut the engine. She stepped out of the car and slammed the door. "Sam!" she called out.

"Not you again," he moaned.

Ashlyn ignored the insult. "I need your help."

"No."

She raised her eyebrows in mock surprise. "I'd hate to arrest you for obstruction to an investigation."

"Why do you always do that?" he asked disgustedly.

"Do what?" She batted her eyelashes in mock innocence.

"Threaten me when you want me to help you out. You don't need to. I know my rights as well as my obligations to this community."

"You live in this community?" she asked, surprised.

"Where else would I live?"

"I guess I never gave it much thought. There are plenty of other towns to live in close enough to drive in to work in Monroe. Do you have a wife or kids here as well?"

"Am I part of your investigation?" Sam growled.

"No. To be honest, I'm not even here on official business."

"Now honesty is something I respect. Come in and let me see how I can help you."

Sam was still snarling, but Ashlyn suspected it was only a facade. "Hold on, I need to grab something from my car." She smiled.

He shrugged and waited for her to rummage through the groceries and pull out some chocolate ice cream. She quickly caught back up to him. She saw a hint of a grin as he replied, "Women and their chocolate fixes."

It was unusual to enter an empty bar. She knew from past experience that this place didn't get booming until later, but it was still unexpected.

Sam walked over behind the bar and pulled out two bowls and two spoons and joined her at a table.

Ashlyn was the first to speak. "You didn't answer my question. Do you have a wife and kids?" She held up her hand to stop his reply. "No interrogation. Just curiosity."

Sam looked at her for a long minute before he looked down at his ice cream and quietly answered, "My Lucy died five years ago of liver failure. My two boys are married but don't get down this way much. The sorry bunch is ashamed of their old man, I'm afraid."

Ashlyn was shocked. Sam had tried to keep up his brisk exterior, but Ashlyn had noticed the hurt in his eyes. "But why?" she whispered.

He looked her sadly in the eyes. "Because I contribute to the degenerates, scum, lowlifes, and criminals in the world—or so they say. But not everybody who drinks alcohol becomes a criminal or drunk. My Lucy is probably rolling in her grave too."

"If you feel that way, why are you doing it?"

"Don't you pass your judgments on me, girl!"

"Trying to understand can hardly be misunderstood for judgments, Sam," Ashlyn countered.

"Sometimes the only way to forget your sorrows is to hear about everyone else's. Not everybody drinks to cause crime. Some do it to loosen up, others to escape. This place is all I have. I don't force anybody to drink. I don't even encourage them. If someone needs a place to battle their demons, well . . . I know that feeling. I don't even drink the stuff myself." Suddenly Sam looked uncomfortable. "I got work to do, so ask your questions and go before somebody sees you here."

"I didn't come here to offend you or judge you. I'm sorry if I gave you that impression. I really am. I guess I've never gotten to know you, but I'm glad that I'm getting to." Ashlyn paused and switched subjects. "Anyway, there was a guy outside with Carl and Terry Wadsworth last night around ten-thirty. Do you know who he is?"

Sam spoke reluctantly, "I only know he's trouble. I don't know his name, but he's mean. He came in and had a few beers. I tried to talk to him and he shoved me off, so I figured he doesn't want any friends. Fine with me. They're the kind best to stay clear of.

Besides that, Carl is up to no good. Anyone involved with him can't be into much good either. That's all I know."

"Can't you give me more?" Ashlyn pressed. "Who is he?"

Sam shrugged. "He ain't a local. At least I've never seen him before. He paid cash, so I can't give you a name. That's all I'm gonna say."

Ashlyn knew that Sam was done with this conversation whether she was or not. There was no point in pushing him and risk losing one of her best sources of information.

She stood up and put her hand on his forearm. "Thanks, Sam. Keep the ice cream for next time." She turned and walked out the door.

* * *

It was almost five o'clock by the time Ashlyn pulled into her driveway. Kerry would be home at any time, so Ashlyn carried in the groceries, put them away, and took a hot shower. She had two hours to pull it together before seeing Tyler at work.

The thought depressed her and thrilled her. At least Shirley wouldn't be there. She might be his secretary, but she had day-shift hours and any work that Tyler wanted her to do was done then. *Poor Shirley,* Ashlyn thought sarcastically. She wasn't quite sure how she felt about facing Tyler, but she knew she didn't want to see Shirley or the two of them together.

Ashlyn heard Kerry call to her as she opened the front door. "Ashlyn? Are you home?"

Ashlyn walked into the front room to meet her friend there. "I'm here, but not for long," she answered, noticing the distressed look on Kerry's face. "You look a little upset, Kerry. What's wrong?"

Kerry sunk onto the couch and leaned her head back. "Nothing that a good dose of arsenic won't cure! Tell me it's not true that Tyler is interested in Shirley."

"Why would you think so?" Ashlyn answered, trying to sound as uninterested as her suddenly dry throat would allow.

"She so casually mentioned that Tyler asked her to lunch tomorrow. I didn't believe it until I overheard that at the luncheon today they couldn't take their eyes off each other. Is that true?"

Ashlyn tried to clear the dryness from her throat. "It appeared that way to me. I left early so I didn't see the whole thing, but he certainly had her undivided attention," Ashlyn mentioned, attempting to sound nonchalant while secretly holding back a sob.

"Well, I still didn't believe it until I talked to Eric. He told me that Tyler had asked about different restaurants. He said he was going to lunch tomorrow but didn't say with who."

"I'd say that's enough evidence to convict then," Ashlyn answered dismally.

"Doesn't it bug you? It's really bugging me! Is he so shallow to go for someone like her? I thought he was a better judge of character. I'm not trying to be malicious. It's just that she's so phony and insincere. I mean, *anyone* in the office would be better than her. The rest of the day she was strutting her stuff like a peacock. I'm so . . . She's so . . ." Kerry's words were lost in her frustration. "It's just that . . . I'm going to make something chocolate."

"You're taking this awfully hard. Were you pining for his heart as well?"

"Not for me! For you! I saw you both dancing together on Saturday night. You were stunning! You hit it off so well. He wants to help you. Doesn't that say something?"

"Yes, it says that he's a really nice man who is willing to help a friend. You know how I feel about my goals, and I can't let the Tylers in the world distract me."

She hesitated before continuing, almost reluctantly, "I'll let you in on something. If anyone has ever tempted me to change my mind, it would be him. No one has ever gotten my attention like him before. I don't know his favorite color, food, anything about his family, nothing. But I feel like we've always been friends. Believe me, I know how ridiculous that sounds. I hear myself say it and I know it's insane. When I look at him or watch him, I feel like I'm going to melt into a puddle of mush. It scares me and it makes me angry. For that reason, I need to keep as much space between us as I can.

"It's for the best to have him interested in someone. Shirley wouldn't be my first pick, but I can't honestly give you a name of *any* girl I'd like to see him with. The sooner he finds a girl-friend and gets married, the better off I'll be. It won't be long before he finds someone, so I'd better get used to it. I say, 'Get him married and good riddance.'"

"What if he's here to sweep *you* off your feet?"

"He can't. My feet are set in stone. If he's interested in Shirley, so be it. Trust me, it's all so complicated, but he never will be mine, so I'll take his friendship, but even then at a distance. It has to be that way."

"I'm sorry, but it's just not right," Kerry said, sitting dejectedly on the couch as the phone rang.

Ashlyn smiled sadly at her friend and picked up the phone.

"Could I please speak with Ashlyn Lawrence?" the male voice asked.

"This is she."

"Ashlyn, this is Dave Parker. How are you?"

"Dave Parker! Well, this is a surprise. I'm doing well. What about you?"

"I'm great! Did I call at a bad time?"

"Of course not! It's been almost a year since you called last. What has happened since then?"

"I'll give you the *Reader's Digest* version. Work has really been booming. The company started out in California. From there I was transferred back east, and now I've been transferred to Salt

Lake. Actually, I'm based there but I cover the surrounding area, so now I'm over the Denver office too, where I'll be spending a lot of time. I was hoping you'd let me take you to dinner. That is, if you're still unattached."

"I'm still unattached. I'm assuming you are too if you're asking me to dinner. I'd hate for some girlfriend to remove my lungs with a spoon for stealing time with her man." Ashlyn laughed.

Dave laughed also. "I would never mess with the long arm of the law. No woman in sight for miles. Are we on?"

"We're on. When is your next trip?"

"This weekend. I know it's short notice, but I'm flying in on Thursday night and leaving Sunday. Do you have any free time?"

"I'm working nights right now, so Saturday is my only free night."

"Sound's great. Hey, by the way, what time is your church on Sunday? I thought I'd try to go before I fly out. It somehow makes me feel not quite so guilty for flying on Sunday."

"Our church starts at 9:00 A.M."

"Dang! That won't work since my flight leaves at 11:00. Maybe next time I can get a later flight and join you. Give me directions to your house, and I'll pick you up around six on Saturday. Will that work?"

"Well, I'm about a half hour outside of Denver. Will that be too much travel for you?"

"Not at all. I'm looking forward to this. It'll be good to see you again."

Ashlyn gave Dave directions and hung up the phone, her emotions mixed. She looked up and saw Kerry watching her.

She looked at Ashlyn and spoke quietly. "That was Dave Parker? You're going out with Dave Parker? What about Tyler?"

Ashlyn felt a little defensive. "Yes, that was Dave and yes, I'm going out with him. Why is that such a bad thing? He even offered to take me to church. There was a time that Austin had to beg him to go. His flight interferes with our church time, but it's nice he's stayed active after all this time."

"Yeah. That's just great. Really impressive," Kerry answered Ashlyn sarcastically.

"What?"

"You've met Tyler now, that's what. Dave may have kept brief contact with you over the years, but he's never even come to see you."

"Give me a break, Kerry. He's been working back east. It's not as if that's right around the corner," Ashlyn reasoned.

"Is that the best argument you can give me in his defense? If so, it'll never stand in court."

"He's not on trial here, Kerry."

"I'm sure I won't like him."

"I'm not marrying him—I'm eating dinner with him. Besides, don't pass judgment on him. He's taken a really bad situation of a life and turned it into something good." It was time to change the subject. "I've got to go or I'll be late for work. Oh, and could you feed Gomer, Gunther, and Gomez?" She looked over at the aquarium in front of the large window in guilt.

Kerry sighed. "Poor babies wouldn't be alive if it weren't for me."

"No wonder they like you better. Thanks, Kerry. Lock the doors and I'll see you later."

CHAPTER 8

Ashlyn walked into the office prompt as usual. She tried to force her eyes from looking to where Tyler might be, but she found herself scanning the room for him. He was in the same clothes as he had been in earlier and sat discussing a report with Officer Harris. When she walked over to her desk, he looked up and smiled. She was never going to get used to that smile.

She sat down and turned on her computer, intending to go over some files and do some research. There was an e-mail waiting to be opened, so she quickly clicked it on to retrieve her message. It was from Shirley, and the message was brief. "Mission Accomplished" in large letters flashed on the screen. It irritated her, but not nearly as much as it depressed her. She sat staring at the screen, and her stomach dropped. She hated the thought of Tyler falling for Shirley. Her stomach turned as she reminded herself there was nothing she could do about it.

"What does that mean?" Tyler asked from behind her. There was no way he could have missed seeing the large bolded words across her screen. Ashlyn quickly deleted the message and turned to look up into his gorgeous eyes.

"You'd better ask Shirley," she said dejectedly. She had been so deep in thought that she hadn't even heard him come up behind her. Fortunately, she was saved from further comment when the office page went off on her phone. Since the secretaries were gone by six, the dispatchers took both personal and emergency calls. Apparently one of the dispatchers had seen Tyler standing by Ashlyn's desk. "Ashlyn, could you tell the sergeant there's a call for him on line one?"

"Will do, Aimee. Thanks."

"Mind if I take it here?" he asked.

"Go ahead." She slid the phone towards him.

"Hi, Kate," he answered. "Everything okay? Is everything still on in three weeks? I'm dying to see Maddie. I've missed her. Don't forget to pack everything. After this time apart, I don't plan to ever let her go again. She's mine for good. Make it clear to him that he'll never have her. Thanks. I'll see you soon . . . Bye."

Ashlyn overheard it all. She was glad that Shirley wasn't necessarily Tyler's new love interest, but this Maddie person only complicated things worse. Ashlyn's hands were shaking, so she clenched them in her lap. *Who is Kate? Even worse, who is Maddie?* The thought sickened her that maybe she'd have to watch Tyler in love with someone else.

"Are you feeling all right?" Tyler interrupted. "You look a little pale. I noticed you left the luncheon early, so I wondered if everything was okay."

"Yeah. Sure. Great," she mumbled.

Tyler looked at her, disbelieving. "I looked through your files, and everything seems pretty much cut and dried except for this Carl Wadsworth character. I wonder if he's the one making the threats? We're missing something here, and I've got a gut feeling that he's capable of a lot worse than some prank calls. Let's first go through that file with a fine-tooth comb, then we can go out and scout his stomping grounds."

"Oh!" Ashlyn said in surprise. "I thought you said today that you wanted to spend time with each officer to go over cases and such."

"That's still my plan, and you're first on my list. I think one of our own being threatened should take precedence, don't you? Besides, I'm right here if anyone needs me, so let's get started."

For the next couple of hours, Ashlyn sat next to Tyler and showed him all the information she had gathered clear up to Sunday night when she saw Carl at the bar. She told him about her visit with Sam, and as she filled out a report about her interview with him, Tyler walked around chatting with his officers and checking in with dispatch. Just as she finished filing the report, Tyler walked back over.

"It's a slow night, and everything is in order here. Let's go check Carl's house and the places he hangs out. Hopefully I'll get to see what he looks like instead of going by this tiny snapshot. Your car or mine?"

"Carl knows my car," Ashlyn said. "How about if we take yours?"

"Let's go. I'm parked around back. I'll go get a radio."

Tyler opened the door of his black Jeep Cherokee for Ashlyn. The interior was soft, tan leather. As he walked to the driver's side, she quickly inhaled, taking in the smell of pine and cologne.

He climbed in the car, then turned to her. "Which way?"

Ashlyn gave directions across town to the bar as well as to Carl's house. As they drove, they talked about their families, childhood, and the schools they had attended. While they sat watching the bar, Tyler spoke about his mission to Canada. She laughed as he told her stories about his mission and his companions, and listened intently as he told her of the experiences that strengthened his testimony of the gospel. She even talked him into speaking French to her. He wouldn't translate, but it sure sounded good. It had been a wonderful evening, except, Ashlyn thought, that they weren't on a date; this was work.

Since they hadn't spotted Carl at the bar or his house, they headed back to the office. Ashlyn glanced at the clock, which read 2:00 A.M. Where had all the time gone? She had enjoyed herself so much she hadn't realized it was so late.

At this hour, the streets were all but abandoned. As they drove down Main Street, a man ran frantically out into the street, waving them to stop. Tyler immediately pulled over and was out of the car in a flash.

"It's my wife!" the man cried. "I've got a flat, and she's having a baby. Please help us!"

Ashlyn pulled out her cell phone and called dispatch. Tyler ran over to check on the woman.

"Hey, Ashlyn!" he called. "There's a blanket and a first-aid kit in the back of my Jeep. Grab them! This baby isn't waiting."

She ran to get the things he asked for, and by the time she returned to the car, Tyler had helped the woman lie down in the backseat. Her husband had her head in his lap and was in a panic, crying.

Tyler calmly spoke to him. "Sir, it's okay. You've got to calm down for her sake because we've got to deliver the baby."

"Please, please help," the man said. "She's been so sick and couldn't get ahold of the doctor before his office closed for the day, so she was going to wait to see him at her checkup tomorrow. But then she couldn't take the pain any longer, so I was taking her in to the hospital. Then we got a flat. Do you know what you're doing?"

"Don't worry, sir," Tyler calmly said. "I've done this before, and the ambulance is on its way."

Ashlyn kneeled at Tyler's side with the blanket, ready for the sweet little baby that refused to be held back any longer from making an entrance into the world. Within seconds, Ashlyn held a tiny, wailing baby boy. His fists were clenched tight, and he stretched his small, spindly legs. She cleaned him as best she could, then wrapped him tight and spoke soothingly. Once he was warm, he calmed down and looked up at Ashlyn with tiny, squinting eyes. He was the cutest thing she had ever seen!

Tyler stood up and looked at Ashlyn. They smiled at each other, obviously moved by the recent event. "Sounds like his lungs are working just fine! Hey, little guy! Welcome to the world!" Tyler said as he leaned over Ashlyn's shoulders. "Look at him! He's just as amazed with you as the rest of us are."

The paramedics arrived at that moment to finish taking care of the mother and the baby, who was taken from Ashlyn's arms. As the ambulance pulled away, she looked at Tyler and felt so empty that she cried. She couldn't stop herself. She cried because she would never get to have that most sacred experience herself, and she cried because Tyler was beyond her reach.

Suddenly without a single word, Tyler stepped over to her and held her while she cried. For one brief moment, she was caught off guard because somehow, being in his arms felt surprisingly right.

* * *

Tyler drove toward his home so deep in thought that as he pulled up in front of his house, he didn't recall driving there. He stayed out in his car for several more minutes before cutting the engine and slowly walking in.

He stood beneath the hot shower until it ran cold, then he got out and slowly dressed. He walked into his room and lay on his bed with his hands behind his head. He stared at the ceiling.

The same thought repeated itself over and over in his head. He had really fallen for Ashlyn. It didn't make sense. He hardly knew her. He was thirty years old and had never experienced these emotions in his life. They talked like they'd known each other forever, but didn't it take longer to fall into lasting love? But how long? It didn't matter. He couldn't love her. It was too complicated.

He thought of her again, then got off his bed and kneeled in prayer. He sincerely prayed to his Father in Heaven, begging for answers and blessings. He felt the need to especially pray that Ashlyn would overcome her struggles. After ending his prayer, he got up and shut the blinds in his room to make it darker, a necessity for anyone working the graveyard shift. Then he crawled back into bed.

Back in L.A. he had prayed about coming here. Several times in fact. He felt sure this was the place he wanted to work and settle down. Was this why? So that he could help Ashlyn? He wanted to settle down and have a family, but he figured it would happen when the time was right. Tonight he looked at Ashlyn as she sat in his car and marveled at how they'd talked and laughed for hours. He didn't want to go back to the office after their surveillance, but felt prompted to leave. Now he knew why. Someone had needed the help that they had to offer. When he stood and watched Ashlyn holding the baby, he could hardly contain himself. She looked so beautiful. He really wanted things to work out with her. He'd gotten hints before tonight, but it hit him full force when she was standing there with the baby. When she started to cry, he was too afraid to ask why since he'd been choked up too. It was an indescribable experience, helping a baby come into this world. Tyler knew he was in trouble. Holding her felt so natural.

* * *

Two weeks later Ashlyn walked into the office at eleven-thirty to see if she could bring Kerry some lunch. She had gone shopping to get the new baby a gift and to finally replace the punch bowl that she and Tyler had broken. Plus, today was payday, her favorite day.

As she neared Kerry's cubicle, she noticed Kerry was taking a call. So she picked up Kerry's check and motioned to her that she'd go deposit it with hers. Kerry nodded, and Ashlyn was on her way. As she began to exit the front door, Tyler was just coming through.

Shirley came running up to greet him. "Couldn't wait to see me, huh?" she gushed. "You're early." Shirley saw Ashlyn and stepped a little closer to Tyler.

He looked at Ashlyn and smiled. "Hey! I didn't expect to see you this early. What are you doing?"

Shirley glared, and Ashlyn relished Tyler's attention. After all, he had hardly even acknowledged Shirley. "Payday." She held up the two white envelopes. "I came in to get our checks to deposit them. I thought I'd get Kerry some lunch, but she got a call." Ashlyn looked back at Kerry, who was still on the telephone.

"We were going to get something to eat too," Tyler mentioned. "For the past few weeks, Shirley's been taking her lunch hour to fill me in on some office procedures. Why don't you join us this time?" Tyler offered.

Ashlyn looked at Shirley as she tried to hold herself back from doing a jig of glee. Shirley asked Tyler to lunch! Not the other way around!

Shirley looked away and sighed with an attitude of boredom.

"I'd love to join you." Ashlyn looked at Shirley and smirked when Shirley jerked her head up to scowl at Ashlyn. "But I'd better get this check in the bank to cover the punch bowl you and I broke."

Ashlyn got the reaction she wanted from Shirley. It was a mixture of shock and anger. Shirley looked dumbfounded as she realized that Tyler had been with Ashlyn outside of the office.

"Let me pay for that," Tyler offered.

"According to some biased witnesses, it was my fault. I still say they were wrongly influenced, or dare I say, bribed. Either way, I'll cover the cost. I insist." She smiled at Tyler and continued, "Thanks for the offer though." Ashlyn turned and walked away.

A few minutes later, she walked into the bank while talking to Kerry on the cell phone. Kerry was laughing about every detail of Ashlyn's conversation with Tyler and Shirley. Ashlyn had just gotten to the front of the line, still talking to Kerry, when she heard the shot ring out. She looked up to see the bank security guard fall where only seconds before he was standing at the only set of doors to the bank.

"Everybody get down. *Now!*" yelled a deep, loud voice.

The elderly gentleman in front of her jumped to get on the floor and slammed his head on the edge of the counter. The sharp edge split his skin, and the wound bled profusely.

Ashlyn slid over to him and put her hand on his wound to slow the bleeding. Quietly she placed her cell phone between them and spoke, hoping that Kerry could pick up her voice.

"Three men. Guard shot. Six employees, six customers—one wounded from fall."

One of the three robbers walked over to where Ashlyn huddled next to the older gentleman. "Hey, beautiful," he said. "Fancy meeting you in a place like this. Tony, get a look at her."

Ashlyn kept quiet but was revolted by his slimy character. She finally spoke. "My father here has been hurt. Will you please just let him go? At least let me help him move away from here. I could put him over in the corner."

"How about we shoot him and put the old geezer outta his misery?" he snickered.

"No, please," she pleaded. "I'll do as you ask, just let me move him."

"Oooh, a beautiful whiner. Get him out of here and then come back. This favor's gonna cost you."

Holding back a shudder, Ashlyn stood the man up, and once their backs were to the robber, she leaned towards the elderly man and said, "Sir, I'm a cop. The police department is on the phone. Lie facing the wall and give this dispatcher every detail you can, but be very quiet."

The elderly man nodded as his eyes glistened. "Thank you, dear," he whispered. "Thank you."

She helped the gentleman down and placed the phone between him and the wall. Then she wiped her bloodied hand on her pant leg and turned to go back. There were half a dozen customers including herself and about that many tellers and bank personnel. She quickly scanned the room, taking in as much as she could.

"Get over here, baby. Come to old Randy."

This idiot was probably a first timer, Ashlyn thought. What criminal in his right mind would come on to a hostage while pulling off a robbery? The fact that he was an idiot didn't make him any less dangerous, however. Ashlyn made quick mental notes. *First guy is Tony. This scum is Randy. Give me the third name.*

"I said get over here, baby," Randy snarled, revealing a roll of duct tape. "You're gonna be mine."

Over my dead body, Ashlyn thought with another shudder.

Suddenly, as Randy attempted to duct tape Ashlyn's wrists, the police came barreling into the parking lot. Ashlyn heard Eric calling through the megaphone, "Monroe Police. Come out with your hands up."

Randy pushed Ashlyn toward the third robber. "Hey, Jim, tape her up and use her as a hostage." Jim followed the orders, which made it obvious that Randy was the leader of the three. "Tony, are you done?" Randy asked in a tight voice. Ashlyn noted that he was getting nervous. Beads of sweat had begun to connect on his forehead. Both Tony and Jim were starting to panic, forgetting to bind Ashlyn's hands. She also noticed the tape around her feet was hastily strapped—a sloppy job she was sure she could use to her advantage. The phone started ringing.

Ashlyn took the clue and spoke evenly. "It's probably the cops. Maybe they'll negotiate." She knew there was no way for these criminals to get away now.

Randy grabbed her by the upper arms and threw her into a chair near the phone. He held his gun to her head and said, "You talk but one false word, and I'll blow your head off and everyone else here one at a time. You tell them I want a direct line with the one in charge."

He picked up the phone and put it next to Ashlyn's ear. She looked at him and spoke carefully. "My name is Ashlyn. We need a direct line with the one in charge out there."

"Ashlyn, this is Eric. We have the whole crew, including Tyler and the captain. Try to assess this for me. I'll try to follow anything you can give me."

Still speaking into the phone, she looked up at Randy and spoke to him. "The gun at my head is hurting me. I can't think."

Randy looked at her. "It'll hurt worse if I blow it off. Tell them to back off."

Eric spoke. "I've got that Ashlyn. You're their hostage and they've got guns. One is pointed to your head. Don't worry. We'll get you out of there."

Ashlyn looked up at Randy and continued talking to Eric. "Call the force off, or the robbers will start shooting one at a time. Can you carry that off?"

Eric's reassuring voice came on the line. "You're doing great. Kerry is on the line with the victim. We have good contact."

She turned to Randy. "Can we negotiate? Let the others go. They'll only be in the way. If you'll let them go, the police will start to back off."

Randy smirked and jabbed her in the head with his gun. "You tell them they ain't got a thing to negotiate with."

Ashlyn tried to think clearly—a difficult task with a gun barrel pressuring her left temple. "They have plenty to negotiate with. Right now this place is surrounded. You kill anyone here, and you'll land on death row. That's if you make it out alive."

"Give me that!" he yelled and yanked the phone out of her hand. "You listen to me, pig. Right now I've got a gun to this beauty's head. You mess with me, and I'll scatter her brains over all these walls—unless, of course, she'd like to negotiate with me personally." Randy laughed.

The laugh made Ashlyn feel physically sick. She shuddered. Anger started to set in. How could these creeps do this to all these innocent people? She knew that once the hostages were out of harm's way, she would take the robbers on or die trying.

Tyler heard what Randy said and groaned in frustration.

Eric put a hand on his friend's shoulder. Tyler turned away and paced back and forth trying to get a grip on his anger and worry.

Randy laughed and taunted. "I'm not too worried about what you'll do with me. A bullet would be worth the time I'm gonna have with her. Don't worry. I'm sending them all out. But this one is a keeper."

Randy turned and ordered two customers to help the wounded men out. Jim opened the doors and allowed everyone out but Ashlyn. Then he quickly locked the doors and stepped back from the door.

The hostages ran to the far corner of the parking lot. The wounded men were immediately rushed into an ambulance. One man walked up to the captain as Eric and Tyler stood making plans to get Ashlyn.

"You've got to get her out of there, Officer. I think the head guy, Randy, is going to kill her. Somebody's got to save her."

Tyler clenched his jaw so tight that his head began to ache.

Ashlyn noticed Randy laid the phone down but didn't hang it up. She still had a connection with her friends. He grabbed her by the arm and whipped her out of her chair. "In the vault, baby. Now!" he yelled. He pushed her over to the vault, where Tony was gathering money.

Ashlyn noticed that Tony had laid his gun down to fill a bag with money.

"Jim, get on the phone and tell them pigs she's gonna die if they don't back off," Randy said, his gun still at Ashlyn's head.

Once they were in the vault, Ashlyn turned to Randy and said evenly, "Tell him to leave." She nodded toward Tony. "No sense in him seeing me die too."

Randy ordered Tony to leave. Just as she'd hoped, Tony left his gun behind. She stealthily tucked it behind her back.

As Randy turned to close the vault door a little bit, Ashlyn cocked the gun and held it to Randy's head. "Shut that and you'll never get out of here alive. The security is set. The vault will automatically lock."

Randy whipped around as Ashlyn caught him off guard. She butted him with the gun on the bridge of his nose and again on his head. She heard his nose break as he yelled and fell to the floor. She grabbed his gun and quickly stepped back as Tony came running in to see what had happened. She held him at gunpoint as she ordered him into the vault. She stepped outside and slammed the door shut.

Ashlyn turned to see Jim pointing a gun at her. "Put your gun down, Jim. You can kill me, but it won't do you any good. The vault isn't going to open. They can't help you. You're all alone. Just give yourself up. Most likely the judge will go easier on you. Come on, let's go outside." Jim looked suspiciously at Ashlyn. "Believe it or not, Jim, I'm a cop."

"You're lying," he answered nervously. His body shook, and he seemed so distraught that Ashlyn quickly kicked the gun out of his hand and held him at gunpoint. She kept the guns aimed at him as she slowly backed away and picked his gun.

"Turn around and head out the door slowly." Jim obeyed and walked out the door in front of her, shaking and crying. Ashlyn held the gun to his back. As she opened the door, she called out, "It's okay. I've apprehended them. We're coming out."

At the sight of Ashlyn walking through the doors, two officers grabbed the man and placed him under arrest. She let the other officers know of the offenders who remained in the bank vault. Evidently, someone had called the media as well as the bank president, and crowds gathered around Ashlyn, asking questions. She smiled wearily and asked that the commanding officer make a statement for her once she had a chance to brief him.

Ashlyn turned and looked for Tyler. She spotted him immediately. He was leaning against the police car with his elbows on the hood watching her. He smiled at her and gave her a thumbs-up as she smiled back. She walked away from the crowd toward him, Eric, and Captain Sinclair.

Eric greeted her with a hug, and Tyler envied him the opportunity. The fear that had gripped him earlier started to dissipate, leaving him with pent-up emotion. He could imagine that Ashlyn's adrenaline rush must have worn off by now because she looked exhausted. He wanted to tell everyone to leave her alone, but although he was her boss, he wasn't in command. The captain and Eric were. So he waited.

After what seemed like an eternity, Tyler got his chance to talk to her. Everyone had wanted details. All he wanted to know was if she would be all right. If she wasn't, Tyler would make the robber pay.

He felt such anger toward the creep who'd tried to kill her. Tyler couldn't remember the last time he'd felt this red-hot anger. Ashlyn wasn't a cop today. She was a patron at the bank and could have been harmed or killed.

Ashlyn walked over to him. "I didn't get my check deposited after all."

"Ever heard of automatic deposits? The office does that, you know." Tyler looked down into her eyes. All he wanted to do was hold her and let her know that he'd protect her.

Ashlyn looked up into his eyes. "That's so 'new age,' don't you think?"

"I think you ought to seriously consider it," he said with a smile.

"It might keep me out of banks. Consider it done. Where do I sign up?"

Tyler smiled. "You look beat. I came with Eric, but I can drive you home in your car and have Eric pick me up and take me back to the office."

"Thanks, but I have to file a report so that Eric can make a statement to the press. I am tired, though." Ashlyn sighed. "A minute ago I would have taken all the press on, but now I'm drained and a little shaky."

"How about if I drive you home so you can get cleaned up and I'll take you back to the office," he asked hopefully.

"There's an offer I can't refuse. My keys are in my purse, and it's still in the bank."

The captain walked over to Tyler and Ashlyn. "Good work, Ashlyn. You did us proud. I need to see you both in my office today. When you're done with your statement, why don't you both come see me right after?"

Without waiting for an answer, the captain turned away.

"Are we in trouble?" Ashlyn asked with raised eyebrows.

"I don't know why we would be," Tyler responded.

"So much for a long hot bath. I guess we're going straight to the office."

* * *

Ashlyn felt ragged and dirty as she looked at her bloodstained jeans. But she was more concerned at her present situation as she sat with Tyler across from the captain seated at his desk. She had a bad feeling about it, but she couldn't figure out why.

The captain spoke clearly. "This is the first problem I've come across as the captain, so I'm a little unfamiliar on how to deal with it. I'll get right to the point. Someone who chose to remain anonymous e-mailed me a letter this morning that concerns you two, and whatever budding romance you two have going here should not affect your jobs."

Tyler's jaw clenched as the captain continued. "Apparently, since Tyler's first night on the job, Ashlyn has had his undivided attention, and it's my understanding you left together for a few hours during your first shift as well. You will get only this one warning. If it happens again, you're both fired. Am I clear?"

Ashlyn was shocked speechless.

Tyler was furious. Through clenched teeth he tried to explain. "I made an announcement my first day that over the next several weeks I would spend my shifts with each officer. I even gave Shirley a schedule so that officers would be notified as to which shift I'd be working with them on, and I've stuck to that schedule. Haley is scheduled for tonight. I plan to go on his routes too. That doesn't mean I intend to have a 'budding romance' with him as well!"

Tyler continued, "At the beginning of that first shift, I checked with each officer before sitting at Ashlyn's desk to go over a particular file. Then, before we went out to patrol her areas, I checked with every one of my officers again, offering any assistance. On the way back from her route, we got a bit sidetracked. It was all in my report. I've also spent a lot of time working with Ashlyn because she received a threatening phone call that appears to be job related. I felt the safety of one of my officers held priority. If this 'anonymous' officer had such an issue with me, why didn't he confront me? I don't like being accused here, and I don't like my morals being questioned, so if that's how this place works, I'll save you the trouble of firing me. I'll quit."

Ashlyn was stunned. Tyler had a right to be angry. He'd done everything by the book, and although Ashlyn had loved the time they spent together, it was all work related. Ashlyn was also embarrassed. She knew that now, every time she looked or talked to Tyler, someone might be questioning her motives. She thought of the officers on her team. Who would pull such a dirty trick? Maybe she needed to be off the team. Hastily she spoke up.

"I don't want to work on this team anymore. I refuse to be questioned every time I talk to the sergeant or have to go with him on a case. I won't work with someone I can't trust, and because I don't know who wrote the letter, I'm suspecting all of my team."

The captain stood and paced the floor. He stopped and faced them both. "Why have you never told me about being threatened?" he asked Ashlyn.

"Because I can't explain it yet. There are a few holes in the Carl Wadsworth file, and Sergeant O'Bryan went with me to look for him or to see if we could make some sense of those holes." Ashlyn was angry, but not as angry as she was hurt and discouraged.

The captain looked concerned. "What goes on between you two is nobody's business. I don't give two hoots about it. But I will not allow it to affect this office. Ashlyn, you have the night off with pay. Maybe we had better separate you two for the sake of the office. Putting you on different teams might solve the problem. I'll let you know in the next day or two. Until then, Ashlyn, go home."

"I'm being suspended? You're suspending me over an anonymous letter?" Ashlyn cried, getting angrier by the minute.

Tyler was seething. "I can't believe that you're taking the word of an anonymous letter over our explanation."

The captain spoke sternly. "Simmer down, both of you. You're not being suspended. You have the night off because of your efforts today. We still have to investigate the scene of the crime. That's how it works, as you very well know. Plus, you've earned it. I'll speak with both of you either tomorrow or the next day over this other matter. And please don't mention this little visit to anyone. You're excused."

Ashlyn stood and walked to the door as Tyler walked behind her. He reached around her to open the door for her.

They took a few steps away from the captain's office and were greeted by Shirley, who looked at Ashlyn and smirked. "Why, Ashlyn, you look positively awful. I don't believe I've ever seen you look so terrible." She dismissed her by looking up to Tyler and smiling sweetly. "Tyler, why don't we go to lunch now? It's a little late, but maybe we can call it an early dinner."

Ashlyn glared at Shirley as she walked past her, not even bothering to stop and reply. Right now she was livid, and if Shirley didn't lay off the snide comments, Ashlyn would say something she'd regret.

Over her shoulder, she heard Tyler answer, "I'm not hungry, and just for the record, it's not a good idea for us to go anywhere. If you want to have lunch delivered here tomorrow, I'll meet with you in my office with the door open."

Ashlyn heard the shock in Shirley's voice. "Why? I thought we had plans."

Ashlyn was out of earshot so she didn't hear Tyler's reply. It didn't matter. She wanted to get out of there as quickly as possible.

CHAPTER 9

As Ashlyn pulled into the driveway, Kerry ran out to meet her. Eric pulled his car up behind Ashlyn's. Kerry, a bit teary eyed, reached out to Ashlyn and gave her a hug. "I was so worried about you! Are you all right? What's wrong? You look angry. Was it the bank episode or is there something else?"

Ashlyn turned to see Eric approach. He had concern etched on his face. "What's wrong, Eric?" Ashlyn asked.

Eric looked at Kerry, who watched him with pleading eyes.

"What's the matter, you guys?" Ashlyn asked impatiently.

Kerry looked at Ashlyn. "I called Eric and asked him to come over. You got a delivery and after the kind of day you've had, I thought maybe he could help."

"What kind of delivery?"

"I left it just how it was when I got home. It's on the porch."

The three turned towards the front porch. Ashlyn walked up the stairs slowly. Lying next to the front door was an old, yellowed program from Austin's funeral along with a wilted, moldy rose. On a piece of paper, the words were typed large and clear:

I'M WARNING YOU
BACK OFF

Ashlyn stared at the yellowed picture of Austin in the program and tears rolled down her cheeks. She stood there for several minutes, looking at the picture and seeming miles away. Slowly she lifted her head, looked at her friends, and walked into the house, clutching the program in her hand. As she did so, she heard Eric say he was going to call Tyler. Ashlyn ran back outside.

"No. Don't tell him anything about this," she commanded.

Eric was surprised. "I thought he was going to help you figure all this out."

"Eric, I'm asking you to leave him out of this." Ashlyn was adamant.

"But why?"

"There are many reasons why, but I'll give you the main one. Tyler *does not* need to deal with me right now. He's got bigger fish to fry."

"What are you talking about? He cares about you. Surely you know that."

"What I know is that we quickly became friends and now someone is out to destroy our friendship. I'm telling you that if we lay this on him, I'll lose that too. He'll even be in danger of losing his job. So just leave him out of this. I'll take care of it myself. But I do need your help with something else. Do you think you could get me on your team?"

"What happened?" Eric asked suspiciously.

Ashlyn sighed and filled them in on everything that had happened since the bank robbery.

Eric whistled between his teeth at the end of the story. Kerry was angry and surprised, then spoke defiantly. "Fine. Have nothing to do with him at work. This is personal, after-hours stuff. He's allowed to do what he wants on his own time."

"But it is work related, and I need to keep a distance from Tyler, period. I know he wants to help, but he can't. If anyone misunderstood his intentions again, we could both lose our jobs. So leave Tyler out of this. The less he knows and the less he sees of me, the better. I may even be transferred to a different shift so that he won't be my boss."

"Isn't that a little extreme?" Eric asked.

"It was at my request. Someone in the group I work with doesn't even have the nerve to take the responsibility for his letter. I don't know who to trust."

"You're making the whole unit take responsibility for the opinion of one officer," Eric tried to reason.

"You tell me how to narrow it down. It's impossible."

"What did Tyler say to all this?" Kerry asked.

Ashlyn sighed. "He's furious. Whoever said the Irish have tempers made an understatement. It's my fault that he got called in. I'm sure he's angry with me as well as whoever is responsible for the letter. I should have never accepted his help. He's only been with the force a few weeks, and already he's been reprimanded, all because of me. Look, I'm tired. I'm dirty. And as much as I love you guys, I just want to be alone."

She hugged her two dear friends. Sadly she walked back inside, holding the funeral program tightly in her fist.

Kerry waited until Ashlyn was out of earshot, then looked at Eric with discouragement. "You know as well as I do that no matter what Tyler and Ashlyn say, they're meant to be together, don't you?"

Eric couldn't help but note again how much he loved Kerry's determination. He said, "Yeah. This is not what they need. Between the two of them, there's already enough to keep them apart. I'm beginning to wonder if they really aren't supposed to be together. The stack against them keeps getting thicker." Eric leaned over and took Kerry's hand. "Hungry? My treat."

Kerry smiled. "Starving. But do you think she'll really be okay?"

"Yeah. Tell her we're going and we won't be gone long. I'm calling Tyler to ask him to pull Ashlyn's file on Carl. I want to take a look at it."

"What if he asks why?"

"I'll tell him the truth. I want to research it."

"Again, what if he asks why?"

"I care a lot more about Ashlyn's safety than I do for her concern of what other officers might think of her and Tyler. We need Tyler's help before this person really does try to hurt Ashlyn. I've talked to him. He wants this guy as bad as Ashlyn does, and I'm not going to write off his help. Tyler's got an unbelievable record. He's good at his job, and he's a good man. Not only that, he's got my respect. I hope someday that Ashlyn will thank me and not resent me, but I'm going to Tyler. She might not realize it, but she does need his help. She needs all of our help. If I lose her friendship over this, at least I'll lose it knowing she's safe."

Kerry looked at Eric with pride. "You're a good friend, Eric. She'll see that."

* * *

Tyler couldn't remember the last time he'd been so angry, not just about the letter but about the way the captain had handled the situation. It was just so unfair. His feelings were so new for Ashlyn that even he didn't understand them, or at least he didn't know what to do about them. Thanks to some insecure, uninformed officer, he had lost any chance he might have had with her. Now if he asked her out, he already knew how she'd answer. She cared about her job too much. He wanted to talk to her after leaving the captain's office, but that obnoxious Shirley had gotten in the way.

Tyler's mood was black as Shirley once again stood in the doorway of his office. "Did you need something?" Tyler asked shortly.

Shirley was unaffected by his tone. "Eric Christensen is on line one for you. My time is up for the day. Would you like me to go get us dinner and we can talk here tonight?"

"Shirley, I've already explained that I'm working with my officers tonight. Have a good night. I'll take that call now."

"But what about dinner?" she pressed.

"Shirley, I won't be eating any more meals with you. Type up the office procedures for me or be patient until I have a minute to come in during the day to talk at your desk."

"But we had plans," she pouted.

"You make it sound like we had a date. It was nothing more than a meeting. I refuse to be alone with any single woman in this unit," he said through gritted teeth.

"Just because Ashlyn caused you to get a bad rap doesn't mean I will. I'm good at secrets. We could see each other and no one would know it."

"I don't think so. I think you're a good secretary, but there isn't and won't be anything personal between us. I'm not trying to be unkind. I just don't want to give you any false impressions. By the way, how do you know what happened with Ashlyn and me?"

"Word travels." Shirley shrugged her shoulders, but her eyes were cold.

"I won't comment on the accusations about Ashlyn. But as far as the *word* that *travels*, I want it to end with you. If I find out you started the word, or chose not to end it, I'll see to it that you don't have the opportunity to make that choice again. I hope you understand me. I'm not in the mood to be gracious, so if you'll excuse me, I've got a call to take. Close the door on your way out."

"I know you've had a bad day thanks to that witch, so I'll forgive you for now. I think we could have something wonderful between us, but for the sake of your job, we need to be careful. We can talk later. Until then, not one word will pass these lips."

Before Tyler could reply, Shirley shut the door and was gone. He didn't think his day could get worse until he talked to Eric. Twenty minutes later, he was fit to be tied.

* * *

The night shift went by without any incidents. The office ran smoothly, and all calls and cases were handled appropriately. Tyler found himself studying each officer, looking for any hint of bad will from any of them. Several officers talked about Ashlyn and her good work at handling the bank incident. Everyone was disappointed that she wouldn't be in to tell the story firsthand. Tyler listened to the conversation but didn't join in. Rather, he took the opportunity to observe each officer. Everyone sang her praises. He didn't find one clue that anyone was upset with him or Ashlyn, or that anyone was seeking revenge. Not only was he still angry, but now he was also confused.

He decided he needed someone to talk to and asked Eric to meet with him in the morning when they switched shifts. He counted down the hours. Eric had told him that Ashlyn received another threat but that she'd asked Eric and Kerry not to mention it to Tyler. It seemed that every opportunity he had of getting closer to Ashlyn was slipping through his fingers. He began to wonder if maybe he was meant to leave her alone, but every time he thought that, he got a depressing feeling. He didn't know what to do next. Pretend he never met her? That wouldn't work, for she was already close to his heart.

The early morning dawned, and the tired officers left the office. Tyler noted that each bid him a friendly farewell. How could such an unprofessional letter be written by one of these guys? It seemed impossible. But still, he intended to find out who the rat was.

Tyler noticed Eric walking in and stepped over to see if he had a minute. The two went in to Eric's office and closed the door.

Eric looked Tyler over. "Buddy, you look beat."

Tyler rubbed his face and felt a day's growth of whiskers reminding him that he needed to shave.

"I'm beginning to feel beat," Tyler said, implying that it was more than work that was getting to him. He looked at Eric. "Did you see anything in Carl's file that raised any questions?"

Eric shook his head. "Other than there's more to him than we have proof of. He may be into organized crime, or dealing, even smuggling. His file indicates that anything is possible."

Frustrated, Tyler ran his fingers through his hair. "We need to get some names of others involved with Carl. We need the supplier or the middleman. The names we have are leaving us swimming in circles. I'll work on that end." He paused. "Did you see Ashlyn again last night?"

"No. By the time we got back from dinner, she was in her room. I was there until after eleven and she never came out."

"What, pray tell, were you doing at a certain young, single female's home until after eleven?" Tyler joked with Eric.

Eric grinned and said, "I never kiss and tell."

"You kissed her and won't tell me about it?"

"That's not what I said exactly. I took her to dinner, and then we went back and watched a movie. We talked until eleven, when I dragged myself to her front door. The rest is between me and her."

"What happened to the part about her not wanting to settle down, no chasing her, she's not interested—"

Eric cut him off. "Okay, it was my battered ego talking. Let's just say I think she might think I'm cute."

Tyler burst out laughing. "Now that's big stuff! What makes you say so?"

Eric turned crimson. "She told me."

"Well, there you go. Honesty goes a long way."

"Yeah. You should try it. It may pay off." Eric looked directly at his friend. "You know, after hearing about your little talk with the captain, I've no intention of letting anyone in on what's going on, or I should say, what I hope goes on, between me and Kerry. But it's not going to stop me from going after what I want. What about you?"

"You know, I sometimes wonder why I ended up in Monroe. I sincerely hope it's so that I can end up with Ashlyn. The day I saw her sitting at my kitchen table, I fell under her spell immediately. I threw my resolve to never date a cop out the window. I knew it even as I vowed to you and Rory that I thought otherwise. But what's worse is that I can't do anything about it. It's not the caveman days where I can grab her hair and pull her over to my cave. What bothers me the most is that she wants nothing to do with me. To be honest, taking that shot for Jessica hurt a lot less than this."

Tyler rubbed his face with both hands in frustration. "I look in her eyes, Eric, and see the pain she's carrying. I was determined to get rid of it, not add to it. Now she's breaking all the little ties I had to her, and it's killing me. I mean, I'm thirty years old. I never intended to wait this long to get married. The right girl just never entered my life. But with Ashlyn, I felt this instant connection that I've never known. I really thought she might be the one, but no. I'll be lucky if I walk away with even a friendship. I don't even know how to explain it because as I sit here listening to myself, I realize I sound like an idiot—"

"Actually, it all makes perfect sense," Eric broke in. "Kerry broke some confidences last night—with the best intentions of helping Ashlyn—so, I'll tell you what I know. But if this gets back to Ashlyn, you'll ruin some really important friendships. So take this in the strictest confidence. It seems that Ashlyn has fallen for you." Eric laughed at the lopsided grin on Tyler's face but quickly became somber as he continued. "But you must realize that Ashlyn feels a sense of obligation to her brother because of his death. No one but Ashlyn knows the reason why. It has some kind of hold on her. Someone needs to get to the root of that problem, and that, my dear friend, is why I think you have come to Monroe—to help her slay her dragons. Until you came along, she never questioned the path she set for herself. Now she sees one thing she wants, but can't let go of the others. If you really want to pursue a relationship with her, it's *you* who will have to help her lift the burden she has carried for so long."

Tyler felt encouraged. "I'll do whatever it takes. Where do I begin?"

"Take her out. She needs to see you outside the workforce. Get her away from the cops and robbers stuff." Eric paused and thought for a moment. "Although don't ask her for Saturday. Unless, of course, you like being rejected."

"Why not Saturday?"

"She has a date," Eric said sympathetically.

"Thanks," Tyler muttered, "I needed to hear that."

"You asked. You better get on it, though. It seems the date she has is with an old boyfriend, a friend of her brother's. Ashlyn does date, you know. She just hasn't gotten serious with anyone. You can change that, but you'd better get on the ball. I don't know what this Dave Parker guy has in mind."

CHAPTER 10

Ashlyn awoke to the sound of her doorbell. She got up and lazily walked to the door, wrapping her robe around her. There on the porch stood a delivery woman from the local florist. She had brought a delivery of flowers for Ashlyn.

After signing for them, Ashlyn shut the door and sat to read the card. It was a larger card than usual, and she wondered who had sent the gift. There were three white daisies with greenery and baby's breath set in a bud vase. Simple, but nice. As she tore the envelope open, she saw that Tyler had sent them. She was thrilled until she started to read the message.

Dear Ashlyn,
I wanted to apologize for the meeting with the captain yesterday. I'm sure it caught you off guard, but in truth, I'm actually glad it happened. I've been trying to think of a way to tell you nicely that I feel like you've come on a little bit strong and although I'm flattered, my interests don't lie with you. Obviously we need to be friends because we work together, but I would appreciate you not bringing this up again. In the future I would appreciate it if you would keep things on a professional level. I'm sorry that it all came about this way, but I hope you can understand.
Sincerely,
Tyler O'Bryan

Ashlyn felt the flush in her cheeks. *Of all the humiliating, insensitive, arrogant—*

Her thoughts were interrupted as she heard a car door slam. She glanced out the window to see Tyler making his way to the front porch. Quickly she threw the flowers and the card into the garbage can and ran to her room.

The doorbell rang, but she refused to answer it. Instead, she called the office to ask for a personal day off. Shirley said she would be only too happy to give the message to Tyler once he came in. The doorbell rang a couple more times before she heard Tyler slam his car door and start the engine to leave.

Alone with her thoughts, she allowed herself a few minutes of self-pity. Tyler wanted nothing to do with her. She should have felt okay. After all, wasn't part of her plan not to get involved with anyone? Then why did his words hurt so much? Her pity turned into anger. Just who did he think he was? *He* was the one who offered his help. *He* approached her at church and at the retirement party. Not once did *she* approach him. But if that was the way he wanted it, fine! She'd give him just what he wanted. In fact, she'd see to it that he didn't have to deal with her again.

She went back to the garbage can and fished out the card and the flowers, then put them in her room to remind her to avoid him at all costs. She didn't have to see him until tomorrow night and even then, for the next two weeks, he'd be working with the other officers, so he would be in and out of the office each night. As luck would have it, she could actually avoid him for a while. Maybe by then, he couldn't hurt her anymore.

Man, what an arrogant jerk! she thought. Then why did she feel so hurt and humiliated?

Taking a deep breath, she fought for control and decided the day would be hers. She had planted a flower garden the spring before and knew that tending it would give her some peace. As she pulled weeds here and there, the cool breeze reminded her that it was the end of summer and soon, her tomorrows would find her gazing at the beautiful fall leaves.

She suddenly felt homesick and knew she needed to go home soon. Besides, autumn up Big Cottonwood Canyon was unbelievable. The array of colors was truly something to behold. She missed her mom and dad and regretted not being able to visit them more at Bob's retirement party. She was lucky enough to be within driving distance from home, but at times those miles seemed to stretch farther away, and she longed for her parents' closeness.

Thinking of her parents naturally made her think of Austin. It wasn't always with sadness and regret that she remembered her brother. At times she thought of the fun they had together as well as the endless pranks and jokes they played on each other. She no longer resented God for taking Austin. Bob's talk had given her much to think about, and she knew Austin was safe and happy, a thought that could sustain her for some time.

Her trouble came when she thought of how she was living a lie. The life she was living was one she would have never picked for herself. She wanted romance but never allowed herself to relish the thought. To have someone of her own, who would always be there for her no matter what, was something she had daydreamed of even as a little girl and now longed for as a woman. She was tired of being alone, and even though she had good friends and family, it wasn't the same. The truth was, she was lonely. But that's just how it was, how it would always be.

She thought about Tyler and how she had allowed him into her daydreams. She no longer could do that because now, she needed to get away from him. The hurt wouldn't disappear, but at least she wouldn't have to feel humiliated around him. She could move away, but there were things she needed to do first. She had to know who was threatening her. After she figured that out, moving—maybe even back to Salt Lake—would free her of the pain of seeing Tyler fall in love and get married. She knew she was determined to be angry with him, but it was too late. She was already falling for him. Falling hard. Falling fast. Falling deep. It was a miserable feeling.

She had no idea how long she'd been thinking, but the cramps in her legs told her it was time to get up from weeding the flowers.

As she stood, Kerry walked through the back door. "I heard you're not up to facing your fellow employees because of being caught blatantly flirting with your boss man."

Ashlyn looked up at Kerry, stunned. "Let me guess. Shirley?"

"Yep. However, it's classified information and it's pertinent that it doesn't get back to the captain that Tyler confided in her about the special meeting between you two and the captain."

"Looks like Sergeant O'Bryan has a big mouth," Ashlyn mumbled.

"Surely you don't buy what she's saying!" Kerry asked in surprise.

"It was either you or Eric or Tyler who squealed. I know you and Eric too well. She would have no way of knowing about that meeting unless Tyler told her. We were told not to discuss it with anyone."

"You did," Kerry reminded her.

"Yeah, with you and Eric. I knew it would never go anywhere. Unless you're trying to tell me that one of you talked to the Queen of Gossip of Monroe City."

"No, of course not. What I was getting at was that maybe there was a special reason he told her."

"Yeah. I'll buy that when donkeys fly."

"Don't be too quick to judge him," Kerry pleaded.

"It really doesn't matter. She'll never have him. He's already been taken. His 'Maddie' comes into town Saturday. You can even ask Kate. That will dry Shirley up."

"Kate who?" Kerry asked, surprised.

"How would I know who Kate is?" Ashlyn exclaimed.

"You just told me to ask her." Kerry spoke slowly, wondering if she had missed something.

"That doesn't mean I know her personally," Ashlyn replied.

"Then how am I supposed to ask Kate?" Kerry asked in frustration.

"Ask her what?" Ashlyn asked, confused.

"Ask her about Maddie! Ashlyn you've been out in the sun too long. Come in and I'll make you some lemonade. Even better, how about some chocolate chip cookies? Sounds like you're having a chocolate kind of day. Then you can tell me everything you know about Kate and Maddie."

"I'll take the drink, but never mind the cookies, thanks." Ready to change the subject, Ashlyn said, "I came up with an idea. Remember how we were going to start family home evening? How about we start on Monday and begin with an activity? I thought we could invite Sam and Annie. And you could casually invite Eric. What do you say? It's brilliant, don't you think?"

"Why don't we invite Tyler too? He doesn't have a family here to have home evening with," Kerry asked hopefully.

"No! He's got Maddie. Besides, I don't want him around here."

Kerry stared at her friend. "That's a bit cruel. He's done nothing unkind toward you. In fact, he's been nothing but sweet to you. This is my house too. Are you trying to tell me that I can only have the friends here that you approve of?"

"*Sweet* to me, you say? Let me show you how 'sweet' he is."

Kerry followed Ashlyn to her room where she saw the flowers on her dresser. She smiled until she read the card. Then she looked at her friend in shock. "You're right, he's not invited," Kerry concluded.

* * *

That evening, Kerry called Annie and Eric while Ashlyn went to Sam's tavern.

As she entered, Sam looked up and watched her walk up to the bar. "You're coming around here too often. It's bad for—"

"Yeah, yeah, it's bad for business. Blah, blah, blah. I'll make this really short and sweet if you'll allow me one request. If you say no, I'll hang around here spouting off all the Colorado laws and codes that drunk people could be cited for until you say yes."

"Yes. Now go," Sam replied sarcastically.

"Very good. It's at my house Monday night at 6:00. Don't be late. I have to work that night and find drunk people to arrest. Here's my address." Ashlyn smiled.

"Whoa! Now just wait a minute! What are you talking about?" Sam's eyes narrowed.

"You just committed to coming to my house for dinner on Monday night. There will be my roommate, a neighbor, and a friend all joining us."

"I'm not going to your house for dinner. I have to work," Sam grunted.

"So do I," Ashlyn stated.

"Why in blazes would I want to do that for?"

"Because I want to be your friend and so do the others. A person can't have too many of those. Now, is the answer yes, or should I start reciting the blood-alcohol-level laws and so forth?"

"Why should I trust you?" Sam glared at Ashlyn as if looking for a hidden secret.

"Why shouldn't you?"

Sam let her comment sink in before finally replying, "Fine. Six. But I can't stay long."

"Alright. See you on Monday. Unless, of course, I have to come in here before then." Ashlyn chuckled.

"Get out of here," Sam growled.

Ashlyn watched Sam walk away but didn't miss the ever-so-slight grin that showed itself on his tired face. Ashlyn felt good inside for the first time that day.

By the time she got back, Eric was at the house. She looked at him and Kerry and grinned. "If you keep coming around so much, we're going to have to start charging you rent."

Eric smiled good-naturedly. "I've got ward council tonight and needed to get some information from you since you're on the activities committee. I tried to call Grace, but she's gone to stay with her daughter, who just had a baby. The elders quorum is planning a party, and I think it's right around the date of our ward temple night. Can you give me that date?" Ashlyn grinned. She knew Eric was looking for a way to see Kerry. Judging by the way she beamed, Kerry was on to him too.

"Sure, sure. I thought you were just looking for an excuse to see Kerry again. I'll go get my planner and get you that date. I'm pretty sure it's two weeks from Saturday."

Chuckling, Ashlyn left both friends in an embarrassed silence.

Kerry ventured a look at Eric, who smiled at her. Once she felt sure that she would have a steady voice, she tried to lighten the silence. "Good old Ashlyn isn't one to mince words."

"She's right. I'm running out of excuses to come here," Eric said softly.

"I'm running out of excuses to get you here." They both laughed, and Eric walked over and whispered something in her ear.

By the time Ashlyn came back, Eric had good news for her. "You did us a great favor. We want you to be the first to know. Actually, due to the circumstances at the office, you're the *only* one we want to know. We've set a date."

Ashlyn stopped and looked at her friends with a sparkle in her eye. "Shouldn't you go out on a date first? I mean, isn't that just kind of a given when it comes to this stuff?"

Eric and Kerry laughed. Kerry hugged her friend. "Thanks to your big mouth, we've set a date for our first official date. It's Saturday night."

"Oh, well, I guess congratulations are in order." She laughed and hugged both of her friends. They always made her smile.

"About Monday night's dinner, I don't want to be tacky here, but do you think we could invite Tyler?" Eric hesitated to ask.

"No!" both girls shouted simultaneously.

Eric raised his eyebrows, looking at one girl and then the other, waiting for an explanation. Neither girl offered one, and Ashlyn left the room. "Ooo-kay." Eric sensed that now wasn't the time for questions. Once Ashlyn was out of hearing distance, though, he asked, "What did Tyler do?"

"Sent her flowers. The big jerk," Kerry answered angrily.

"Of all the dirty things to do! Remind me to never do such a thoughtless gesture."

"No, it was the card he sent with them," Kerry said. "He basically told her that he was sorry about the whole captain episode but that it was good that it happened because he was searching for a way to tell her to back off. There was something about how important his job is, and on and on. It was pretty insulting. Ashlyn plans to do everything she can to get off Tyler's team, and I don't blame her. Boy, did I have him pegged wrong! May I just go on record to say I think he's a dirty rat?"

"Huh? No, that can't be right! He's not a dirty rat, but I think I'm beginning to smell one. Who delivered them?"

"Impressions, why?"

"How late are they open?" Eric glanced at his watch.

"I think until six. Why?"

"I've got fifteen minutes."

"To do what?"

"To get to the flower shop," he said, and took off running.

CHAPTER 11

Tyler went in to work early in hopes of pulling Ashlyn aside to talk to her. He'd been to her house twice that day to see her. The second time he was sure she was gone because her car wasn't in the driveway, but the first time he could have sworn she was there. He thought he saw movement by the window, but he had rung the bell several times, and nobody answered. He had a sick feeling she was avoiding him, and his nerves couldn't take much more. He was going to ask her out if it killed him. He just had to see her first.

Once he was in the office, Shirley greeted him a little too warmly and, of course, in plain view of the captain. The captain rolled his eyes and walked into his office. Tyler felt like he was sinking in an ocean of problems in Monroe.

Shirley dragged him to her desk to go over several instructions he had already spoken to her about. He was angry that she had wasted his time this way, and even angrier that she was doing everything she could to make it appear there was something going on between them. She had called him several times that day at home asking silly questions or saying she wanted a chance to make him happy. The only thing she could do to make him happy was to disappear. He was ready to slam the door in her face when she gave him his messages.

"Ashlyn called and said she wasn't coming in tonight and if you didn't like it, too bad. She said if you couldn't find someone else to fill in for her, she'd be on call if you needed a detective. Otherwise, don't bother her." Shirley smiled a sour smile and continued, "She was really rude. Somebody ought to get that smart mouth fired. I gave the message to the captain thinking maybe he could find someone to cover for her. He couldn't, and now he's upset that she put you in this predicament."

"Why did you give the message to the captain? Isn't it *your* job to find people to cover the officers? Isn't that number twenty on your list of office procedures?" Tyler asked, his anger growing.

"Yes, it is. I didn't know who to call," Shirley innocently replied.

"Who would you normally call?" Tyler asked.

"One of the other detectives."

Tyler was ready to pull his hair out. Ashlyn's job was already on the line, and now his insane and terribly annoying secretary was stretching that line even thinner. "And did you call them?"

"No. I've been really busy today."

"You've been . . . ? You called me five times today! Three of those were to ask me out!"

"Sshh! You're talking so loud! It's our secret, remember?" Shirley batted her eyelashes.

Tyler clenched his jaw and spoke through his teeth. "Go home right now before I tell you that you have no job to come back to."

"But Tyler, I—"

"Go!" he cut her off. He knew he should have been ashamed for talking to her that way. His parents had ingrained manners in him from the time he pushed Stacey Andretti in the mud in sixth grade. He knew he was supposed to treat each girl like a lady. Until now he had tried to remember that lesson, but he found it difficult to treat someone like a lady when she wasn't one.

Erasing that thought from his mind, he concentrated on the fact that he wouldn't be seeing Ashlyn tonight, and he was sure that she was avoiding him. His personal line rang as he sat down in his chair. He answered it, and immediately Eric's voice came on the line.

"Why in the world did you tell me one thing in my office today and then do exactly the opposite? Did you change your mind or are you just out of your mind?" Eric blurted out.

"Whoa, slow down there. What are you talking about?"

"The stupid flowers and card thing."

"I don't know what you're talking about."

"Are you trying to tell me you didn't send Ashlyn flowers and a card today?"

"No. Would I have gotten a better response than I did going to see her in person? Because that was sure a hit," he said ruefully. "I think she's avoiding me."

"Buddy, I was ready to avoid you. After those flowers and card, I wasn't sure I wanted to even know you."

"What flowers and card?"

"Someone is trying to sabotage you. Could it have been Maddie?"

"Maddie? What has she got to do with this? She's in California, and I highly doubt she's capable of sabotaging me."

"So you don't deny there is a Maddie?" Eric asked, surprised.

"No. Why? Eric you're talking in circles. Forget Maddie. What about Ashlyn?"

"Since Maddie's coming to Monroe to stay, don't you think she plays a role in all this?"

"Don't you think Ashlyn will like Maddie? She hasn't even met her. I think Ashlyn and Maddie will be great friends."

"You're bringing one female to town to introduce her to the other female you're chasing. Are you nuts?"

"I didn't think about it."

"Don't you think you should have?" Eric was obviously angry.

"If Ashlyn doesn't like her, other arrangements can be made. She's really good to have around though. She obeys every command."

"You make her sound like a dog." Eric sounded disgusted.

"She is," Tyler laughed.

"Now you're just being insulting. Every time I think I know you, you throw me for a loop."

"No, Eric. I mean Maddie *is* my dog. She's a longhaired golden retriever. I trained her myself. I got her through the LAPD."

"Then who is Kate?"

"Rory's wife. They're coming up this weekend to a baby blessing in Denver, and they're bringing Maddie with them. I didn't bring her with me because it would have been hectic trying to situate her while moving in and such. Rory was taking care of her until I got settled in. Why? What's all this about?"

"Ashlyn thinks that Maddie is your girlfriend."

Tyler sighed. "At the rate things are going, she may be my *only* friend. What about the flowers and the card?"

Eric took the next several minutes to tell Tyler about the flowers and card. Tyler couldn't believe it. He *had* to talk to Ashlyn, but how? He couldn't leave, and he knew getting her to come to the office was impossible, especially after the captain's reprimand.

Eric told him that the person who sent the flowers was male and had paid cash. That was all the florist could remember. Was this connected to Ashlyn's threats? Somehow he didn't think so. The letters and flowers didn't seem to be the same kind of threat as the others that Ashlyn received. Someone obviously wanted to be sure that Ashlyn and he didn't get together. What was going on in this strange town? He thought he had moved into Mayberry, but instead, he'd entered the Twilight Zone.

He and Eric racked their brains, but neither could come up with anyone who might be behind the letters and flowers. Unless . . . Shirley? Eric said a male had ordered the flowers, but couldn't Shirley have gotten someone to do it for her? That had to be it! Tyler was sure of it. She might not be capable of the threats to Ashlyn, but she was in a great position to cause her some trouble at work. Now he needed to catch her in the act. Better yet, he needed the captain to catch her in the act.

Tyler raced to the captain's office, hoping he hadn't left yet. The captain was just locking up his office when Tyler caught up to him. "Could I ask you for a favor?"

"You can always ask," the captain replied.

"You have the password to Shirley's computer, right?"

"Yeah. But I won't give it out. You know that."

"I know. I don't want it. I was going to ask if you'd pull up her e-mail list. I need a specific letter for work tonight. I was hoping she might have saved it. She left and I hate to make her come all the way back to retrieve it for me."

The captain grunted and unlocked his office. "Let's make it quick. Meet me at her desk and I'll look up her password."

"Thanks. I'm sorry to do this to you on your way out." Tyler kept his fingers crossed. *Please let me be right and let this work,* he silently prayed.

The captain retrieved her e-mails, and there were no messages. Tyler's heart sank. He'd always been so sure. He looked a little closer. "Wait a minute. She's thrown an e-mail away. Can you retrieve it? That might be what I'm looking for." The captain pulled up the letter. "Bingo!" Tyler called out.

"What's this? Why is this letter on Shirley's computer?" the captain asked as he read over the letter. Sure enough, it was the same letter that had been sent about Ashlyn and Tyler's "involvement."

"Captain, meet your anonymous officer. I don't know when she went through the academy, but unless I'm mistaken, Shirley just misrepresented herself to the captain of Monroe's police department. Her little trick could have cost you the best detective you've got, not to mention one of your sergeants."

The captain was furious. He had lost two days' work interviewing Tyler's officers trying to find the guilty party. Now, as he was finding out, some foolhardy secretary had played some sort of sick game for reasons known only to her.

"Let's go in my office," the captain said. "When is Ashlyn scheduled to come in? This involves her too."

"She took a personal day, but I bet she'd come in for this. Should we call her?"

"Yes, and while we're waiting, maybe you'd better tell me how you figured this out. I'd like to clear this up."

* * *

Ashlyn walked towards the captain's office. So far she'd been lucky and hadn't run into Tyler. She wanted to be in and out before he knew she had even been there. She knocked on the captain's door and heard him call out to her to come in. As she entered the office, there sat Tyler. *Great,* she thought. She looked at the captain. "You wanted to see me?" she asked hesitantly.

"Sit down, Ashlyn. I owe you an apology."

Twenty minutes later, the captain excused them both. As they left the office, Ashlyn felt marginally better. Sure, Tyler had solved the letter mystery, but that didn't change the insult of the flower and card.

"Ashlyn," Tyler reached out and took ahold of her wrist, "I know about the flowers and the card, and I want you to know that I didn't send them to you. I came to your house twice to apologize for what had happened with this anonymous letter. I also know you've been avoiding me. I don't blame you. I would have avoided me too. I'm really sorry. This whole letter incident was embarrassing and insulting for both of us. After our chat with the captain the other day, I have no intention of jeopardizing our jobs." He stopped for a moment and took a deep breath. "But what I do on my time is up to me. Having said that, I thought that Sunday after church we could get together with Eric and Kerry and have dinner at my house—if you're interested. There's someone I want you to meet. Do you like dogs?"

Ashlyn didn't know whether to panic or shout for joy. "I love dogs, and I'd love to come over for dinner. I'd also love to help cook.

"That'd be great. We'll make them dinner and they can return the favor another time. Can you go grocery shopping with me on Saturday?"

Ashlyn's spirits fell as she remembered her date with Dave on Saturday. Tyler noticed the change of expression on her face. "I can do the shopping myself if Saturday doesn't work for you," he offered, afraid she'd back out.

"No. It's not that. I'm going to dinner with an old friend on Saturday night. I forgot about that."

"That's all right. We can go in the morning or afternoon to get groceries. Unless, of course, you want to reschedule."

"No. If Saturday works for you, it does for me."

"Works for me. We work on Friday night, so what time would be best for you on Saturday?" Tyler smiled as he did a mental victory dance. Ashlyn had said yes to a date. Now if he could just get this Dave character out of the picture.

"Is eleven okay? I'll treat you to lunch," she offered.

"Eleven is great, and I'll buy lunch."

"Eleven it is, and it's *my* treat." Ashlyn grinned.

"You're not going to back down are you? Your mother was right. You *are* stubborn."

* * *

Ashlyn floated all the way home and then started to panic. What was she going to wear? She wanted to look good but didn't want to appear too eager.

She pulled into the driveway and noticed Eric had left. She ran into the house and grabbed Kerry. "We've got to go shopping! Grab your purse. We're running out of time!"

"Running out of time for what?" Kerry asked.

"I've got two dates this weekend, and I have nothing to wear—well, three if you count Dave Parker—but I need something really good for Saturday and Sunday."

"Who with and where are you going?" Kerry asked excited.

"With Tyler to the grocery store!" Ashlyn shouted with glee.

Kerry laughed. "Gee, how romantic. Couldn't think of anything better to do than that? Your options of clothing may be a little limited then," Kerry answered sarcastically.

"Kerry! I need to look great!" Ashlyn cried, then stopped, suddenly remembering. "By the way, Shirley sent the card and flowers and the letter to the captain. I don't know what's going to happen to her, but whatever it is, I can't wait to find out!"

Kerry grinned, realizing that her first impression of Tyler had been right. She exploded with excitement. "You're going out twice with Tyler this weekend? How romantic!" she said dreamily.

"Kerry, focus! I need to find something to wear. I need my hair trimmed, and I need a manicure. Oh, I wish I could lose a few pounds by Saturday. You and your darn 'chocolate days' have done me no favors, you know."

Kerry was trying not to laugh at Ashlyn's panic. "All this to go to the grocery store?"

"No, Kerry! It's to go out with Tyler! Who cares about the location?"

"I thought he was taboo."

"I can go out with him. I just can't marry him. He asked me out! I never dreamed that possible. Look at him! He's wonderful! Help me! We're wasting time. What do you wear when making dinner for friends?" Ashlyn was rambling, but she was too excited to notice.

Kerry giggled. "The possibilities are endless. Why?"

"We're making dinner for you and Eric on Sunday."

"The dinner is for us? Why didn't you say so? I haven't got a thing to wear if Eric is taking me to your dinner! What are we waiting for?"

The next few hours were spent going from store to store trying on everything that caught their eye. Ashlyn settled on light blue jeans and a blue pullover with a white T-shirt under it. It was a classy ensemble, but not overstated. For Sunday she picked a pair of tan khakis and a ribbed white shirt with a scoop neck. Because she was running a little low on money, she decided to wear her old dark blue blazer and flowered skirt to church on Sunday.

Kerry picked out two outfits as well for her two dates. Eric had already called her on her cell phone and asked her to the dinner on Sunday. The women drove home feeling like Christmas was just around the corner.

As they drove past Sam's tavern, Ashlyn noticed that a black limousine was parked out front. A man stood beside it, talking to Carl Wadsworth. Ashlyn whipped around to the back of the gas station as she had once before and watched. The man handed Carl an envelope and got into the car before Ashlyn had a chance to see his face. Quickly she memorized the license plate number. Once the car left and Carl was out of sight, she took off after the car to get the name of the limo service, but it seemed like it had just disappeared. It didn't matter, though. She had the license plate number, and tomorrow she'd research it at work.

"You're really good about this whole spying thing, Kerry. Does it worry you when we do this?" Ashlyn looked over at her friend, who sat quietly in the car.

"Of course it worries me. But I understand the life of a cop and the risks that they take. I admire them."

"You'll be a great cop's wife," Ashlyn smiled.

"From your lips to God's ears. May He bless me with that opportunity." Kerry smiled.

CHAPTER 12

Ashlyn spent part of Thursday getting her hair done and having a manicure. She was splurging a bit, but it had been a long time since she had allowed herself the luxury.

When she went into work that night, Shirley was just leaving. She walked past Ashlyn without saying a word. Ashlyn raised questioning eyes at Tyler as he walked out of his office.

"Hey, you're early." He smiled.

"I have some information to research and couldn't wait to get started. Did Shirley have a bad day?"

"I hope so. She's certainly given me my share of them lately. She's mad at me right now, but she has no idea that she's been caught. Tomorrow when the captain comes in, he plans to question her, and then she's out of here."

"So why is she mad at you?" Ashlyn asked.

"I told her to stay away from me before I turn her in for harassment."

"Ouch!"

"It seemed to work. I've had peace all day for the first time since before I started. Did you know she started calling me in L.A. before I even moved here?" He grinned. "What information do you have?"

"It may not be anything, so let me research it and see what I turn up. If I find something, I'll let you know. Who are you working with tonight?"

"Winters."

"Sounds good. I guess I'll talk to you later."

As she turned to leave, Tyler stopped her. "Did you get your hair cut?"

"Uhh, yeah. It needed it." She smiled shyly.

"It's pretty," he said quietly.

Ashlyn grinned. "Thank you."

He smiled back. "You're welcome."

When Ashlyn got to her desk and booted up her computer, she put in the license plate number and got the name of the company the limo was registered with. When she called it, she found it was already closed for the day. But she did find out it was run out of Denver. That was all she could do for the night. The evening was busy, and soon her thoughts of Carl and the limo were put on the back burner. Yet Tyler's compliment carried her through the whole shift, and although she didn't see Tyler again that night, she thought of him nonstop.

* * *

Friday, Ashlyn called the limo service in Denver and found that the person renting the limo was someone by the name of Martin Crosby from California. She entered the name into the computer and found two aliases: Daniel Parks and Drew Perkins. Martin Crosby's sheet was clean, but the other two names each had rap sheets all having to do with drugs. She knew it! Carl was into drugs. So was Martin—or whoever he was— the supplier or the middleman?

Toward the end of her shift, Tyler walked in with Officer Winters. After he checked in with his other officers, he walked up to Ashlyn. "Ready to call it a day?"

"I think I'm on to something here," she said, staring at the computer screen.

Tyler sat down next to her and listened intently as she showed him the information. When she showed him the names, Tyler stopped cold. "I know Daniel Parks. He's a big drug lord in California. Remember Rory? Earlier this year he got a lead that there would be a shipment coming in. It would be our big chance to bring them down. There was a shootout. Parks wasn't there, but we brought down one of his guys instead. I don't know all the facts because I wasn't there, but Rory probably would."

Tyler spent the next hour telling Ashlyn about different cases he'd worked on in L.A. Before she knew it, their shift was about to end. Tyler left her desk as Ashlyn reluctantly wrapped things up for the day.

A few minutes later, Tyler came sauntering up to her desk as she turned off her computer. He held a package of miniature doughnuts from the break room's vending machine. "Well, now that the sun's up, I guess I'll go to bed."

Ashlyn chuckled at his reference to the backward schedule the graveyard shift was famous for. "I know what you mean. I don't know who is more confused in the morning—me or the roosters."

Tyler offered her a doughnut. Ashlyn looked at the thick, dark frosting. It looked nothing short of sickening to her. Tyler noticed her reluctance.

"Come on," he coaxed. "It's the breakfast of all champion cops. It's the good kind that tastes like lard and leaves a waxy residue on your teeth."

* * *

At five minutes to eleven on Saturday morning, Tyler pulled up to Ashlyn's house. His hands were shaking as he knocked on the door. *Get a grip,* he chided himself. When Ashlyn opened the door and invited him in, he decided that no one in their right mind could look at Ashlyn and get a grip. No one had ever looked so good for a trip to the grocery store.

"Is everything okay?" Ashlyn asked innocently as she noticed the admiration in his eyes. She mentally patted herself on the back. His expression told her she had done well at getting ready.

"Yeah. Sorry. You look great. Nice outfit." Tyler tried to gather himself.

"Thanks. I just threw something together," she replied with a twinkle in her eye.

Tyler peeled his eyes away from her to look around the front room. "This is a great place. Have you lived here long?"

"Three years. Kerry moved in a little less than a year ago."

"I like it. It reminds me of my grandma's house." He smiled as he held out his arm. "Well, are you ready?"

Ashlyn nodded, and Tyler turned to open the door for her. He walked her out to the Cherokee, which he had washed and polished for this special occasion. It shone in the sunlight. After he helped her in, he walked around to the other side.

"Where to first?" he asked as he climbed in. "If you're hungry, we can eat first, or we can get the groceries, take them back to my house, and then eat. Which do you prefer?"

"I'm starving. Can we eat first?"

"Sounds great. My stomach's growling."

* * *

They decided to eat at a local restaurant. As Tyler drove, Ashlyn kept stealing glances in his direction. He wore a white T-shirt and jeans. As his arms turned the steering wheel, she watched his muscles tighten and loosen with each movement. She was impressed.

Tyler noticed her watching, and when their glances met, he grinned. She pretended that she was watching the road on his side of the car. As they drove along, the conversation flowed easily, and Ashlyn noticed she had no first-date jitters. *At least none that are too obvious,* she thought.

Before they knew it, they were at the restaurant looking at the menus. They narrowed the selections down to two and decided to split them with each other. As they ate, they talked about their friends and family and growing up. Tyler chuckled as he related incidents from his growing-up years. "Okay, I've got one for you. I'll tell you about my criminal record. As a teenager, I was charged with breaking and entering and trespassing."

Ashlyn was shocked. Suddenly this knight had a chink in his armor. "I take it this is something you left off your résumé?"

Tyler laughed. "Okay, it's not quite as bad as is sounds. We lived in a house that was across the fence from the church. The building had these doors in the front that if you grabbed onto the doorknobs and yanked them just so, they would open. My friends and I decided it was sort of our unofficial pass to basketball land."

"Is that it? I thought you had a great story coming." Ashlyn giggled.

"See, that's where the plot thickens. The singles' ward always had their choir practice there, which constantly conflicted with our game plan. So one night, we came up with a brilliant idea to rid ourselves of the spiritual glee club. If they didn't have a piano, there could be no song practice. If there were no song practice, they would have no reason to infringe on our playing time. After all, what was more important?" Tyler leaned back and chuckled but continued on.

"In our underdeveloped teenage minds, it was the perfect plan. There was a large men's bathroom that could house a piano for weeks without being noticed. We rolled the piano into there and, voilà! Problem solved. Now our hoop dreams could be realized.

"We congratulated ourselves on a job well done, but when I looked back at the barren Relief Society room, I felt like the Grinch who stole Christmas. However, being the mastermind behind the project, I figured that was not the best time for regrets. We left the building only to come face-to-face with a police officer. He escorted us to his car and drove us to the station. I had never ridden in a police car before, and it was the longest ride of my life. When the cop asked us what we had been up to, I tried to explain but he interrupted me right in the middle and said, 'Son, I've heard a lot of crazy ones in my day. But when they start getting too far, I stop the person right there and tell them if they don't give me the truth, I'm taking them in. Now why don't you start again, and this time give it to me straight.'" Tyler rolled his eyes and shrugged. "I was released into my mom's custody, and it wasn't long before I wished I was back in the police car."

By this time Ashlyn couldn't control her laughter. "Serves you right!"

Tyler winked at her and started laughing too.

She loved those eyes. They were so expressive. By now he had stopped laughing and was watching her. She reveled in his gaze and gave him a big smile.

Tyler reached over and held her hand, still silently watching her. Finally breaking the silence, he spoke.

"Are you ready to go shopping?"

Ashlyn grinned lazily. "I am so full I don't think I can move."

"We can stay here as long as you like."

"No, really, I better get moving to burn a few of these calories off."

Still holding her hand, Tyler helped her up. She grabbed the bill and went to pay the cashier, then slowly walked back to his car. Tyler helped her in and walked to the other side to get in.

"What sounds good for tomorrow's dinner?" he asked. "I can barbecue a mean steak."

"Sounds perfect. I can make a Danish caramel cake for dessert. How does that sound? It's topped with whipped cream."

"The more whipping cream, the better. Speaking of Danish things, tell me about your Danish heritage. Have you ever met your relatives?"

"My grandparents have come here a few times, and my parents have gone there a few times. I've been there once. When we went there, my grandparents invited the whole family to a formal, seven-course meal to welcome us to Denmark. There were relatives there—none of whom are members—that we had never even heard of. My dad, brother, and I sat at one end while my mother, the guest of honor, sat down at the other end with my grandparents. We were given these bottles of soda pop to drink since everyone else was drinking wine. Throughout the dinner, everyone kept raising their wine glasses in salute and calling out 'Skaal!' which means, 'To your health.' They 'skaaled' so many times that I ran out of soda pop and asked for another. My grandma gave me this lemonade kind that had pulp floating in the bottom. It grossed me out. Being eleven at the time, I was no dummy. I knew that if I shook up the soda, it would explode everywhere, but I reasoned that if I put my finger in the bottle, shook it, and removed my finger very slowly, no harm could be done. I went through with my plan, and sure enough, it didn't work. The pop flew everywhere—down the walls, down our faces, dripping off our relatives' hair. After that, my mother was determined to make a lady out of me or die trying." Ashlyn laughed at the memory.

Tyler listened to her laugh, unable to do anything but start laughing himself. By the time she finished her story, they had pulled into the grocery store parking lot. He opened her door for her and held her hand as they walked into the store.

Soon they were walking down the aisles as Tyler pushed the cart along. Within a short time, they had gathered all the groceries they needed and stood behind a young mother in the checkout line. She had a baby in the cart and a small toddler who stood nearby. The little girl tugged on Tyler's pant leg.

"Hey, I have a trestion." Tyler looked at Ashlyn in question. She shrugged her shoulders, and Tyler looked back to the little girl. "You have a what?"

"I want to ask you a trestion," she repeated.

"Oh, you have a question. Okay."

"What dooning?"

"I'm shopping for food. What are you doing?"

"We buyning a tookey. Mommy is going to sew the bottom up. Then the stuff won't come out. Baby Oliver can't have some because he was borned with no teeth. Maybe he will grow some though. He eats the smelly stuff in jars."

The mother looked up and called to her daughter, "Jamie, don't bother the nice people. Come and stay by Mommy so you won't get lost."

She called back to her mother impatiently, "I just have a trestion for her." She pointed a chubby little finger at Ashlyn.

Ashlyn smiled at the mother and reassured her the little girl was fine. "So, Jamie, what's your question?"

"You are so pretty. Do you have a Jamie at home?" Whatever Ashlyn was expecting, this was far from it. She recovered quickly.

"Uh, no. But if I did, I would want her to be like you."

"Don't you want a Jamie?"

"Uhhh, sure." Ashlyn turned red, but probably not as red as the mother. Tyler burst out laughing, lessening the tension a bit.

As the mother sincerely apologized and dragged the little girl away, Jamie called out, "Bye, mister! Bye, pretty lady!"

Ashlyn was speechless. Luckily the cashier started to ring up the groceries. It wasn't until after Tyler paid the bill that he broke the silence. On their way back to the car, Tyler jokingly asked, "So pretty lady, how many Jamies and Olivers do you want?"

Ashlyn decided to be honest. "I always wanted to have at least one or two of each, but I'm afraid it was only a dream."

"Why is it only a dream?"

"Because of the career I chose. I'll let you in on a little secret—I never wanted to be a cop. I wanted something else entirely, but then my life changed and I put my dreams away."

"What were your dreams?"

"You'll laugh."

"I guarantee that dreams are not something to laugh about. Tell me your dreams and I'll tell you mine." Tyler opened the car door for her and quickly moved to the other side. Ashlyn stared straight ahead as Tyler drove toward his house to drop off the groceries.

"I wanted to have someone to grow old with, to sit on a porch swing and hold hands with. I wanted children running all around, the whole scenario of puppies, fishing poles, buckles and bows, ribbons and lace. I wanted family reunions and a beautiful wedding. I wanted that one person who would not leave me alone. But," Ashlyn sighed, "as it is, life happened and now all my wishes are just dreams." Tears had welled up in Ashlyn's eyes, and one rolled down her cheek.

Tyler reached over to hold her hand as he pulled up in front of his house. After helping Ashlyn out of the car, he stood closely in front of her. He pulled her chin up with his finger so that he could look into her eyes. "Those are very real and noble desires. Why are they only dreams? You can have them all."

"No. I can't have any of them." She shook her head slowly. "I'm a cop."

"But you can have that too."

"That's my whole point. I don't want to be a cop. But if I chase after my dreams, they'll prevent me from accomplishing what I have to."

"What is that, Ashlyn? What do you have to accomplish?" he asked softly.

Ashlyn took a deep breath. "I'm sorry. I don't know why I'm telling you this. You're so good to talk to. Let's change the subject before I bore you with my problems."

"Come on, Ash, tell me what you have to accomplish," Tyler persisted.

Ashlyn's head jerked up to look at him in shock. "What did you just call me?"

"I'm sorry. I called you Ash, but I didn't mean to offend you."

"My brother, Austin, always called me that. It was his nickname for me."

"It fits you. But I didn't mean to hurt you by it."

"No, you're welcome to call me that. It seems right, and it's actually so good to hear it again."

"Talk to me. What do you need to accomplish that stops you from going for your dreams? I promise I won't say anything."

Ashlyn surrendered her desire for secrecy. She had kept everything locked in for so long, but she was afraid of losing Tyler. Yet she wanted him to understand her. "The police never found who killed Austin. I have tried to make up for that. I need to make a difference."

"You can make a huge difference in this world by achieving your dreams. They're honorable and sacred."

"I don't deserve them." A single tear rolled down her cheek.

"Why?" he coaxed her gently.

Suddenly Ashlyn burst out, "Because it was my fault he was killed. It's because of me that he's not here to have someone to grow old with. So why would I deserve anything different? If the police had caught the shooter, and he had been brought to justice, maybe my goals would have been different. But it's my fault. Now I have to somehow try to make up for it."

"You didn't pull that trigger, Ashlyn. How can it possibly be your fault? Surely you know that."

"But Austin had more to offer people than I do. I know I didn't pull the trigger, but I sent him into the line of fire. We were playing Frisbee, and I made him run all over chasing after it. As long as I live, I'll never be able to change that. It should have been me who died that day. This world would have been a better place with Austin in it."

Tyler couldn't believe that Ashlyn had carried that burden with her for ten years. He held onto her as she sobbed in his arms. While she wept, he prayed silently. *Please give me the words to help her and to comfort her. Help her to understand Thy will. Please lighten this horrible burden.*

"Ashlyn, come and sit with me." He led her to the porch and sat down with her on the front step. "You are a very courageous woman. You have dealt with things that other people's nightmares are made of. But I think you know in your heart that the rules you have set for yourself go against everything the gospel teaches us. Otherwise, you wouldn't be constantly torn between your job and your dreams. There is nothing new that I can teach you, but I want to ask you some questions. Have you let go of the anger over your brother's murder? Have you forgiven the person who killed Austin? Have you forgiven the police for not finding the guilty one? And most important, have you forgiven yourself for what you misunderstand to be your fault? I don't think so. If it's a difference you want to make, you can truly accomplish that even more so by living your dreams than by being a cop. But you need to start with forgiveness."

Tyler took Ashlyn's hand in his. Then he looked at her and spoke quietly.

"On my mission I had a companion named Elder Costas, who was from Chile. His family was extremely poor. He had saved for years to have enough money to send himself on a mission. He was much smaller than I was, but he had the testimony and faith of a giant.

"We met a family who lived on our same street. The father was a bitter, angry man and hated 'them Mormon boys.' So every time we passed by their house, he'd make a point to yell and cuss at us. As time went on, he began to cause a big scene. We'd usually just cross the street and all but run past his house to avoid him. He'd spit at us, squirt us with his hose, and call us dirty names. One time he hit my companion square in the back with a large, jagged rock. He threw that rock so hard that it tore my companion's white shirt and cut and bruised his back. The rock hurt him and I knew it, but he just smiled at me and said, "I'm okay, friend. Let's go teach now." I looked at him, amazed. His family had probably given up a few meals for that shirt! I'd had it with this man. It took everything I had not to punch him out. I started to cross the street, but my companion grabbed me by the arm and said, "I am strong. I am not hurt. Let's go teach now."

Ashlyn stared at Tyler and easily imagined the anger Tyler must have felt. "What did you do?" she asked, horrified at the cruelty of this man.

"We had to go back home so my companion could change his shirt. I cleaned up his wound and bandaged it. Then I prayed. I prayed probably the most sincere prayer I had ever prayed in my life. I felt so angry that someone had done such a horrible thing to a person I respected so much."

Tyler put his arm around Ashlyn. "I took the problem to the Lord day after day, but the harassment continued. One day the man crossed the street, got right up in my face, and called me every name in the book. I politely tried to step aside, but he stepped with me. Quite a crowd gathered, and some were cheering him on while others tried to get him to back off. Up to that point, I had been angry that the Lord wouldn't get this man off our backs so that we could get His work done. After all, I reasoned, we were there to do *His* work. But as I stood there that day, I looked into this man's eyes and saw pain as well as anger. I asked him why he was hurting so bad. Guess what? It took him completely off guard. He spit in my face and walked away."

Ashlyn became angry. "Why that awful, horrible . . ."

Tyler cut her off with a chuckle. "Yeah, but get this. After we got home, I got down on my knees again. Instead of praying to get this man off our backs, I prayed for a way to reach him and to let go of my anger, to forgive and understand him."

Tyler looked at her sincerely. "The longer I prayed, the less angry I became. The less angry I became, the easier it was to forgive him. As I knelt in prayer, there was a knock on the door. It was this man's oldest son. His mother had sent him to get us. His dad had become violently ill and was throwing up blood. We called our president and the bishop to ask for his help and ran over to the man's house. He looked up at me as I walked in and said, 'I'm sorry, son.' We gave him a blessing, and as we did, I grew to love this man who had spit in my face only hours before. That day I learned that forgiveness replaces anger and hurt. Now, Ashlyn, I realize that to forgive someone for spitting on you doesn't compare to killing someone, but no matter the sin, forgiveness is what the Atonement is all about. Most of all, for the Atonement to apply to you, you have to let go of the hurt and the anger and forgive."

Tyler slipped his arm away from Ashlyn and took her hands in his. "You have to trust God. He had a greater plan for your brother. If Austin had died in another way, who would you blame? Let the Lord take care of you. He's willing to carry the burden if you'd let Him."

Ashlyn had been listening silently to Tyler and knew that he was right. She had never forgiven anyone. She knew that Austin would be disappointed that she'd given up her dreams. She felt obligated to let them go; she'd never find peace in the police force. She could find it with God. Never once had she considered the possibility of finding her peace in forgiveness. After all this time, was it possible?

She looked at Tyler and realized she loved him. She'd waited a long time to find him. She wanted him to love her. Was that possible? For the first time, she cried tears of hope. Through her tears, she smiled at Tyler. He felt the knots in his stomach loosen, and he smiled back at her.

They looked into each other's eyes. He reached out and cradled her chin with his thumb as he tilted her head back. Her eyes closed as his lips touched hers softly and ever so gently. He started to pull away for fear he had pushed her too far. He looked at her and slowly leaned over and kissed her again, this time more firmly. They drew apart, and for one long moment, they looked at each other and smiled.

He sat back and took her hand. He kissed her palm softly and rubbed it with his thumb. "Do me a favor?"

"Anything." She smiled.

"Don't let him kiss you."

"Who?" Ashlyn asked, confused.

"Your date tonight."

"Oh my gosh! I forgot about that! What time is it?"

"Four. I guess I ought to take you home. I'm meeting my friends for dinner at six."

"Any chance there'll be anyone there you might kiss?"

"Only Maddie. But she's usually the aggressive one. I promise not to kiss her. Now, reassure my insecure soul and promise me the same."

"I promise," she laughed.

"Really?"

"Really. Really."

Tyler drove Ashlyn home and lightly kissed her good-bye. He opened the front door for her and then returned to his car and left. Ashlyn floated into the house. Today, Ashlyn had given her heart away.

CHAPTER 13

The doorbell rang at ten after six. Ashlyn opened the door to see Dave standing on the porch.

"Hi, Dave. Come in," Ashlyn greeted.

"It's so good to see you again. I've looked forward to this all week. I've missed you." Dave tried to lean in to give her a kiss, but Ashlyn took a step back.

"Are those for me?" Ashlyn asked, eyeing the flowers in Dave's hand.

Dave showed his reluctance at having missed his kiss, but he handed the flowers to her with a grin.

"How nice," Ashlyn replied. "Thank you. Let me put these in water. It'll only take a second and we can be off." She wanted to get the dinner over as quickly as possible so her thoughts could rest solely on Tyler.

"Is Kerry home tonight?" Dave called out from the front room.

"No. She's out on a date. You just missed her. Her boyfriend is a sergeant and a good friend of mine, so he's here a lot." Since Austin's death, Ashlyn always felt the need to make it clear that she wasn't alone or wouldn't be for long. She figured it was a safety tactic she couldn't shed.

She put the flowers in a vase and brought them into the front room. Placing them on the table, she replied "There. They're lovely. Thank you again. Ready to go?"

Dave lingered a bit. "I thought we could visit for a minute if that's all right with you. I've been so busy that it'd be nice to sit for a while. Do you mind?"

"Not at all. Have a seat."

Dave walked over to the couch leaving plenty of room for her, but she chose the chair facing him, obviously keeping a friendly distance.

He smiled at her. "There's something I need to say. I feel like I owe you an apology for skipping out on you ten years ago, just when things were getting good between us."

"Is that how you see it? Skipping out on me?" Ashlyn asked surprised.

"Well, I know how you felt about me and you know how I felt about you. I just wish we'd had more time together. I know you could have used me to lean on at that time."

"I did have a schoolgirl crush, but I hardly think that moving away with your mother would be considered skipping out. I didn't think you had an option. Besides, I had many good people to help me out."

"Did you resent me?" he asked bluntly.

"No, I didn't resent you. I *was* hurt at the time, but I certainly understood your reasons for leaving. You've been kind to keep in touch with me throughout the years. We've both changed, but I still consider us friends."

"They never caught the person, did they?" Dave asked out of the blue.

Ashlyn didn't want to discuss Austin with Dave, but she knew it was inevitable that the topic would arise. Tyler's words came to her mind. *"You need to forgive."* She had to start now. Taking a deep breath, she plunged in.

"No, they never found out who did it. Guess that was the hardest part for me to deal with. That and the fact that I have no idea why it was him."

"Maybe he was tied up with the wrong people," Dave suggested.

"Oh, come on. You were one of his friends. Austin hung around with good people, and he was always trying to help others." Ashlyn suddenly stopped and eyed Dave. "We've never really talked about this, have we? Why do *you* think someone would do it?"

Dave shrugged his shoulders. "I don't know. Maybe he knew something or saw something he shouldn't have. Did he ever tell you anything like that? If he'd tell anyone anything, it would have been you."

"What could he possibly have to tell me? Austin was a good person who died for no reason. There is some creep out there who has the blood of an innocent man on his hands."

"I can see this is still hard on you. Is that why you became a cop? Are you looking for the guilty man? You still seem angry."

"Maybe, but I'm really trying to forgive whoever did it. I have no idea who it could be, but he knows where I am. I think he's close by."

"What makes you say that?" Dave asked, the shock evident on his face.

Ashlyn told him about the threats she had received.

"You better take him seriously. He sounds like he means business," Dave said worriedly.

"I guess so, but I have no idea what I'm supposed to back off from."

"What cases are you working on?"

Ashlyn didn't want to talk about any specifics on her cases, so she spoke generally. "There are a few dealers I know of, but I think they're small stuff. I want to bring down their supplier. I want the big guy."

"Why is that?" Dave asked with curiosity.

"Because I have a gut feeling they're all connected to the threats. I have nothing to go on. I can't get the evidence, or even a lead for that matter, but someday I'll bring them all down."

"There's the determination I remember. How do you propose to bring them all down?"

"For now, I'm waiting. The day will come when someone is going to blow it. It's probably right in front of my face. But I won't give in. One guy has already messed up once. He's only free on bail."

"Right now, it doesn't seem like you have much to support your case. Why not give it up for something else? Can't another detective work on it? Maybe the threats would stop." Ashlyn could see that Dave was genuinely concerned.

"I'll stay on it for a couple of reasons. The other detectives don't have as much training. Plus, it was my arrest to begin with, and I've asked my superiors not to take me off the case."

"Why? I mean, no offense, but it seems like your revenge could cost you your life."

"Because I have this unexplained need to bring them down, I guess." Ashlyn sighed.

"What if they bring you down instead?" Dave asked, getting fairly worked up.

Ashlyn spoke with determination in her voice. "Then I'll go out knowing I did my best."

"That's crazy! Get out now or you might get killed!" Dave stated bluntly, making Ashlyn flinch.

"Can we please change the subject? I know what I'm doing. It's my job, and I know the risks."

Dave took a deep breath. "I'm sorry. It's just that I'm scared for you. Look at your brother. He had everything, and look where that got him. These guys may be out for the big stuff, and a small-town cop certainly won't get in their way. I lost Austin, and I don't want to lose you too. I think you know how much I care about you."

"I can't give it up now. I'm too close."

"You're playing with fire, and you're going to get burned. You should get out now while you can."

"Running scared isn't going to fix the problem. It just makes the bad guys think they have power. I want to bring them down for all the lives they've destroyed and are still destroying."

"Your revenge won't do it. They have power whether you think so or not."

Ashlyn sensed Dave's anger and frustration. Tyler's words came to mind. *Forgiveness. Atonement.* She hadn't forgiven anyone. Did her anger and frustration portray itself like Dave's did? Was it Austin's death that had destroyed her life? Or was it the anger she carried around because of it? She suddenly knew the answer, and the knowledge floored her. Giving up her anger was not giving in. It was leaving it in Heavenly Father's hands.

It was time. It was time to say good-bye to the anger and the resentment. It was time to truly live knowing that the Atonement was meant for *everyone* no matter their station in life.

And it was time to say good-bye to her brother for now.

She could live her dreams knowing that the way she raised her children, supported her husband, and lived the gospel would leave a bigger mark than how many people she arrested.

The recognition and understanding of this blessing lifted such a weight off her shoulders that she felt she could fly. She wanted to stand up and scream, "I finally get it!" Her unexplainable joy caused her to begin weeping. Suddenly, she remembered that Dave was talking to her. "I'm sorry. What did you say?" She smiled.

"I said I didn't mean to make you cry. Did I scare you?"

"No, of course not. Could you excuse me for just one minute?"

"Yeah, sure," Dave replied.

Ashlyn got up and walked quickly to her bedroom and picked up the phone. Knowing that Tyler wasn't home, she left a message on the answer machine. "Hi, Tyler. This is Ashlyn. I just wanted to tell you that I think I understand the Atonement more now than I ever have. You were right. I *can* live my dreams. I intend to start now.

"Oh, and one more thing—my mother would pass out if she knew I was going to say this because it goes against every rule in the *Ladies Book of Proper Etiquette*—but . . . okay . . . here goes . . . I hope you like me, because I like you . . . a lot! See you tomorrow in church. Bye."

Ashlyn said the last sentence so fast she wondered if Tyler would think she said it in Danish. She had never done anything like that in her life. She looked at the phone. There was no taking it back now. She'd have to deal with the consequences of her actions. Ashlyn laughed. She couldn't wait to see what those consequences would be.

Then she remembered Dave and realized her rudeness. He was in the front room, sitting there while she was on her path to self-discovery.

Ashlyn walked into the room, smiling and more composed. "I'm sorry about that, Dave. Can we talk about something else over dinner? I'm starving."

Dave stood and smiled. "After you."

* * *

Ashlyn gave directions to Grizzly's as they drove through town. Although the topic had been dropped, Ashlyn could still sense Dave's tenseness. As it was, her new discovery put her in a great mood. After all, she'd just lost ten years' worth of weight. She smiled to herself.

Finally she turned to Dave. "I know you're still angry." She wanted to make amends. "Can we agree to disagree? If I do stop being a cop, it'll be for a bigger, better reason than for some druggie. How's that? Now, let's talk about you. You left Utah and moved to California. Why?"

"Mom had a friend there who helped us get back on our feet. He opened up a whole new world for us. My mom dumped my dad and hooked up with her friend. I went to school, and when I got out, I went to work for him. That's when I was transferred back east, importing from foreign companies."

Ashlyn sensed he was letting go of his frustration as he talked about himself. "So why would they send you to Utah of all places? It doesn't seem like a typical place for foreign imports."

"Now I'm involved in distribution."

"Do you enjoy your work?"

"It pays for all my toys," he laughed.

"So why did you never marry? It couldn't have been for a lack of prospects."

"I guess I just got too busy." Dave paused and looked over at Ashlyn.

"Too busy for women?" she asked in disbelief.

"No, too busy for marriage. Listen," Dave said as they pulled up to the restaurant, "I didn't mean to get angry earlier. Forgive me? I was trying to talk some sense into you. I do hope you get your guy before he gets you. I was just concerned about you."

Ashlyn grinned, thinking of Tyler. "I do too. It seems that suddenly I have even more to live for."

They walked into the restaurant and were seated at a table. Ashlyn glanced up and unexpectedly saw Tyler with Rory and a woman she assumed was Kate. *Of course,* she thought, *there are very few restaurants in Monroe.* But still, she was surprised to see them. She turned her attention back to Dave. "What is the name of the company you work for?" she asked as she looked over the menu.

"D.P. Imports."

"D.P. . . . *Dave Parker* Imports?"

"Yep. Ever heard of me?" he grinned.

"I have. Not your company though. Wow! How did you manage that?"

"I worked my way up into a partnership. The owner died recently, leaving me his share of the company. The business is booming, and I'm set for life."

Ashlyn looked over at Tyler again, and this time he spotted her and smiled.

"Someone you know?" Dave's glance followed Ashlyn's.

"My boss actually."

Tyler stood and walked over to greet them. He put his hand out to Dave for a friendly handshake. "Hi, I'm Tyler O'Bryan. I didn't expect to see you here tonight, Ashlyn," he said looking at her.

"Tyler, this is Dave Parker. He's in town this weekend from Salt Lake."

"Nice to meet you. Let me introduce you to some friends. They're out-of-towners too." Tyler led them to his table. "Rory, Kate, this is Ashlyn and her friend Dave Parker." Rory stood to shake hands, studying Dave's face. Dave turned away under his scrutiny.

Rory spoke. "I have this uncanny feeling we've met before."

"No. I don't think so. You don't look familiar to me. Maybe I just have one of those faces."

"Do you ever get to L.A.?"

"No. I haven't been there for a few years, unfortunately. Beautiful beaches . . . it was nice to meet you, but I have so little time with the lovely Ashlyn tonight that I think I'll steal her away. Again, it was nice to meet you. Good night." He graciously shook their hands, then took Ashlyn by the arm and led her back to their table.

She looked back at Tyler and Rory, who watched them walk away with questioning looks on their faces. Ashlyn raised her eyebrows, shrugged her shoulders, and smiled.

"Are you always on first-name basis with your commanding officers?" Dave asked.

"It depends on the commanding officer. Tyler's on first-name basis with his officers, but not all precincts are that way."

"I've never seen his friend in my life. I felt like he was staring at me."

"I don't know that I'd call it staring. Like you said, you probably just have one of those faces."

"It was bothering me. Who is he?"

Ashlyn laughed. "Why would it bother you? Have you got something to hide?" she asked teasingly.

Dave watched her laughing, and rolled his eyes and chuckled as well. "Of course not, but no one likes to be stared at. Who is he?"

"He's a friend of Tyler's. He's a cop from the LAPD."

"Oh. So what's he doing here?"

"Just visiting. They're on their way to see family, but I don't know where. I only know they're just passing through."

The waitress came and took their order and was back within minutes with their sodas. Ashlyn sat watching Dave. He hadn't changed much. His sandy brown hair had thinned a bit, but his face showed very few wrinkles. He had a casual stance, but his personality appeared domineering and controlling. He wasn't muscular like Tyler, but seemed fit.

"Why are *you* staring at me now? I'm starting to get a complex here." Dave grinned.

"I wasn't staring. I was watching you." Ashlyn giggled. "You haven't changed much. The years appear to have been good to you."

The waitress brought their dinner and the conversation resumed.

Dave chuckled. "I don't know that my looks show it, but they have been good to me. Things are a lot better for me now than I would have thought possible ten years ago."

"Where are you living in Salt Lake?" Ashlyn asked.

"Upper east side, of course."

"Why do you say 'of course'?"

"Because that's where the rich and classy live."

Ashlyn laughed. "There are rich and classy people throughout the city. Besides, being rich doesn't always mean classy, just as classy doesn't always mean rich. Is that why you live there, though? I have to admit there are some beautiful homes in that area."

"I'm not there for beauty. I'm there for prestige," Dave stated matter-of-factly.

"Tell me you're joking. Surely you're not that shallow."

"Ashlyn, you have to understand something. I never thought I'd see the day I'd own a house, let alone live on the upper east side. When I'm up there, I'm reminded that I have arrived. You don't know what it was like. When I was young, I saw my mother work two jobs to support our family while my dad sat in front of the TV, drinking until he'd throw up and pass out, when I'd clean him up. He'd repay us by beating my mom and me. My mom worked so we could have a meal, and my dad drank it up. I vowed I'd never be in that position. Now I can buy anything I want or go anywhere I want. You should come back to Utah and join me."

"You almost sound serious." Ashlyn chuckled.

"I am. It took me a long time to get to the position I'm in today. Now I'm above your boyfriend standards instead of below them like I was ten years ago. We can have a good future together, you and I. I'm here in hopes of talking you into going home with me. I want you to be my wife. Anything you want is yours. Will you at least think about it?" Dave seemed too arrogant and confident, like he was used to getting his own way.

Ashlyn wasn't impressed. "Money won't make me happy," she replied straightforwardly.

"What will? Avenging your brother's murderer?" he asked in anger.

Ashlyn was unaffected by his cruel words. "Until recently I believed that, but now I think I'd rather leave that up to the Lord and get my happiness by living my dreams." She smiled confidently.

"But Ashlyn, I have the means to make your dreams come true. Think about it. I worked ten years for the day that I could come back and show you that I'm good enough for you," Dave pled.

"Why do you feel you weren't good enough for me ten years ago?" Ashlyn asked in surprise.

"Austin let me know it. He was always trying to change me, by giving me religion, lessons on how to be a good friend, talks about respecting your elders, the list goes on and on."

"You misunderstood him if that's what you think. Did he ever say you weren't good enough? I know that Austin always felt bad because you never seemed to get a fair break. He wanted to help you, not change you."

"He had it all. Why would he want to help me?"

"Because he thought you were worth helping. Is it so hard to believe there are good people in this world?"

"I didn't see it that way. I felt like he was always trying to change me." Dave paused. "You didn't answer me before, so I'll ask again. Will you leave this small-town stuff and come with me?"

"You can't be serious! You know I can't do that—not at this point in our relationship. I've got goals to accomplish. My life is here now." This time Ashlyn paused. "I'm not in love with you, Dave. I'm sorry. I don't want to hurt you, but I don't believe we have much in common. Money means very little to me. I'm so happy that you made something of yourself, and I wish you all the happiness and success in the world. I've enjoyed renewing our friendship, but that's all I feel for you—friendship. I apologize if I gave you the impression I felt anything more than that."

"You still think I'm not good enough for you, is that it?" he asked rather irritably.

"Dave, believe me, I don't have a problem thinking I'm too good for anyone."

"Look, I'm not good at expressing myself. I hoped that tonight we could rekindle an old flame, and I have failed miserably. I was hoping you felt the same way, but I can see that you don't." Dave stopped and smiled. "I want this evening to end on a good note. Let's finish dinner and enjoy each other's company. And I don't want it to be another ten years before we see each other again, even if it isn't on a more personal basis. By the way, this was a good choice in restaurants. This food is great."

"It's one of my favorites." Ashlyn smiled, glad that the conversation had a lighter tone.

The rest of the dinner went off without a hitch, but Ashlyn felt bad knowing she had hurt Dave.

When dinner was over, Dave drove her home. He pulled up to the house and walked her to the door.

Ashlyn knew it would be an awkward moment and wanted to get it over with quickly and call it a night. "Thank you for dinner. I enjoyed seeing you again. Take good care of yourself," Ashlyn said pleasantly, although a bit uncomfortably.

"Wait, before you go in, I want to apologize again for being obnoxious and rude. Someday I hope you'll let me make it up to you. When you're in Utah, I hope you'll look me up. And about those threats—be careful. I lost one of the best friends I ever had. I'd hate to lose you too." Dave smiled at Ashlyn.

"It really has been good to see you again and to find that life didn't beat you. Thank you for the evening. Good night, Dave."

"Good night." He turned and walked away.

Ashlyn watched him drive away in the Mercedes he had rented at the airport. He really had come out ahead in life—at least temporally. She was ashamed to admit she was relieved that he wouldn't be joining her again tomorrow. They had little to say to each other, and she knew they were both aware of it.

Ashlyn felt drained as she walked into the front room. There sat Kerry, grinning like a cat that had just caught a mouse.

"I really didn't mean to overhear you, but from the sound of things, I take it your 'hot' date wasn't so hot."

"Nope. He stopped being 'hot' ten years ago. Tonight I was *not* impressed," Ashlyn answered.

"You don't seem very broken up about it."

"Kerry, tonight was rough, but that's okay because today was probably the greatest day of my life."

"Okay, you've got my attention. Do tell!"

Kerry and Ashlyn sat up and talked until almost two in the morning. Kerry was thrilled for Ashlyn, and Ashlyn was ecstatic about Kerry's approval—and about Kerry's budding relationship with Eric. Ashlyn felt young and alive.

CHAPTER 14

Kerry woke Ashlyn up screaming, "Church starts in one hour!" Both women raced around the house bumping into each other with one goal in mind—to be to church on time. Amazingly enough, they accomplished the feat with very few bumps and bruises, and each gathered her composure as they walked through the front doors of the Monroe stake center with five minutes to spare.

Ashlyn went to Relief Society while Kerry taught her Primary class, and when Ashlyn walked into the cultural hall for Gospel Doctrine, she spotted Eric and Tyler on the back row. Unfortunately, Stephanie occupied the chair next to Tyler. Once again, she was putting forth a great deal of effort to keep Tyler's attention.

There was an empty chair next to Eric, so Ashlyn made her way over to take the seat. "Good morning, Eric," Ashlyn said breezily. When he heard Ashlyn's voice, Tyler—who hadn't seen her yet—quickly looked up and smiled, and she smiled back. Throughout the lesson, Ashlyn continually stole glances at Tyler, her mind more on him than on the doctrine. She also continually thought of how to get Stephanie as far away from Tyler as she could.

It wasn't until the end of class that she remembered about the message she had left for Tyler. Suddenly her nerves took over, and her mouth felt like it was filled with cotton. Just before class ended, Ashlyn all but ran to the water fountain and into the rest room. She berated herself. She would be facing Tyler soon and would have to think of a way to ease the butterflies in her stomach. Until then, hiding from him seemed like a good, safe, immature plan.

Several minutes later, Ashlyn gathered her wits and headed toward the chapel for sacrament meeting. Eric, Kerry, and Tyler had saved her a place on the back row. Ashlyn looked at Tyler and took in a deep breath. Did he have to look so darn handsome in that black suit and crisp, white shirt? It was time to face him. Praying she wouldn't do something brilliant like tripping in front of him, she made her way towards her friends and slipped down in the seat next to Tyler.

"Was this saved for anyone? Like Stephanie or Shirley or . . ." she asked innocently, batting her eyelashes jokingly.

"Only for you." Tyler smiled. "Where is your friend from last night?"

"Should be halfway to Utah by now."

"I'm not sure I want to know, but how was your date?"

"In a word, *icky.*"

Tyler smiled. "Just as I hoped. My evening was icky too as I wondered how yours was going."

"I'm sorry. Did you keep your promise about no kissing?" Ashlyn asked unsympathetically.

"I'll tell if you will."

"You first."

"Maddie came on a little strong, but I've spoken to her and I think she understands that there is another woman in my life. She wants to meet you. And you?"

Ashlyn smiled with excitement. She was the woman in his life? She did all she could to stay seated instead of running to the pulpit to let the world—especially Stephanie—know. Instead she played it seriously.

"He proposed."

Tyler's face fell. "He what?"

"He proposed that I leave this small-town stuff and go back with him so that he could make me a rich, happy girl." Ashlyn shrugged then looked away, prolonging Tyler's curiosity.

"Keep talking," he insisted.

"Well . . . I didn't kiss him."

"Normally, that would make me happy, but I'm a bit concerned about this proposal thing."

"He wanted me to think about it."

Bishop Norton began to conduct the meeting, and soon the organist began playing the opening hymn. Still, Tyler didn't let the subject go. "And? Come on, you're killing me here."

"And I thought about it."

"And?" Tyler pressed impatiently.

Ashlyn grinned. "And I told him it depended on just how mean that steak was today."

"You're basing your future on my culinary skills? No pressure there."

"He got unhappy with me."

"Gee, how sad. Why?"

Ashlyn turned and looked Tyler in the eyes. She whispered softly, "I told him my life was here."

Tyler gazed into her eyes and took her hand. Grinning smugly, he replied, "Poor guy."

Ashlyn felt wonderful sitting next to Tyler during sacrament meeting. At one point, he took the program out of his scriptures and wrote her a quick note:

> *Hey Ash,*
> *I got this great message on my answering machine last night! I saved it and I've listened to it over and over again. It's from this girl that I'm really starting to fall for. At the end of the message she said something so fast that I didn't quite get the words. Any idea what she might have said? Ty*

Ashlyn turned red. She leaned over and whispered in his ear, "How would I know who left that message on your machine?"

"Well, you left it!" he whispered back. Ashlyn loved the tingling feel of his whisper in her ear. She could also smell his cologne and was sure she was going to float off to heaven. She knew she was in love. She hadn't planned for it, but Tyler had come along and stolen her heart. The thought of telling him that made her blush even more.

Tyler quietly chuckled. "You're beautiful when you do that."

"Do what?" she asked, not trusting herself to look at him.

"Blush." He reached over and took hold of her hand again.

During the rest of the meeting, they sat quietly holding hands and listening to the speakers. Ashlyn stole a glance at Kerry, who sat holding Eric's hand. Ashlyn grinned to herself. Life was getting good, and she was feeling lighthearted.

While they stood after sacrament meeting, Ashlyn thought Tyler would let go of her hand, but he didn't. As Stephanie walked up and saw that Tyler held Ashlyn's hand, she quickly turned and walked away.

Ashlyn leaned over to Tyler and spoke softly. "Your harem is diminishing rapidly. First Shirley, then Maddie, and now Stephanie. Holding my hand can't be good for your social life."

Tyler brought her hand up and kissed the back of it. "I was just thinking how dramatically my social life has recently improved."

After finalizing dinner plans with Kerry and Eric, Tyler and Ashlyn drove to his house to prepare the meal.

When they went inside, Tyler brought Maddie in so Ashlyn could see her. She was a well-behaved dog who followed his every command. Ashlyn was impressed and took the dog outside so Tyler could prepare the steaks.

Through the back kitchen window, he watched Ashlyn laugh as she played with his dog. He had truly seen a transformation in her eyes. The pain was replaced with a look he couldn't describe. Hope? Anticipation? Relief? He knew better than to think he was responsible. He had prayed many times to find a way to help her ever since she confided in him, and he knew the Lord had answered his prayers.

That's not all he prayed about. He prayed that she might be his. A part of him felt like he was watching his wife out the window, but part of him feared that he wasn't following God's will. He knew his feelings for Ashlyn had come on fast and strong, but he wasn't sure of hers.

After several minutes, Tyler heard the door shut and looked up.

Ashlyn's hair was windblown and her cheeks were red from the exertion Maddie had commanded of her.

"I hate to say this, but I think Maddie likes me more than she does you. She is such a great dog! She was so friendly and fun to play with!" Tyler remained silent as he started to wash the potatoes at the kitchen sink.

"You're awfully quiet." Ashlyn said with concern in her voice. "Are you okay?" She looked at him. He had removed his suit jacket, loosened his tie, and rolled his shirt cuffs up. Once again, her heart beat faster as she realized how handsome he was.

Slowly he turned and faced her. He set the potato down and leaned back against the counter. Folding his arms across his chest, he sighed deeply. "Ash." His voice cracked, so he cleared it and tried again. "Ash." He ran a hand through his hair in frustration and then gripped the counter behind him.

Ashlyn became worried at the look on his face. "Tyler, what's wrong? Whatever it is, you can tell me."

He rubbed his face with both hands and looked over to her. "I'm going to lay all my cards on the table and pray you don't bolt out of this kitchen and out of my life."

"You look like you're going to pass out. What's wrong?" Ashlyn felt her heart sink. *He's going to tell me he just wants to be friends,* she thought.

"Ash, I'm falling in love with you. I want you to know that because I don't want to play games. I know we hardly know each other. We both need more time to really learn about each other, but I wanted you to know where my feelings are headed. If that's not the direction your feelings are headed, I need to know. There, I've said it."

Tyler ended with a big sigh, a worried look on his face. Ashlyn had to smile. That hadn't been easy for him. She was struck at how truly wonderful she felt when he had said he loved her. It was a feeling she never imagined she'd feel. Now that the moment was here, she felt humbled and blessed that this could happen to her.

"Ash? Talk to me. Say something. Anything."

Ashlyn took the few steps to close the space between them. She looked up into his eyes and spoke softly. "I'm heading in the same direction as you."

He slowly smiled and brought his arms around her waist, pulling her toward him. Ashlyn pulled on his tie, bringing his head toward her. The kiss was lasting and sweet and somehow different from the one they shared the day before. This time they were both secure in the knowledge that they were on the road to becoming one.

* * *

The potatoes were in the oven, the green salad was made, the rolls were rising, and the steaks were marinating. Ashlyn stood in the kitchen making the dessert, and Tyler was setting the table. The two had gotten into a round of twenty questions.

It was Ashlyn's turn. "What is one of the dumbest things you've done in your adult life?"

"Easy. I got shot chasing a girl."

Ashlyn dropped the mixer, and it whipped cake batter all around the kitchen. Tyler grabbed the mixer and turned it off. He looked at Ashlyn's pale face and wide eyes.

"You've been shot?" Ashlyn asked, horrified.

Tyler took her by the hand, led her to the kitchen table, and sat her down. Then he kneeled before her.

"Oh, Ashlyn, I'm so sorry I threw that at you." He spoke sincerely. "I wasn't thinking. It wasn't life threatening, but maybe now is a good time to tell you about it and Jessica."

Her stomach felt like it was tied up in knots. Someone had tried to kill him? Tears welled up in her eyes.

Tyler sat in a chair facing Ashlyn and took both of her hands in his as he told her the whole story, including his resolve to never date a cop again.

"I'm a cop," Ashlyn said, stating the obvious.

"Yeah, but you weakened me. I can't resist you."

Ashlyn asked quietly, "Did you love her?"

"At the time I wanted to, but it was a fleeting thought. I cared about her, but I was never in love with her. I knew that almost from the beginning."

"But you put your life on the line for her. If you got shot going after me, I could never live with myself! I carried blame like that for years. I could never go back there again."

"Ash, it's not the same thing. You put your life on the line every time you step into the precinct. You do that for me and for everyone else you work with. Jessica was way too selfish. As far as my feeling for her, things were over long before they began and way before I even thought about leaving the LAPD. I wasn't in love with her, and she wasn't in love with me, although I think we both wanted love and stability in our lives. As it turned out, we just didn't want it with each other."

Ashlyn tried to swallow the lump in her throat. She had to admit that she was afraid for Tyler as he filled her in on the details of the shooting, but mostly she was jealous that Jessica had gotten Tyler's attention for even five minutes.

"Should I be jealous of Jessica?"

Tyler laughed. "Nah. She's got nothing on you." He winked at her and kissed her on the tip of her nose.

The doorbell rang, and Tyler kissed Ashlyn gently on the lips before he stood to answer the door. He greeted Kerry and Eric and asked them in.

They walked into the kitchen and saw Ashlyn cleaning the batter from the walls, floor, and counter.

"Looks like Ashlyn is attempting to cook again," Kerry joked. She was met with Ashlyn's glare and the men's chuckles.

Ashlyn quickly finished cleaning up as Tyler put dinner on the table. It was as good as he had promised. Afterward, the women sat in the family room as the men did the dishes, talking.

"I think it's safe to say they'll be at it for a while," giggled Kerry.

"How heavenly is it to not have to do the dishes for once?" Ashlyn agreed. Then she remembered her earlier conversation with Tyler and grew serious. "Tyler shocked me with some really bad news, Kerry. Would you believe he's been shot?" Ashlyn waited for a reaction from Kerry and was stunned when she realized this wasn't news to her friend.

"Ashlyn—"

Ashlyn interrupted Kerry before she could continue. "You knew? You already knew and you didn't tell me? Why in the world would you even think to keep something like that from me?" Her anger was rising.

"Because I'm your best friend and I love you," Kerry replied calmly.

"What in the world do you mean?"

"It's the truth. Ashlyn, what kind of friend would I be if I didn't hurt when you hurt? I may not fully comprehend the devastation you felt when you lost your brother, but I do feel and understand your pain to some degree when I see you hurting. In all the time I've known you, you have never once smiled the way you have since you met Tyler. You seem to be more alive, and you have a sort of glow. What kind of friend would I have been if I took that away before you had a chance to explore those feelings?"

"You should have been up front with me."

"You're right. Maybe I should have. But you need to understand that if I had told you Tyler had been shot, you would have thought of your brother and run from Tyler for fear of being close to someone whom you could lose. You would never have given Tyler a fair chance." Kerry walked over and sat next to Ashlyn, putting her arms around Ashlyn's shoulders. She looked her directly in the eye as she continued, "What kind of friend would have spoiled any chance you had at happiness? I just wanted to see you free of the burdens you carry," she finished.

Ashlyn smiled ruefully and then hugged her friend. "I am so blessed to have a friend like you. Sometimes I think you know me better than I know myself."

* * *

"Nice job volunteering us for the dishes! You're not trying to impress someone, are you?" Eric asked with a hint of sarcasm.

"I don't know what you're talking about," Tyler laughed.

"Okay, what gives?" Eric grinned.

"I can't help it. I'm falling for her, and I finally got up enough courage to tell her so. And I do believe my wit and charm are casting a spell on her too." Tyler spiked the dishcloth into the sink, sending a splash of soapy water into Eric's face.

"Whoa, hold on a minute. It can't be your charm—you don't have any." Eric snapped the dish towel at Tyler.

"I most certainly do, evident by my graciously consenting to do the dishes. You and I need to do all we can do prove to those two that they simply can't live without us!"

"We might need some help—that's going to take nothing short of a miracle."

* * *

As the afternoon wore on, Eric and Kerry announced they had to leave. Eric explained that Kerry had challenged his younger brother to a round of Nintendo, claiming that the Christensen men didn't go down easily. Tyler walked them to the door and bid them farewell. He then walked back in and sat next to Ashlyn. "Are you okay with everything I've said today?" he asked hesitantly. He put his arm around Ashlyn, and she snuggled into him.

"I'm worried about you," she admitted openly.

"Maybe if the position becomes available, I can try to become a lieutenant. Rumor has it that Don and his wife might have to move back to New Jersey to take care of his mother. I'd hate to see him go. He's a good man and a good cop. But if his job became available and I got it, I'd be in the office more. But that doesn't solve my worry about you."

"I have thought about turning in my badge," Ashlyn admitted. "Many times actually. Up until recently, I didn't think it was an option. I just want to get Carl off the streets. Maybe I'm wrong in suspecting him. It's just that he's the only one I can think of from my files that would want me gone. If I quit, perhaps the threats would too. But I just don't want to leave the force under those conditions."

"Just be careful. I don't want to lose you." He looked in her eyes and smiled.

"I don't want to lose you either." Ashlyn looked at Tyler, who seemed to be in another world. "Penny for your thoughts."

"I was thinking how good my house looks with you in it." He lightly kissed her forehead.

Ashlyn looked up and grinned. "And I was thinking how good it looks with *us* in it."

"I think you're right."

"I hate that the weekend is almost over. Now we have to go to work and act like nothing has happened. By the way, what happened to Shirley?"

"The captain fired her, of course, but before he let her go, he reprimanded her like you wouldn't believe. You know the captain—he's not one to mince words. He was spouting off rules and codes that she'd broken left and right. Some I'm not sure I've ever heard of!"

"They were probably found in *The Ladies Book of Etiquette.* I know she broke a couple of big no-no's in there," Ashlyn replied sarcastically.

"Either way, she got it good. If I hadn't been so mad at her, the soft side of me would have felt almost sorry for her. Almost."

The ringing telephone interrupted their conversation. Tyler walked into the kitchen to answer it.

Ashlyn sat back on the couch and looked around the room. If this house were hers, she'd have so much fun decorating it! Tyler had done a good job, but it lacked a woman's touch.

Tyler came back in shortly. His eyes revealed worry and concern.

"What's wrong?" Ashlyn sat up and looked him in the eye.

"Carl was arrested this morning. Officer Bennett came up on a handover and got enough stuff on Carl that he won't see the light of day for years."

"Did they get his supplier?" Ashlyn asked hopefully.

"No, it was a drop-off and so Carl and the buyer were the only ones in sight. Bennett was at the end of town and saw Carl driving out to the abandoned mill. He called for backup, and then followed him. Carl never knew what hit him until Bennett and Crawford were on him. They apprehended Carl and the buyer. But why Carl and the buyer went alone is beyond me. They usually have someone on watch. Doesn't matter, though. It was the slipup we were waiting for."

Ashlyn looked at Tyler and noticed the look of concern still on his face. She was confused. "Isn't this cause for a celebration then? You don't look like you're in the partying mood," she noted anxiously.

"That was Eric on the phone, Ash. He and Kerry stopped by your place on the way to his house, and there was another threatening message on the answering machine for you. Ashlyn, Carl was arrested at eleven this morning. The message was left at five. Carl isn't your perpetrator."

Ashlyn fell back against the couch in confusion. "Then who? What do they think I know or am close to finding out?"

"Everything pointed to Carl. Now that he's off the streets, we need to start again. We're missing something."

"What message did he leave this time?"

Tyler hesitated, then continued, "He said, 'Get out of town before people find you dead.'" He hesitated again. "Ash, this is serious. Maybe you should take a leave of absence until we can get to the bottom of this."

"And do what? Sit in my house staring at the walls? No. I don't scare off that easy. When I get to the bottom of this, I'll quit, but until then, I'm going to try to get them before they can get me." Her voice was determined, but her mind was a mass of confusion.

She looked at Tyler. "What do I have that they want? What am I missing?" she asked.

"Look, Ash, I'm really worried about you." He looked at her with pleading eyes and sat down facing her. She knew he wanted her to quit, but she couldn't. This was her last case. She would leave the force, but not under these circumstances. She'd worked too long and hard to go out like this.

"I'll be okay. And hey, we're having dinner tomorrow night for a couple of friends. Do you want to come?" Her abrupt change of topic made it clear to Tyler to close the subject.

"That would be great. Who will be there?"

"Annie—our next door neighbor—Eric, Kerry, and you, if you'll come." She smiled. "Oh! And Sam."

"Sam from the bar? Are you seeing him too?" he asked teasingly.

"I *have gone* to see him a few times. Are you worried about a bit of competition?"

"Nah. You're a one-man woman." He winked at her.

"Flattery will get you everywhere," she laughed.

He reached over to kiss her. She returned the kiss with full force. When they drew apart, he kept her face in his hands and told her quietly, "I accept."

She looked at him in confusion. Her heart was racing so fast from the kiss that she forgot everything that happened before.

He smiled at her look. "The dinner? Your house tomorrow night?"

"Oh, yeah." She giggled.

"Let's go say good-bye to Maddie, and then I better take you home. You kiss too good."

CHAPTER 15

Monday morning came bright and early but not early enough. Ashlyn already missed Tyler.

She spent the day cleaning the house and preparing dinner for that evening. Tyler called to see if she was okay and cleverly offered his help—an excuse to see Ashlyn before work. He showed up an hour later. Ashlyn wondered what had taken him so long.

The two spent the time enjoying each other's company—laughing, joking, and at times being serious. The concern about the threats lingered between them, but somehow there was a silent agreement to not let it ruin the moment. However, now and then Ashlyn would glance at Tyler and see the worry on his face.

Everyone arrived on time except Sam. He showed up a few minutes late, but when Ashlyn opened the door, she saw him in a way she had never quite imagined. He stood before her polished to a shine. His hair was combed back, and he wore a suit. He stood before her holding flowers and a gallon of milk.

Ashlyn looked questioningly at the milk.

"I knew you didn't trust me to bring the drinks along, but I wanted to show you that I know how to pick a beverage when I see one. It's one-percent milk—the best of its kind!"

Ashlyn laughed and gave him a hug. She took his arm and led him in to the front room.

Annie came walking into the front room and gasped in surprise. "Good heavens, Sam! Is it really you?" she asked in shock.

"Dear Annie! How are you? I haven't seen you in a coon's age. Last I heard you'd run off and married Hank the Crank!"

Annie burst out laughing. "You were always so jealous of him!" She stopped and became serious. "I heard about sweet Lucy, that dear woman. I'm so sorry. After she passed away I never heard anything of you again."

"What ever happened to ol' Hank?"

"He passed away as well, almost eight years ago. I almost left this town—the memories were so strong—but staying ended up being the best for me; otherwise, I'd never have these girls to keep me young." Suddenly, both became aware that there were four pairs of eyes all staring with raised eyebrows at the interchange that had just gone on.

Ashlyn was the first to recover. "Looks like you two have met before." She smiled. Her plan was working better than she had imagined.

"Met?" Sam laughed. "Monroe isn't *that* big! Annie was my high school sweetheart. Darn near married her until she decided that Hank the Crank would be better for her."

"You and Lucy only had eyes for each other long before Hank the Crank, er, ah, I mean, Hank and I ever eloped." Annie laughed.

"Sounds like this could be good. Let's hear the whole story over dinner," Ashlyn suggested.

Eric offered a blessing, and they all began eating while Sam told the whole story. Sam had been a football hero in high school. Annie was a cheerleader, and he constantly had to beat her admirers off.

"The old football player–cheerleader story," Tyler quipped.

Sam laughed and continued, "There was this guy named Hank that was after my girl and couldn't seem to understand the words *taken*. He was a smarty-pants. Always got high marks in everything except sports." Sam paused, grinning. "He had the grace of a pup. Finally one day we made a bet. His friends got together with mine and made a puzzle for both of us to figure out. Kind of like a road rally. First one to solve it would take Annie to the last school dance."

Annie broke in. "I was furious that he'd put a date with me up on the bargaining block, so I changed rules. Each guy could have one person ride with him in the car, and I asked Hank if I could ride with him. That would teach Sam to have a little more respect for me. Boy was Sam was livid!" Annie smiled. "On the day of the race, I showed up looking my absolute best. I even wore the sweater Sam had given me for Christmas just to add insult to injury. Sam looked the place over and grabbed Lucy, who had been pining for him since the first day she ever met him, and we were off."

Sam took over the story. "Poor Lucy did everything she could to help me figure out the puzzle, but we kept going in circles. By the time we figured it out, it was near midnight. Almost everyone had gone home. But there stood Annie and Hank back at the football field, holding hands and talking. I could tell she liked him, and I'd had such a good time with Lucy that I didn't mind so much."

"Afterward, Sam figured since we both had such a good time with others, maybe we needed to give those others a chance. We both decided it was time to break up." Annie smiled at Sam.

"So how did Hank get his nickname?" Ashlyn couldn't resist asking.

Sam laughed. "That would be my doing. He finally found out what it was like to have to beat every male admirer off this pretty lady. He especially resented me. Every time I got within two feet of Annie, Hank would come unglued. He became so ornery that I gave him the name." Sam smirked over the memory.

Annie blushed. "We both figured out who made us happy, and we all lived happily ever after, didn't we?" Annie asked smiling.

Sam looked at Annie in admiration. "That we did, Annie girl. That we did."

Ashlyn smiled dreamily. "Everyone loves a good love story."

Amidst more laughter and recollecting, the group enjoyed a leisurely dinner. Afterward, they all sat down and visited while eating cookies and drinking the milk Sam had brought.

Soon it was time for Ashlyn and Tyler to leave for work. Sam offered to walk "Annie-girl" home, and Ashlyn and Tyler left in separate cars. The night had been a complete success.

* * *

Over the next couple of months, Tyler and Ashlyn spent as much time together as possible, but they spent very little time together at work. However, they'd secretly smile or wink and talk if they could find any reason to at all. The months flew by.

Ashlyn continued to receive threatening phone calls. Tyler contacted Rory and asked him to check up on the names that were linked to the rented limo that Ashlyn had seen. Rory worked on it but couldn't find any connections. Tyler was becoming more discouraged, and he just wanted to get to the bottom of the investigation.

One Sunday after church, Ashlyn and Tyler found a threatening note on her front door. The note was heart-shaped, and a bullet was torn through it as if it had been shot through. The words were once again typed. Chills ran through Ashlyn as she read the words.

**YOU WERE WARNED
BUT YOU WOULDN'T LISTEN.
WATCH YOUR BACK. WE'RE COMING AFTER YOU.
PREPARE TO JOIN YOUR BROTHER.**

Tyler, upset, immediately called the precinct. "Hey, Don, I need to get your permission for some protection on Ashlyn."

He talked with Don for a while as Kerry and Eric walked in. Ashlyn explained to them about the threat. When Tyler was finished, he joined them. He knew Ashlyn needed to make an announcement. She said, "I think now is a good time to go home for a visit. I need to gather my wits and think things through. Maybe they'll see that I've gone, and Kerry won't be in danger."

There was a knock on the door, and Kerry jumped. It was Annie. She brought over some cookies because, she said, she'd made too many. Would anyone be willing to take them off her hands? Annie's smile immediately disappeared as she took in the looks on everyone's faces. Tyler glanced at Ashlyn, who nodded her head. He explained everything to Annie, who, as soon as she heard it, walked over to the phone and called Sam, hoping he could help with possible suspects from the bar.

Sam arrived in no time, angry and confused. "Why didn't you tell me?" he asked Ashlyn. "All this time I could have been paying more attention for some kind of clue. Everyone's tongue gets a little loose when it meets up with a little alcohol." He sat down and put his arm around Ashlyn in a fatherly fashion.

"What can we do to help?" Annie offered.

The room was silent for what seemed like an eternity. Eric cleared his throat. "Actually, this is probably not the best time for this announcement, but I think it's relevant, considering the situation. Kerry and I are getting married. I don't want her to be here alone, and it probably wouldn't be appropriate for her to stay at my house. Annie, if we try to offer adequate protection, do you think Kerry can stay with you?"

Despite the depressing situation, Ashlyn squealed in delight over Kerry's news. She grabbed her friend and gave her a big squeeze, bombarding Kerry with all kinds of questions.

Annie was thrilled to have Kerry stay with her. In no time, plans were made and put into action. Sam would keep in close touch with Tyler and Eric.

The newly engaged couple left a few minutes later to make the announcement to his family. Tonight Ashlyn would stay with Annie and leave early in the morning for Utah. She wasn't going to tell her parents that she was coming or they'd worry. She would just plan on surprising them.

A couple of hours later, everyone had left except Tyler and Ashlyn. They sat on the couch, saying very little. Tyler's arm was around Ashlyn, and she snuggled into it. Both were contemplating the upcoming separation. They'd seen each other almost every day since they'd met in Tyler's kitchen. Now they were being forced apart, and the thought was a difficult one for Ashlyn.

Tyler, on the other hand, was angry. Finally he spoke. "How would you like to meet my parents? They'd love to visit Salt Lake, and since you'll already be there, I can drive there and meet up with all of you. We could go to lunch or something. Are you up for it? Comes with a free meal and excellent company."

"If it'll give me an excuse to see you, I'll do anything." She hesitated and then asked, "What if they don't like me?"

Tyler laughed. "My dad will be proud that I have such good taste. Mom will hope that we get married and fill her home with grandchildren." Tyler paused and then continued, "It's getting colder now. Won't be long until the first snowfall. Do you want to go for a ride? I found a really neat place."

"Yeah. If I stay here much longer I'm going to cry knowing that I'm leaving you tomorrow." She sighed and then stood up slowly.

"We won't think about that right now. Come on. I wanted to do this earlier, but we got sidetracked." Tyler stood and helped Ashlyn to her feet.

Tyler drove along a winding road up the canyon. The leaves had turned an unbelievable array of colors, announcing that fall had arrived. Tyler parked the car on the side of the road near the top of a mountain and helped Ashlyn out. He took her hand and led her up a small winding path that unexpectedly opened up to a beautiful view of the valley below. As the sun set, it flashed glorious colors throughout the sky: pinks, oranges, and yellows.

Tyler stood behind Ashlyn and wrapped his arms around her waist. He rested his chin on top of her head and whispered, "This is the most beautiful place I could find to bring the most beautiful woman in the world."

Ashlyn turned around in his arms and kissed his cheek. "But you had to settle with me instead, huh?"

"Ashlyn, you've become a major part of me. The place you have in my heart grows every day, and the love I feel for you at times overwhelms me. I need you. I don't think I've ever been so afraid of losing someone as I am right now. I know you have to go for your safety. I believe that, but I feel frustrated and even angry about it. While you're in Utah, please think about marrying me. I swear to love you and respect you and treat you the way you've always dreamed, not just for now but for eternity. I'll make your dreams my priority. After all, your dreams are mine as well. Will you think about it?"

Ashlyn looked up at him. Tears streamed down her cheeks. "I don't need to think about it, Tyler. I've prayed and fasted about you so many times, and every time I've received some sort of confirmation that you and I will do fine together. I have loved you from the moment we met, and I promised my Father in Heaven if I were blessed to have you in my life, I would spend it trying to live worthy of that blessing. I want to be your wife, and I promise you that I will honor, cherish, and love you forever."

Tyler leaned down and gently sealed their promises with a lasting kiss. Then they stood in each other's arms until the sun set and the night air turned chilly.

Back in town, Tyler told Ashlyn he had something to give her. They drove out to his house, and when they arrived, he led her to the kitchen. "I'm glad you said yes," he confessed, "because I was hoping I hadn't jumped the gun." He tied a dish towel around her eyes and led her out the back door onto the porch. Tyler made the sound of a drum roll as he slowly untied the towel. Before her sat a beautiful, wooden love seat swing. On the back panel Tyler had engraved the words "To my darling Ashlyn, who wants to grow old sitting on a porch swing. From Tyler, the man who will always sit beside her."

Tears filled Ashlyn's eyes as she hugged Tyler. "It's the greatest gift I've ever been given. Thank you."

"Care to try it out?" Tyler asked as he took a step forward and sat down. Ashlyn sat next to him. With his arm around her, they silently sat and rocked the swing until they both shivered from the cold.

* * *

Later, back at Annie's, Tyler, Ashlyn, and Annie sat and visited. Annie had thoughtfully made hot chocolate to go with her cookies. All too soon, Tyler had to leave. Ashlyn, cuddled under a big quilt, walked him to his car.

Tyler held her close. "I'll call you first thing every morning and last thing every night. Then this weekend I'll come and see you. If you don't change your mind before then, I'll ask your father for your hand in marriage."

"Start practicing your speech, because you're stuck with me. I love you."

"I love you too, sweetheart. Call me when you get to Salt Lake so I'll know you made it okay." He laid his cheek on the top of her head as he held her in his arms. The wonderful smell of her hair washed over his senses while her hair tickled his face.

"Don't worry about me, Tyler. I'll be fine. You be careful too." They kissed good-bye, and Ashlyn watched him drive away. She tried to choke back the tears. She'd never cried so much in her life as she had the past few months. Slowly she walked back to the house.

CHAPTER 16

Ashlyn felt rejuvenated as she entered the Salt Lake Valley, but even more so as she entered the front door of her parents' home. Neither was at home, but she could smell the roast that her mother had in the oven. When she was young, Sunday dinners often consisted of a roast with new potatoes, and although today was Monday, the smell took her back in time.

She walked into the family room and set her suitcase down. Not much had changed. The family photos on the wall were the same. She loved that wall and was happy that one more picture would soon be added.

Ashlyn thought of Tyler and realized he'd be leaving for work soon. She picked up the phone to call him as she had promised. The sound of his voice brought with it a longing she was sure she'd never get used to as long as the state border separated them. They talked for a few minutes, and Tyler promised he'd call when he got off work the next morning.

Ashlyn put the phone back in its cradle and walked over to the big sofa. She loved to sink down into the old, worn couch. On the coffee table were the family photo albums. Ashlyn picked one up and turned each page lovingly, glancing at the snapshots of baptisms, birthdays, graduations, and holidays. There were also photos of the simpler moments, like hugging each other on the couch. Austin's face was ever-present, and although she missed him, Ashlyn could now look at these pictures and smile.

As she turned each page, she felt strongly that family was what life was all about, the sacred link to heaven. She thought about how much she loved Tyler and wanted him to be a part of all this. She felt so much peace and love at that moment that she never wanted it to end.

The front door closed with a slam, interrupting her thoughts.

"Ashlyn? Are you really home?" her mother called. She walked through the front room and into the kitchen.

Ashlyn met her there with a big hug and a smile. "Hi, Mom! Care to have a visitor for a few days?"

Her mother, with tears in her eyes, squeezed her daughter tightly. "Nothing could thrill me more."

The two women started talking as they walked up the stairs to Ashlyn's old bedroom to unpack her things. When they were finished, Laura sat on Ashlyn's bed and patted the space beside her. "Come and tell me all about him."

"Who?" Ashlyn asked, surprised.

"The man who put the twinkle back in your eyes. The man who has made such a change in you."

There was much to be said about her mother's intuition.

Ashlyn sat beside her mother and told her all about Tyler. Her mother was pleased. "I believe I love him already!" she exclaimed.

As they walked downstairs to fix dinner, Ashlyn told her mother how much Tyler had helped her learn to forgive and trust in the Savior. She finally ended with Tyler's proposal and the porch swing. Her mother laughed and cried at the same time.

The phone rang, and Laura turned to answer it. She smiled widely as she thanked Tyler for all he had done for Ashlyn. She giggled and handed the phone to her daughter.

"Tyler? You now have a fan in my mother."

"I thought I felt my ears burning. Have you told her why you're there?"

"No. I will when I can tell her and my dad at the same time. I didn't think I'd hear from you so soon. Is everything okay?"

"Do you remember the name that we found on the registration for that car rental? It led us to two names in California."

"Yeah," Ashlyn said. "Daniel Parks and Drew Perkins, right?"

"That's right. I called Rory and he traced the names for me. He already knew about Daniel Parks. He's the supplier I told you about several months back. Rory couldn't recall if he had seen any mug shots of Parks because, like I told you before, he wasn't there the night of the bust. He said he'd try to come up with a picture of him and fax it to me. Then I figure I can show it to Sam and see if he recognizes him. If my suspicions are correct, he just may be Carl's supplier. That doesn't clear up the threats, but it may give us something to go on. Also, I called Bob Bradley. He wants to help out, so he's going back through some information from Austin's investigation. It seems that one of Austin's friends is a cop there."

"Yeah, Brett Reynolds." Ashlyn moved the receiver to the other ear. "He and Austin all but used to live together. I worked with him for a short time before I moved to Colorado. Maybe I can contact him in the morning and see what information he can pull up for me."

"What about that Dave character? He was a friend of Austin's too, right?"

"I talked to him about it. All he could come up with is that maybe Austin saw or heard something he shouldn't have, which was ludicrous. Dave's dad was in prison at the time of Austin's death, and his mom moved him to California. Once he got out of college, he moved back East and earned his way up to a partnership in an importing business. Now he's involved in distribution."

"What's the name of the company?" Tyler asked.

"D.P. Imports. It stands for Dave Parker Imports. His partner died, leaving him his share of the company. That's all I know."

"I'm typing his name in as we talk," Tyler told her. "It's not coming up. Must be clean. To be safe, I'll dig a little deeper. Check with Brett tomorrow to see if he can come up with anything."

"I'll do it first thing in the morning. I may as well check to see if Dave's company is reputable too."

"That's my girl. Hopefully Rory will have a picture and some leads for us by tomorrow. Anyway, I just wanted to fill you in on what we've got going."

"Please keep me up to date. I miss you. I'd much rather be with you than sitting here waiting for something to turn up."

"I'd love it if you'd come home, but I need you to be safe. I love you, Ash. I miss you. I'll call tomorrow when I hear something."

"You don't have to wait to hear something. You can call me anytime."

"I'll call first thing in the morning, then. If you need me, call, okay?"

"If you say that, I may as well not hang up. I love you."

"I love you too."

Ashlyn hung up the phone and turned around. Laura stood behind her with a panicked look on her face. "Dear girl, what was that about?"

"Mom, I think we better have a talk." Ashlyn silently berated herself. She had forgotten her mom was within hearing distance.

"Don't leave anything out," her mother demanded, the quiver in her voice betraying her resolution to be strong.

Ashlyn took a seat at the table as her mother sat across from her. She began the long story.

When her dad came home, she repeated the story again over dinner, and it broke her heart to see her parents' grief—both over her and Austin. It was hard for them to learn that Austin's death was actually a murder. It was also difficult for them to understand why she hadn't told them about the threats. But they were slightly relieved when they realized that she'd found Tyler.

For the first time that night, she saw her father smile. "My baby girl is in love. He must be someone good if he's won *your* heart. When can we meet him?"

Ashlyn became a little giddy. "That's the best part, Dad! You have met him! You met him at Bob Bradley's retirement party. Remember the fishing, sports, and outdoors talk you had with my boss? That's him! He's coming to visit this weekend. His parents are coming too, and he wants to introduce me to them."

Laura perked up. "Company this weekend?"

"Not here. We thought we could go to lunch or something."

"Nonsense! Invite them for dinner. We want to meet his parents too."

Ashlyn laughed. Her mother loved to cook.

"I'll talk to Tyler and see what he can arrange."

The conversation turned back to the threats and the leads that Tyler had come up with. They talked for an hour or more. Finally, Ashlyn knelt in family prayer with her parents and asked that everyone would be kept safe. It had been a long day with a long drive, and Ashlyn was exhausted. She fell asleep on the couch watching the late night news with her parents.

Laura covered her daughter with a quilt and kissed her on her forehead. Her daughter was no longer her baby but a grown woman. *When did that happen?* Laura thought wistfully.

* * *

Ashlyn woke to the sound of the ringing telephone. She heard her mother talking and laughing, so she got up stiffly from the couch to join her in the kitchen. Ashlyn secretly stole a moment to watch her mother. Laura had aged but grew more beautiful every day. Everyone said Ashlyn had her mother's features, and she prayed they were right.

Laura turned and saw her daughter. Speaking into the phone, she said, "Just a minute. She just woke up. I'll get her."

Her mother handed her the phone and spoke loud enough for the caller to hear, "It's your Prince Charming!"

Ashlyn turned red. "Oh, for Pete's sake, Mother! You're going to scare him away!"

Ashlyn put the phone to her ear. She could still hear Tyler laughing. "Say one thing, dear prince, and I'm hanging up."

"What could I possibly say? She loves me. Who am I to argue with that kind of compliment? By the way, tell me what you look like."

"Huh?"

"I want to know what you look like first thing in the morning. If I'm going to see you that way for eternity, I need a fair warning. Besides, I miss you. It's been so long that I've seen you that I don't know if my memory serves me correctly. So tell me what you look like first thing in the morning."

"Okay, although the color is different, my hairstyle resembles a carrot top. I have one eye in the middle of my forehead, and my breath could kill weeds. How's that?"

"Just as perfectly beautiful as I remember you."

"Now you do the same for me," she insisted.

"Well, since I haven't shaved for twenty-four hours, I've got Sherwood Forest growing on my face. I need a shower—you know, 'sweat stains' from being at work all night and from incompetent deodorant. I also need a bed, but even more than that I need you. Come home."

"Okay. I'm on my way," she answered brightly.

"Don't you dare. I'll be seeing you in about ninety-six hours and counting. I'm just calling to tell you that I love you. I'll call you tonight unless something new comes up."

"Sleep well."

"Kiss your mom for me. Sounds like she's in my corner." Tyler chuckled.

"I love you more than she does."

"Then kiss you for me too, until I can do it myself. Bye, love."

"Bye." Ashlyn hung up the phone dreamily and sighed. *What a great wake-up call!* She turned to see her mother smiling. "Ashlyn, I'm so happy for you! Let's go buy you a new outfit to wear when you meet his parents. My treat!"

"You don't have to do that." Ashlyn smiled, feeling grateful.

"It's a mother's prerogative," Laura insisted.

* * *

The two women had a great time shopping and going out to lunch. They made appointments for the following Friday to get manicures, pedicures, and hairstyles.

Ashlyn cherished her day with her mom. As they pulled into the driveway, she asked if she could borrow the car. She wanted to go see Austin's grave.

Her mother gave her a kiss and got out of the car. "Dinner will be ready in a couple of hours. Call if you'll be late!" Laura called out to her daughter.

Ashlyn nodded and waved to her mom.

Laura walked into the kitchen and put the packages down. The first thing she noticed was the blinking red light on the answering machine. Five messages had been left. She pushed the button and walked to the refrigerator to begin fixing dinner. All the messages were from Tyler.

Laura became alarmed as she listened to his last message. "Hey, Ashlyn, call me immediately. Rory called. We have the picture, and it's urgent that I talk to you."

Laura stood still. Something was wrong—she could feel it. She jumped as the phone rang again.

"Laura, this is Tyler. Is Ashlyn home?"

"No, she went to Austin's grave. I expect her back in a couple of hours. We've been out, so she hasn't been able to call you back."

"Laura, I know who is threatening Ashlyn. I just don't know where he is. He could be here, in Colorado, or possibly in L.A. But, Laura, he could be in Utah. He probably knows that she's there."

Laura dropped the phone.

CHAPTER 17

Ashlyn slowly walked up the small hill in the Salt Lake City Cemetery. She felt such peace as she leaned over and put flowers next to her brother's headstone and sat down.

For a long moment, she sat in deep thought. Finally, she spoke quietly. "Hey Austin, I'm home—for a day or two anyway. I wanted to stop by and let you know how my life is going. You promised me that someday you'd introduce me to my future husband. Ironically, in a way you did. He's a cop, and he's wonderful. He's helping me to put this all behind me and be forgiving. Who would have dreamed that forgiveness was vital in doing that? Tyler taught me that. Or rather, I guess he reminded me of its significance. Austin, I thought I had to be a cop to make up for your death and to make the difference we talked about. Instead, I'm going to make a bigger difference by being his wife and a mother. I'll for sure teach my children about Uncle Austin. I'm sorry it took me so long to realize the most valuable concept of the Atonement. Then again, maybe I needed this whole learning process to meet Tyler. I love him so much. I can't believe he's going to be mine. You probably already had this figured out long before it finally sunk in for me. Anyway, I wanted to come today to really say good-bye. Good-bye to the anger, good-bye to the revenge, and good-bye to you—for now. You'll always be in my heart. Never doubt my love for you."

Ashlyn heard a deep voice over her shoulder. "Well, isn't that just priceless?" Before she could turn around, Ashlyn's world went black.

* * *

Sometime later, Ashlyn started to gain consciousness, but her thoughts were misty and confused. She couldn't recall what had happened. She was in a dark, musty room that was cold, oh so cold! She tried to get her bearings as she realized the coldness came from the cement floor she lay on. She realized her hands were tied behind her back and her feet were bound at the ankles. The ropes were tied so tight that the flesh stung where it had been rubbed raw. The pain in her wrists and arms couldn't compare to the one in her head. Her left temple throbbed, as did the back of her head.

Suddenly, she heard the muffled sound of voices. The sound came from too far away to be in the same room, and Ashlyn couldn't figure out how many were speaking or what was said.

She opened her eyes slowly. Her left eye was swollen almost shut, but through her right eye she could see a light coming from under a doorway. Something felt caked on the side of her face. Could it be blood? She was almost sure it was.

Where was she? Just thinking made her head throb. She felt nauseated and tired. Ashlyn closed her eyes, hoping the headache would subside if she lay very still.

Ashlyn awoke again when a light came on in the room, wincing at the brightness. She was sure the light would cause her head to explode, so she kept her eyes closed.

Someone walked over and kicked her in the leg. "Wake up, tramp."

She immediately recognized the woman's voice. Ashlyn opened her good eye to see Shirley. Slowly, thoughts started to sink in. Were the threats from Shirley? If so, why? Shirley was talking to someone else. Ashlyn tried to focus on what she was saying.

"I told you I wanted her dead. Can't you morons do anything right?"

"Boss said he wanted to see her first and then we could take her out," an argumentive voice replied.

"He's a fool, a sentimental idiot. There's more risk to being found out this way."

Ashlyn tried to speak. Her voice came out rough and squeaky. "Why?"

"With all your smarts, you could never figure it out, could you?" Shirley replied hatefully. "I knew about you long before you ever came to Monroe. We just didn't plan on your sick obsession with bringing Carl down once you got here." Shirley glared at Ashlyn before she continued. "We figured you'd be easy enough to get rid of though. All we had to do was throw out a few threats, and you'd get out of our way. I have to tell you, it got a little fun messing with your mind and your relationships. It was not only professional, but you can bet it was personal as well.

"But you wouldn't listen, would you? Oh, no. Our little Ashlyn was too busy trying to seek retribution in behalf of her dead brother. Look where it got you. You got in the way, and now we're going to remove you from it permanently. Just for the record, your pretty-boy cop is dead too. I needed that job to get inside information, and he got me blown off, so I settled that score and got someone to do the same to his head." Shirley chuckled mirthlessly. "If it weren't for you, he might still be alive today."

Ashlyn gasped. She looked at the deranged woman in front of her and fought with all her might to hold back a sob. Shirley was lying. Ashlyn could feel it. Tyler had to be alive. He just *had* to be!

"You're lying," Ashlyn said. "You're a lousy liar!"

"Am I? Well, soon enough you'll meet him on the other side—"

"Woman, shut your mouth!" a familiar voice boomed into the room. The voice was filled with fury. "I told you I wanted to handle this alone. Have you got some kind of learning disability? Get out of here. I want my time with her, and then I'll take her out myself. I've waited too long for this to give someone else the pleasure."

Shirley was enraged. "Finish her off already, and let's get out of here," she shrieked.

Dave Parker stepped into Ashlyn's line of vision. His look was evil and menacing as he grabbed Shirley by the wrist. Bringing her arm behind her back in one quick motion, he glared in her face. "Are you threatening me?" Although he was angry, Shirley was not intimidated.

"You could have had me," she said quietly.

"Get out of here! I've got business to take care of." Dave shoved her across the room, and her head slammed against the wall. Shirley crumbled to the floor, passed out cold.

Ashlyn shuddered as she looked up at Dave. He was staring down at her. He paid no mind to Shirley lying in a heap on the floor.

"Sit up!" he yelled at Ashlyn.

She tried, but her muscles had stiffened, and she hurt all over. She took so long that he lost his patience and forced her against the wall. She now had a better view of the room, which appeared to be a small office area in an abandoned warehouse. The walls were paneled, and the room smelled musty and dank. The room wasn't much bigger than a large closet and was quite crowded with the four of them in it. The brown and yellow stains in the once-white ceiling showed signs of a leaky roof, and the bulges gave promise of a cave-in.

Ashlyn looked down and saw blood on the cement floor, assuring her that she had been bleeding. Then she looked to Dave. "What day is this?" she croaked.

"Middle of the night on Wednesday. Now shut up. I'll do the talking, and you'll do the answering. You're a stubborn little witch, you know that? We tried to tell you to back off, but you wouldn't leave well enough alone. Do you have any idea how much you cost me when Carl got arrested? Millions of dollars! That makes me really mad. In fact, I intend to kill you for it."

Ashlyn summoned her strength to speak. "I didn't arrest Carl. Why are you doing this to me?"

"Carl wouldn't have been followed around so closely if you hadn't put out a warning to every dang cop in Colorado. You said you just *had* to bring him down, didn't you? It's your fault. When I met him in California, he was a scared rabbit, but he had the makings of a good employee. A little more time with me, and he would have been one of the best. He was just too greedy to be smart."

"He slipped up," Ashlyn said. "I told you that sooner or later someone would slip up. They always do."

Dave slapped Ashlyn's face so hard that her head reeled.

"Don't argue with me! You and your brother have been a menace to me since the day I met you. Guess what? I'm gonna be real good to you and give you a gift—all the answers you were too stupid to figure out. However, it's gonna cost you your life." Dave smirked and looked at his gun.

Ashlyn tasted the new blood from her newly cracked lip. The taste was nauseating, and she felt light-headed. Once again she tried to focus and speak. Her voice wasn't much louder than a whisper, and she tried to swallow a sob. "It was you. You killed my brother, didn't you?"

"Not that you'll live long enough to do anything about it, but it was an expert hit man who got your brother. How else do you think he got away without a trace?" Dave smirked.

Just then, the nameless man brought in a chair from the other room for Dave to sit on. He was large, but not much larger than Dave. He turned and walked out the door without saying a word.

"You hired a hit man?" Ashlyn asked incredulously.

"No, I wasn't the one who had him killed. My good buddy Martin Crosby was, may he rest in peace. Of course, he double-crossed me, so maybe he's not resting so peacefully."

"*The* Martin Crosby from California?" Ashlyn's mind was becoming clearer and her thoughts more coherent. If he was going to kill her, she first wanted answers to her questions.

"That's right. He and my momma were smitten with each other. She met him when she got into dealing back when we lived here in Utah." Dave smirked at the memory. "I was right about Austin, you know. He hung out with the wrong crowd. I was the 'wrong crowd,' wasn't I? I was never quite good enough for your high and mighty morals. If Austin had stayed out of my business, he'd still be living. I tried to tell you that maybe he saw or heard something he shouldn't have. I knew you were dying to know. And now you really are going to die." Dave laughed at his own joke.

Ashlyn watched him and could feel the evil emanating from him. She was truly afraid.

"Why are you doing this to me?" she asked. "Why would you come back to finish the job ten years later?"

Dave answered, "Austin came to my house the morning after our first date. Your innocent, protective brother walked into my room when I had a five-pound bag of heroin on my dresser. I was on my way to make a delivery for Martin. I don't know if Austin saw it, but after talking to Martin, we couldn't take that chance. After all, back then all it took was one phone call on my part and big brother is gone just like that. For years I wondered if Austin had said anything to you, but as we kept track of you, it became obvious you didn't know anything. Once you got on Carl's trail, however, you became too big of a liability. With your record and determination, we knew it would be just a matter of time."

Suddenly she looked up at Dave. "You're Drew Perkins and Daniel Parks! You were doing Martin's dirty work and keeping his record clean. As long as you had two aliases, you kept *your* name clean as well."

Dave laughed. "You're not very quick. It only took you ten years to figure it out. But you know, we could have avoided this little incident if you'd come home with me. You could have joined me and had it all. But you refused, and look where it got you. You're sitting there sloppy and weak while I have a gun in my hand with one bullet meant for your heart. I vowed long ago I'd break it one way or another. Looks like we'll have to break it this way."

Ashlyn shivered and then tensed with anger in spite of her protesting muscles. "What about Shirley? How does she fit into all this?" Ashlyn looked over at Shirley as she started to come to.

Dave looked at her in disgust. "One lonely night when she was in the depths of despair and couldn't find a man who wanted her, poor thing, she met up in a bar with Carl. He gave her some stuff that made her forget her troubles and introduced her to me. She has been a wonderful informant. Small world, don't you think? Now you know my story, and now you're going to die." Dave cocked the gun and aimed it at Ashlyn's heart.

Ashlyn closed her eyes in fear when the shrill sound of a phone broke the silence.

Cursing, Dave answered it abruptly. Ashlyn couldn't hear the conversation, but judging from Dave's body language, she could see he was livid. Dave hung up the phone, swung on his heels, and headed out the door, slamming it behind him.

Ashlyn heard angry tones, but the words were discernable. A few minutes later she heard a car start up, peel out, and pull away. Then . . . silence.

She took time in the silence to say an earnest, heartfelt prayer. She begged for Tyler's safety as well as for the safety of her family, friends, and any officers that might get involved. Then she prayed for a chance to get out alive. Nevertheless, in trying to show her trust and faith, she whispered the difficult words, "Thy will be done."

Ashlyn heard the door to the room click open. When she looked up, the nameless man was kneeling on the floor next to Shirley, talking softly to her.

"Don't worry, baby. I'm going to kill him, and then we'll get out of here with the money and the goods."

Shirley sat up slowly. "If you don't kill him, Nick, I will. I swear I will." Shirley spoke between gritted teeth.

Nick helped her up and looked over at Ashlyn.

Shirley followed his gaze and spoke with fury, "Why isn't she dead yet?" She walked a few steps closer to Ashlyn.

Nick pulled her back, exasperated. "I told you—Castillo called before Dave could finish her off. He was so mad, but before he walked out, he said he wanted to have the pleasure of killing her when he got back."

Shirley, in a rage, slammed her foot into Ashlyn's shoulder as hard as she could.

Pain tore through Ashlyn's shoulder as a scream escaped her lips. Tears burned her eyes as she fought to deal with the agony of a dislocated shoulder.

"Leave her alone," Nick said. "If Dave comes back and sees we've messed with her, he'll turn on us and we'll never get out of here alive. We'll leave when he comes in here to finish her off." Nick tried to pull Shirley towards the door.

"Wait!" Ashlyn cried. "I need to use the rest room."

Shirley laughed. "Gee, how inconvenient." She turned to walk away.

Thinking fast, Ashlyn called out, "If you don't help me out here, I'll tell Dave about the affair between you two. I'm going to die anyway, so I may as well bring you down with me." Ashlyn prayed her plan would work.

"I'll get the gun," Nick said to Shirley reluctantly. Then he looked at Ashlyn and said, "Let her go, and we'll bring her back in here before Dave gets back. Untie her feet but not her hands." He walked out of the room. Within seconds he returned and pointed a gun straight at Ashlyn's head.

"To buy my silence about your fling here, I want one more thing." Ashlyn tried to sound stern but the tremble in her voice gave her away.

"Who do you think you are?" Shirley asked. "You're in no position to bargain! Maybe you've forgotten who is in control here."

"All I ask is that you tie my hands in the front. I know you're in control here, but may I remind you that Dave will kill you both if I tell him that you're both conspiring against him?"

"We're wasting time here. Let her go and get her back in here before Dave returns," Nick demanded.

Ashlyn noticed he was getting antsy and nervous and thought maybe she could exploit that weakness. He ordered Shirley to tie her hands in front. After a small debate, Shirley gave in and did as Nick said.

Perhaps in answer to her prayer, both Shirley and Nick turned their backs to the door as Shirley removed the ropes from Ashlyn's wrists. Ashlyn looked to the door and gasped. In a panic-stricken voice, she tried her best to scream her plan. "Dave, you're back!"

Her plan worked. Ashlyn had created a diversion just long enough to knock the gun from Nick's hand.

Ashlyn slammed the heel of her palm up under Nick's nose and then kneed him in the groin, rendering him incapacitated. Shirley dived to retrieve the gun, but Ashlyn stomped on Shirley's instep and dragged her down. Quickly, Ashlyn grabbed the gun and pulled it on her.

"Don't move!" Ashlyn yelled.

Ashlyn hit her over the head and watched Shirley slump to the floor. Then she fled through the door to find herself in a larger room with an exit at the far end. She ran as fast as her muscles would allow.

Just as she made her way out, she heard a car in the distance. Ashlyn knew it would be Dave. She had gotten away just in time. Ashlyn knew it was another answer to her prayer as she ran into the dark.

CHAPTER 18

Although one eye was almost swollen shut and her body ached from head to toe, fear had pumped enough adrenalin in her to run. The darkness and the thick foliage were to her advantage. The terrain indicated she was in the mountains.

Ashlyn ran until her lungs burned. Tree branches whipped her in the face and ripped scratches in her arms. Still, she ran on, but never in a straight line. She did her best to run in a weaving pattern to make her harder to track. The moon gave enough light to see, but the thick roots and lower vines constantly tripped her and caused her to fall. Her shoulder was jarred during the fall, sending an agonizing pain down her back. She braced her arm and held it tight against her, but she had never been in such pain.

Finally she slowed her pace as her expanded lungs craved air. She listened for any indication that she had been tracked but heard none.

Just up ahead, Ashlyn spotted a thick pine tree several feet high. She crawled under the huge branches and sat against the trunk to rest. Soon her heart slowed to a normal pace.

Again Ashlyn prayed. She begged for the strength of body and mind to see this through. She asked for endurance so that perhaps she could be with Tyler, her family, and her friends once again. She thanked her Heavenly Father for His help and closed her prayer by saying, "Thy will be done."

Then she sat and thought of all the events over the past few months. Tears escaped her eyes as she thought of Tyler. *What if I don't make it through all this?* she thought.

I will.

She felt weak from the abuse and exhausted from the exertion of her getaway. Her head pounded, and her shoulder throbbed. She felt dizzy and thought she would pass out. She almost wished she would so that for a time she wouldn't feel the pain and fear.

Ashlyn lay down on the hard ground and waited for the spinning to stop. Before long, the cold set in. Her body was racked with chills, and she shook. She waited until she could stand the cold no longer.

Quietly she dragged herself out from under the tree and gathered together small, leafy branches to put on the ground underneath her and a few more to put on top of her. She went back under the tree where the large pine branches provided protection, pausing frequently to listen for any noises that might indicate she would be caught again, but finally the task was complete. She tried to lay in a fetal position and took her arms carefully out of her sweatshirt sleeves and wrapped them around her body. Then she put her face inside her sweatshirt to try to warm her face. Shortly thereafter, she drifted off into a light sleep.

She felt like she had only slept for a minute when she awoke. When she opened her eyes, she noticed some of the swelling had gone down in her eye. She could even see a little bit out of it.

Immediately the hair on the back of her neck stood on end as she realized someone was near. Suddenly, she heard a gunshot and a scream that came from close by.

In a panic, Ashlyn took off and ran in the opposite direction. She ran blindly through the dark as fast as her stiffened body allowed her. Within a short distance the ground beneath her seemed to open up and swallow her, and Ashlyn went careening down a ravine. As she tumbled, she smashed her face against the dirt and the leaves. Her knee hit a boulder as she rolled, but she couldn't stop. Something hard and massive brought her to an abrupt halt, and once again, her head slammed into something. Everything went black.

* * *

When Ashlyn came to, the sun was beaming bright and clear. She must have been unconscious for some time because her aches and pains had left her, and she didn't feel so exhausted. She looked around at the area and felt at peace. Perhaps the nightmare was over and all she had to do now was seek help. She felt comforted.

Ashlyn looked up at the ravine she had fallen down the previous night. Then she saw him. Joy filled her as she screamed, "Austin! You're alive! You didn't leave me!" Tears of true happiness fell from her eyes as Austin's handsome face peered over the edge of the ravine.

He smiled.

Ashlyn tried to run up the ravine, but she noticed the distance to Austin, never lessened.

"Austin, help me! I can't reach you!"

From far away in the distance below, Ashlyn heard Tyler's voice.

"Ashlyn, come back to me. Please don't leave me, I love you. I need you," he begged.

Ashlyn tried to answer, but he couldn't hear her. She turned back to Austin and once again, he smiled at her. How many times had she dreamed of that smile? It was the smile that told her all would be fine. She looked at her brother and felt his joy and peace.

Tyler called to her again.

Austin looked at her. Still smiling, he said, "Go to him, Ash."

An indescribable good feeling consumed her as she looked back in the direction of Tyler's voice. She turned to follow it but stopped and looked back at her brother.

"Are you going to leave me again?" she asked.

"Nah. According to the plan, we'll *all* be stuck together for eternity." Austin chuckled and stood as though to leave. "Go to him, Ash," he repeated.

"Wait," Ashlyn called back to him. "I love you, big brother."

"Don't I know it, Ash. Don't I know it!"

Ashlyn's eyes filled with tears as she blew him a kiss, waved, and then turned to run as fast as she could back down the ravine in the direction of Tyler's voice. It was getting closer as she ran. She was thrilled. She ached for him.

CHAPTER 19

Tyler sat in the dimly lit, silent room. Tears flowed down his cheeks as he sat in the chair next to Ashlyn's bed. He held her hand, rubbing the back of it with his thumb in a gentle caress.

"Please don't leave me, Ash. Come back to me. I love you. I need you."

Tyler shifted her hand so that he held it in both of his as he bowed his head to pray once again.

A nurse walked in and gave Tyler a smile as she checked Ashlyn's IV and vitals. Then she spoke quietly to Tyler. "You should go home and get some sleep. You've been here since they brought her in last night, and there's been no change. If there is, we'll be sure to call you."

"I'm not leaving here until she leaves with me," Tyler said adamantly.

The nurse smiled again and nodded. She walked out of the room and shut the door behind her.

"I mean it, Ash. I'm not leaving you, so please don't leave me," Tyler pleaded.

"Tyler," Ashlyn whispered softly. "I can't find you."

Tyler jerked his head. Had he imagined it? In an instant he jumped up and ran to the door, calling for the doctor. He ran back and grabbed her hand. "I'm right here, Ash. Open your eyes for me. Come on, Ash. Come back to me. I'm right here."

Ashlyn's eyes fluttered open just as the doctor walked into the room. She squinted her eyes, and Tyler came into focus.

Although her face was swollen, she managed something similar to a smile. "I've been looking for you."

Tears wet his cheeks as he laughed and kissed her forehead. "I'm right here. Always."

The doctor walked over to the bed to examine her, and Tyler turned to call her parents. Even though they had barely left a couple of hours before, they were planning on coming back in about an hour.

Ashlyn's condition had been critical for a while. When they brought her in, she had been badly beaten and couldn't respond to people around her. Tyler believed in miracles, though, and when he and her father gave her a blessing, he knew everything would go according to Heavenly Father's plan.

Tyler glanced over at her as she talked to the doctors. Ashlyn met his gaze, and he winked and smiled. Her face was cut, bruised, and swollen. While he had never seen someone so beat-up, to him she never looked more beautiful.

The doctor finished his examination and once again, Ashlyn and Tyler were alone.

"Welcome to Utah," she spoke quietly.

Tyler laughed. "This isn't exactly the welcome I envisioned."

"I promise to make it up to you."

"I promise to hold you to that." Tyler looked at her tenderly. He walked over to the bed, sat on the edge, and took hold of her hand. "You scared me. I thought I lost you. Where did you go?" he asked as he kissed the back of her hand.

Tears welled up in Ashlyn's eyes and spilled over onto her cheeks. "Somewhere close to heaven," she whispered.

* * *

The next morning, just as she awoke, Ashlyn heard a soft tap at the door. She called for them to come in, and Tyler's smiling face poked around the corner of the door. He asked if she was up to having visitors. She nodded, so he called for them to enter. Brett and the Bradleys walked in with flowers and smiles. Brett was now a grown man, but he still had the same boyish grin.

He slapped Bob on the back and said, "See? I told you she was hardheaded enough to survive this."

Ashlyn looked at Tyler and tried to grin. "Don't listen to him. He's still sore at me for a harmless little joke I played on him and my brother years ago."

"What did you do?" Tyler asked.

"I spray painted 'Austin loves Brett' on our barn. He's still holding a grudge."

Tyler looked at Brett for confirmation. Brett nodded and smiled at Ashlyn. "How could you do anything so rotten?" Tyler asked.

"Because they wouldn't let me join their secret boys' club. Huh! Some secret it was too. No one even knew about it because the whole club consisted of just those two. The barn was their secret hideout." Ashlyn tried to roll her eyes but her left eye was still quite swollen and bruised.

Brett broke in. "Yeah, justice was served when she had to repaint the whole barn herself that summer. It never dawned on her that the operative word was *boys'* club. What girl in her right mind would want to join a boys' club? She vowed she would hate all boys for the rest of her life. Looks like she changed her mind." Brett looked at Tyler and grinned. "Buddy, you're in for a real adventure with this one."

Ashlyn gave Tyler a crooked smile. "In case you can't tell, I'm winking at you."

"Until some of that swelling goes down, I think that wink is stuck." He leaned over and kissed her on the tip of her nose.

The guests stayed to visit until it became obvious that Ashlyn was exhausted. Once they left, though, Ashlyn asked the question she'd wanted to ask but was afraid of to.

"Is the nightmare over, Tyler?"

"Honey, it's all over. Rory found out that Daniel Parks and Drew Perkins were aliases for Dave Parker. That's why he recognized him at the restaurant. Rory never put the two together until he searched out those names and came up with a picture. I called Bob, who then called Brett, and that's how the SLPD got involved. By that time, Bob and I were already on our way here."

Tyler settled himself on the edge of Ashlyn's bed and put his arm around her. She snuggled into his side. Then he continued. "Brett knew of the old warehouse you were taken to. He also knew of a few other places that had been staked out as drop-off sites. So it took a bit of time to check them all out. When we got to Salt Lake, we met up with Brett and eventually we got to the warehouse." He kissed the top of her head.

"There was a guy there named Nick. Shirley was there too."

Tyler's eyes narrowed, and she could sense his anger. "Nick shot Dave in an attempt to clear out of there. It seems he and Shirley were playing lovers behind Dave's back, but accomplices to his face. There was another guy involved too. His name was Devon Castillo, Dave's right-hand man. He killed Nick when he saw that Dave was dead because he wanted everything for himself. Shirley then killed Devon for killing her lover. This all happened outside the warehouse and took place in a matter of minutes. It was a pretty ugly scene."

"What happened with Shirley, then?" Ashlyn asked.

"She went back into the warehouse, probably looking for the money and enough drugs to supply her with even more money. She wasn't bright enough to consider that we were there waiting for her. She ran quite a ways before she was caught. But now we have so much evidence on her that for the rest of her life the only daylight she'll see will be obstructed with bars. That's it in a nutshell. The details are a little more complicated than that, but we can go over them when you've recuperated. The police need your statement as soon as you're up to it, though. But, Ash, it's all over. It's time for us to start celebrating life." He kissed her gently.

Ashlyn had cried quietly as Tyler spoke of the whole horrid tragedy, but she knew he was right. It was time to celebrate life and love. She looked at Tyler. "Sergeant O'Bryan, I quit. My letter of resignation will be given to you shortly."

Tyler looked at her for a moment then spoke carefully. "Ashlyn, you don't have to decide that now. You don't even have to quit. You can still have it all."

She looked at him softly. "I have it all. I'm going for my dreams. That's what I want. It's what I've always wanted. Are your dreams still my dreams?"

"Ashlyn, all my dreams begin and end with you."

ABOUT THE AUTHOR

Jeri remembers learning at a very young age that her dad wrote a book. At that time, the desire to do the same was instilled in her. The youngest of four girls, Jeri grew up in the Salt Lake Valley enjoying the great outdoors and all it had to offer.

She now resides in West Jordan, her old stomping grounds, with her husband, Brad, and her two sons, Tyler and Bryan. Besides her love of reading and writing, she enjoys woodwork, crafts, scrapbooking, gardening and yard work, cooking, being with family, and working with her friends at the Jordan River Temple. Jeri enjoys corresponding with her readers, who can write to her in care of Covenant Communications, P.O. Box 415, American Fork, Utah 84003-0416, or e-mail her via Covenant at info@covenant-lds.com.

EXCERPT FROM

CONFLICT OF INTEREST

If one had to choose when to die, this Friday evening in late September would have been a beautiful choice.

Yet dying was the furthest thing from Jennifer Sterling's mind. She gazed out the screen door at the sunset that filled the low western sky with fiery clouds, tinting those hovering higher in several shades of pink. A slight breeze stirred the wind chimes on the deck, evoking a sweet melody from them. She drew a deep breath, drinking in the pleasant scent of the afternoon's light rain that still lingered in the cool air. It had been a lovely day. And it was a beautiful evening. Too beautiful, perhaps, considering the unpleasant task ahead of Jennifer—a task that might render the day's conclusion dark and unsettling, rather than the perfect close it hinted at now.

She turned from the window as darkness settled in, a sinking feeling of despair in her heart as she thought of what she must say when Rob returned tonight. And surely he would be home soon. She had a confession to make to him, and it would be one of the hardest things she'd ever had to do. She really did love Rob, and she knew he adored her. Why she'd let herself spend time alone with another man, especially when she knew that man was attracted to her, seemed both strange and foolish to her now.

Perhaps it was because she'd had certain expectations when she married Rob. He came from a wealthy and prominent family, so it was only natural that she'd expected him to lavish her with the finer things that money could buy. But he had rejected his father's business in order to become a cop, and his father had basically disowned him for it. What he had now in the way of possessions were bought with his meager salary, and now that he was in law school, the only money he had was from student loans and what little he made working a few shifts as a reserve deputy. They had been pretty much surviving on her salary as a legal secretary, and that wasn't much.

She'd begun to flirt with Dan partly because she was lonely. Rob spent long hours at school and at the library studying. She missed him when she was home alone in the evenings, and she resented his being gone so much, but she knew that was no excuse for flirting and spending time alone with another man. Oh, it had seemed innocent at first. She hadn't really done anything but have lunch and dinner with Dan a few times. And he'd seemed like such a nice guy, his attentions no more noticeable than what she was used to.

As a former Miss Utah, Jennifer had been admired by many men. The fact that she had chosen and married Rob had not stopped her admirers. Dan, she had thought, was simply one of those. She had enjoyed his company, but after a while she realized that she was attracted to him. That was when she started to think about what she was doing.

Now, as she reflected, Jennifer realized that she had not been faithful to her marriage covenants. She remembered complaining to Dan about how Rob spent so much time away from home in the evenings. She'd even whined about being scared because she was alone so much wondering if she really *was* alone.

Dan offered to come over and spend those disturbing times with her, but she'd quickly redirected the conversation, telling him that she'd be fine as long as she stayed near a flashlight and a phone at all times. "But can you get to them quickly enough?" he'd asked.

"Oh, yes. We keep a flashlight in the kitchen cupboard near the back door. It's small, but it's bright. And I keep the cell phone by my side."

"Use it if you need me," he said, and she'd promised she would.

They talked about a number of things when they went out. Dan often kidded her about going to church, and now, as she reflected, she realized that spending time with him and listening to him had adversely affected her activity in the Church. Rob had been hurt, maybe even a little angry, when she'd insisted that she was just too tired to get up on Sunday mornings lately. The truth was, she didn't want to go. That was what her association with Dan was doing to her. She had finally made up her mind that morning, when Rob left early for school without even giving her a kiss, that it was time to change all that.

* * *

Martin Ligorni got very excited as he watched Jennifer moving around the living room. She cleaned and straightened things up, the motions of her body a work in perfection. She was so lovely to watch. He'd talked to her as often as possible over the years, and he loved her voice too. He was sure she'd been impressed by his as well—he'd seen it in her eyes. He had such a smooth and melodious voice, even if he did say so himself. He also loved the way Jennifer moved, the way she smiled and the way she flipped her gorgeous blond hair from her eyes. As he watched now, he memorized the way she crossed her legs when she sat on the recliner for a few minutes to watch TV. Every move she made caused him to love her all the more.

Jennifer got up and walked into the kitchen. Martin had to hurry around to a different window. When he peeked into the kitchen, Jennifer was just pulling a glass from the cupboard next to the back door. She left the door to the cupboard ajar when she stepped to the sink to fill her glass with water. Martin strained to see if anything valuable was in the cupboard, not that anything more valuable than Jennifer herself graced the house. She drank about half the glass, set it down, then returned to the cupboard. She picked up a flashlight from the cupboard, opened the back door, and began shining it into the yard. Martin dropped down, hiding himself. *What is she doing?* he wondered. Had he made too much noise?

But a moment later he heard the door close, and he again peeked into the kitchen window. She had just put the flashlight back in its place and then checked the back door and locked it. After that she returned to the living room. He hurried as fast as his chubby legs would carry him back to the main living room window.

Martin suddenly became angry, his thin lips quivering as Jennifer walked to the mantel and took down the large framed picture of her and Rob on their wedding day.

What right did she have to choose Rob Sterling over him? Martin had loved her since the time in high school that he'd been assigned a seat next to her in a math class. He'd helped her a little with her math because she wasn't very good at it. But even after that it was all he could do to get her to notice him. It was Rob's—money his family's money—Martin thought, that made her marry him. She didn't love Rob, she just loved his money. Well, when he, Martin Ligorni, got to be a successful lawyer, he'd have plenty of money, he reminded himself. He could provide Jennifer with the lifestyle she wanted.

But Martin became increasingly frustrated as his lovely Jennifer traced her fingers over Rob's profile in the portrait. It was making him furious. All she had to do was get the guts to leave Rob. Martin would take her in anytime. He'd seen her toying with the idea over the months, could see it in her behavior. He loved her, and he'd be better to her than Rob. He wouldn't leave her alone almost every night like Rob did.

Martin was suddenly forced to turn away from the window and drop behind Jennifer's shrubs when he saw headlights turn onto the street. His visits to see Jennifer had to remain his little secret until he was ready to tell her himself, to present what he had to offer.

As Martin thought about the months he'd spent getting to know Jennifer, he still couldn't believe the coincidence that had occurred when he and Rob ended up in law school together. It was so convenient to be able to come here when Rob was studying late. And tonight . . . Martin smiled to himself as he waited for the car to pass. Tonight Rob would be real late, at least Martin hoped he would, since Martin had arranged it so that he could watch Jennifer for several hours.

He stood up and peeked back in the window. What he saw made his blood run cold with the anger born of betrayal. Jennifer was kissing the picture of Rob! *How could she?* he wondered. He turned away, too angry to watch anymore. She'd just ruined his whole night. Fuming, he walked away from the house and back to his car. *What is the matter with her?* Martin wondered as he hoisted his heavy, pear-shaped body into the driver's seat. Why couldn't she see that she was meant for him? He shook his thick jowls in disgust. She *was* meant only for him.